SEEDS OF PLENTY

by

Jennifer Juo

Juo

_07/13_

For my father

Prologue

On the night Sylvia went to the hospital, the baobab blossoms were in full bloom. These flowers that open at dusk and die by dawn were said to be spirits.

Sylvia followed the Nigerian policeman through the crowded hospital. The hallway was a living obstacle course, and she had to concentrate on every step. Patients paced up and down, their rubber slippers slapping the tile impatiently. Bare-shouldered women in batik wrappers lay sleeping on the terrazzo tile floor. A gloveless man shoved used bandages and syringes into loose, plastic bags. She knew they would end up in the mound of burning garbage and ash that lined the road. A hospital in this state, how could her husband survive? She tried to focus on the dueling paint on the walls, light green above and forest below, but the color could not hide the dark stains.

Sylvia stumbled as she entered Winston's room. He lay on a bed, connected to an IV, a plastic respirator covering his face. His body seemed so small, deceptively calm, no sign of the chaotic struggle occurring within. The only clue was the IV piercing his skin. Seeing the needle, she panicked. Sylvia scanned the room in vain, searching for discarded packaging, any evidence of a sterile needle. Her eyes stopped at Winston's things in the corner—his worn leather satchel, vials containing soil in various shades of ochre and brown, his clothes lying in a rust-stained heap on the floor. She felt her legs turn soft, and she sat down, breathing heavily.

She should have been prepared. She had been warned. The juju man with yellowed eyes had told her this would happen. Years ago, he had stood under the dying baobab tree in the center of the Ibadan market and shouted to her— *I go give him spell, I go kill him.* Why Winston, she had wondered then and still wondered now? Why when her husband was helping his people?

The Nigerian doctor came into the room and sat down next to her, as if sitting would somehow soften the blow.

"Mrs. Soong," he said quietly. "Your husband was shot in the chest."

"Shot?" Her voice faltered.

"The bullet punctured his lung, and I performed emergency surgery." He let a little time pass to be sure she understood.

"Was the needle sterile?" Sylvia asked in a small voice, even though she knew it was insignificant now. There were the operating instruments to worry about as well.

The doctor ignored her question. "He's lost a lot of blood and we've run out of Type O. I need you to go back to your compound and round up some donors. Can you do this?"

There wasn't enough blood, she thought, when so much of his blood was everywhere. She tried not to look at his blood-stained clothes in the corner of the room.

"Can you do this?" the doctor repeated.

"Yes, doctor," she said. "Yes."

"Go then. There isn't much time."

Sylvia ran outside into the dark, tropical night. She wanted more than anything to save her husband's life. She wanted to make amends, to right the wrong she had done to him, to be a good woman, at least in her own eyes.

PART ONE

1973-1977

SYLVIA

Chapter 1 1973

Many years ago, Sylvia had given birth at this same hospital. The labor had not been easy, and during the seventeenth hour, the spirit children tried to take her baby. They wrapped the umbilical cord around her daughter's neck. But the American missionary doctor realized this, and she cut Sylvia open to save her. A Yoruba nurse swaddled the baby in white cloth—to protect her from the spirits. But white was the Chinese color of funerals, and when Sylvia saw this, she ripped the cloth off. The baby screamed, flailing her arms and legs. This was the first time they tried to take her child, but it would not be the last.

Winston missed the birth. An overturned lorry, scattering shards of Coca-Cola bottles on the one-lane, orange dirt road, had prevented him from reaching the clinic. When it had been built two decades before, there had been no road, only a leafy footpath through the bush. But it didn't occur to Winston to walk and instead, he turned his car around and went home.

After the birth, Sylvia waited for him in the maternity wing with its sloping tin roof and dusty courtyard of violet bougainvillea. When Winston failed to come, she couldn't help interpreting this as doubt. The disappointment hurt more than the labor itself— that had been a sharp, but temporary physical pain while this was a dull, emotional one that slowly twisted inside of her. Without her husband or family by her side, she instinctively held her baby closer. This tiny, warm body was all she had. After months of not wanting her, suddenly Sylvia clung to her.

· · ·

The evening Sylvia returned home with baby Lila, she ate dinner with Winston on the teak dining room table that came with their house. They ate food that was not theirs—boiled potatoes, dry roast chicken, and green beans prepared by their Nigerian steward, trained only in colonial English cuisine. Like their marriage, the house and the servants had been handed to them without courtship or deliberation.

Sylvia and her husband lived on a compound for expatriates in the town of Ibadan in southwestern Nigeria. Ibadan was known as "between the forest and plains" because it straddled the southern tropical rainforest and the northern dry savannah. The largest village in West Africa, its auburn tin roofs stretched for miles in every direction. The compound was situated on the edge of town, connected by Oyo Road, the same tarmac route that led to the north of the country. Along this road, there were houses with fiery galvanized roofs, cool cement floors, and silhouettes of chickens.

Royal palms and manicured lawns graced the driveways of the expat compound, swimming pools were kept full, and golf courses were watered even during the dry season. They had their own power plant, reservoir and dam, water treatment facility, and a road wide and long enough for emergency evacuation by plane. The streets were laid out on a small grid with identical houses, each fitted with modern Danish furniture, white terrazzo tile, granite stone walls, and glass sliding doors that led to screened porches. Every piece of the house was imported from the West, down to the plumbing in the bathroom, so every time Sylvia flushed the toilet she saw the brand name, *American Standard*.

After nursing her newborn at the dinner table, Sylvia gave Lila to Winston. He seemed to hold her as if she weighed his life down somehow. Was it the roundness of her eyes or her light brown hair? He didn't say anything. But Sylvia felt those words he didn't say. The metal fork in her mouth suddenly seemed sharp, biting against her cheek.

Lila started crying, and Winston hastily gave her back.

"I leave tomorrow morning. First thing," he said.

"Tomorrow? So soon?" Her stomach knotted up into tiny, sharp stones.

"We need to distribute the seeds before the planting season begins." He avoided her eyes. Winston had come to Nigeria bearing "miracle" seeds that promised to triple harvests. It was 1973, and he truly believed these new hybrid seeds, bred in the lab in the West, could wipe out hunger in the children of Africa. Developed by an American scientist, the seeds had successfully eradicated famine in parts of Asia and Latin America.

"How long…how long will you be gone?"

"Three weeks, maybe four."

"The baby…?" Is this why you are leaving, she thought?

"We've hired Patience to help you. She came with the best references," he said curtly. "I'm going to be travelling quite a bit. For my work, as you know."

"Of course," she said, her voice fading. "I just hope ..."

"I must pack." He stood up abruptly from the dining table.

She felt a quiet sadness swirling inside her, slowly gaining momentum. Since the arrival of the baby, she sensed a subtle shift in him as if he were taking a step back, reassessing their relationship and his role in it.

Sylvia looked down, pushing the bland English food around her plate. She wanted to share her thoughts with him, but the paper-thin walls of their relationship were not filled with the cheery, noisy comforts of their mother tongue. Although they were both Chinese, Sylvia and her husband spoke different dialects, forcing them to converse in English. Using adopted English names, they had begun their relationship in a borrowed language.

Sylvia sat alone at the table framed by the tropical garden beyond the screened porch—lush green lawn, majestic gray palm trees, white frangipani blossoms, and leafy banana trees. But the sky was the color of black bats hovering at dusk, and the evening was filled with their eerie chorus.

Chapter 2

Nigeria in 1973, the year of her baby's birth, was full of surprising optimism. In the wake of the Biafran Civil War, the country was still recovering from the massacre of several million Igbo people. But Nigeria was salving its wounds with black gold flowing out of its Southern river delta—the sweet, low-sulfur crude oil, *Bonny Light* that was in high demand by Western oil companies. This sudden influx of cash buoyed the confidence of the new, fledging nation.

The first few weeks after Lila's birth, Winston travelled all over the country, trying to harness this newfound enthusiasm. While her husband was out evangelizing his miracle seeds, Sylvia was left with a crying, colicky newborn. The days blended into nights. Most mornings, when her maid Patience arrived, Sylvia was still in her nightdress, hair uncombed and shadows under her eyes. Sylvia had not wanted motherhood, but now she was in the thick of it, she desperately tried to be a good mother. She responded to her baby's every cry as if trying to overcompensate. She felt Patience watching every misstep, compounding Sylvia's insecurity.

"Give her to me, madam," Patience said one morning, setting her broom against the granite wall. She was a middle-aged, heavyset woman. Her batik wrapper dress was decorated with the smiling faces of a blonde Jesus.

"I don't know if she'll let you," Sylvia hesitated.

"Just give her to me, madam," Patience said in a commanding tone, a servant used to giving orders to less-competent mistresses.

Her baby seemed to disappear into Patience's big arms. Using her wrapper, Patience tied Lila onto her back in snug bundle. Then she gently swayed, continuing to sweep the floor, and within a few minutes, Lila was asleep.

"Dey like to be warm and tight like dat, like in the mama's stomach. Dey don't like dere legs to be free, comprend?" Patience said. "I go take care of so many babies. I know about de babies." Patience spoke a mix of English and French patois, reminiscent of Cote d'Ivoire.

Despite Patience's knowledge of babies, Sylvia had heard through other wives and their gossiping house girls that Patience could not have children herself, so no man in her village wanted to marry her. She had left the remote forests of Cote d'Ivoire to find work in the city of Abijan and was soon hired by a French family. As a young girl, the French family brought Patience to Nigeria because their children were attached to her. Sylvia didn't know why Patience stayed on, even after the children were long grown, and the French family had left. Perhaps, she had been away so long from her Beng tribe in Cote d'Ivoire that she felt she couldn't go back. Like Sylvia, she had adopted an English name, her given Beng name, discarded.

"Why does she cry so much?" Sylvia said. "Is this normal?"

"When she cry, she speak de language of bush spirits," Patience said.

"The bush…?" Sylvia couldn't say the word.

"De babe dey travel de road between de spirits and de living. When a babe is born, my people say it is de return of an ancestor. Comprend?"

Sylvia nodded, even though she did not want to understand.

"She cry because dis earth is worrying her. She want to go back," Patience added.

"Go back where?" Sylvia asked in a small voice.

"To de spirit world. You know about de spirits, madam?"

"Yes," Sylvia said, quietly. "I've seen them before."

Sylvia felt a dull pain radiate out from her stomach. She had witnessed the power of the spirits as a girl in her family's large Shanghai English-style manor. She remembered coming home from school, flinging her satchel on the kitchen table, the cook scowling at her. She ran upstairs to her three-year old sister's room. Mei Mei had been sick with tuberculosis for several weeks, but that day, Sylvia opened the door and found her bed empty, stripped of its linens beneath the open lattice window. Then she saw her mother crouched in the corner, rocking herself, her eyes glazed. "The hungry ghosts took her," her mother whispered hoarsely. After her Mei Mei's death, Sylvia and her siblings were raised in the shadow of these hungry ghosts.

"All de little babies, dey are still spirits," Patience continued, but her voice seemed far away to Sylvia. "Dey will want to go back. You have to work work to keep dem here, you hear? Make dem happy, *non*?"

Sylvia knew she didn't deserve to be a mother, not after all her negative thoughts while the child had been in the womb. She felt the spirits judged her for this.

"Give me Lila," Sylvia said, suddenly panicking. She didn't like that her baby had disappeared into a bundle in Patience's wrap.

Until Lila's umbilical cord fell off, Patience explained, Lila was still fully in the spirit world. In parts of West Africa, if a newborn died, no funeral was arranged. Still a spirit, the baby was not yet considered part of the living world. During these precarious first few weeks, mothers watched over their babies closely, making sure they were still breathing. Sylvia held Lila, slept with her, and picked her up when she made the slightest cry. Those first few weeks when Winston was gone were the most difficult. Lila was not gaining weight, and the doctor was worried. She had difficulty nursing and she cried from hunger. Sylvia sensed Lila's hold on life was weak, and this made her hold onto her baby more.

When Lila was two weeks old, her umbilical cord still had not fallen off. Sylvia was sitting on the screened porch overlooking the garden. Lila had just woken up from a nap, and Patience handed her over. Sylvia noticed her baby was uncommonly quiet. This eerie silence was like the eye of a hurricane, a warning of something raging inside her child.

"She's burning up," Sylvia said, feeling her forehead.

"I will go get de thermometer. Try feed her, madam. De milk is good for her." Patience spoke calmly while Sylvia's nerves verged on the edge of calamity.

Sylvia tried to nurse her baby, but Lila threw up the milk. She was shriveling up before her eyes, losing weight quickly. Patience put the thermometer under Lila's arm, then held it up in the light. The mercury registered 102 degrees. Sylvia knew it was dangerous for newborns to contract a fever in the first month of their lives. If something happened to Lila, what would happen to her? Sylvia's life and Lila's were intertwined now.

"Her spirit is still strong, but her earthly body is weak, *non?*" Patience said. "De babies, dey cross over from de spirit world to de earth. Every day, dey are less spirit and more earth. But sometimes de crossing is not easy."

Sylvia feared the spirits were punishing her. She would have to use all the tools of modern medicine to fight them. She drove to the small clinic on the compound with Patience sitting in the backseat holding Lila. Her baby was barely moving or crying now.

At the clinic, the Nigerian nurse turned to Patience, "You go wait here, you hear?"

"She's coming with me," Sylvia said, grabbing Patience by the hand. They went together into the doctor's office with the nurse following, annoyed at this infraction of an invisible rule.

"Sit down, love," the doctor said to her, ignoring Patience. He was an older, English man who had worked in Nigeria for over twenty years, a relic from colonial times.

Sylvia explained Lila's symptoms to the doctor.

"It's probably malaria. I'll do a blood test to confirm." He checked Lila's vital signs.

"Malaria?" Sylvia stood up suddenly. She and Winston took bitter white pills every Sunday to ward off this dangerous disease. But as a newborn, Lila was vulnerable to these bloodthirsty mosquitoes.

"Don't worry, love. It'll be alright. It's early in the process." The doctor put his hand on her shoulder as if forcing her to sit down. "The chloroquine should stave off the malaria, but she's dehydrated from the fever and her inability to hold food down. I'm going to put her on an IV. She'll need to stay here for a few nights."

Sylvia knew dehydration could kill babies. Her own mouth felt dry and parched in this heat. She glanced over at Patience for some kind of reassurance. Patience nodded at her, as if to confirm the doctor's words, but seemed uncomfortable speaking with the doctor in the room.

The nurse took them to another room. She laid Lila in a plastic crib and pierced her translucent skin with an IV needle, nourishing her with sugar water. Sylvia sat there, twisting her long locks into knots, falling back into this childhood habit. Ever since Lila's birth, Sylvia's hair had looked ragged and shorn haphazardly because of the knots, her once beautiful hair cannibalized by her anxiety.

"Madam, don't worry. De doctor will help her, *non*?" Patience said.

"And the spirits?"

"Dey will have to fight de doctor. Dey will have to fight you."

"Me?"

"You and God. I will pray. Pray to our almighty God and sweet Jesus to help her. I know dey will help."

"I'm not Christian. I'm Chinese...Buddhist."

"God go help everyone. He no care you be Chinese, Nigerian, Budd whateva. He help. I go pray."

Patience got down on her knees and closed her eyes, muttering.

Sylvia wasn't sure about this Western God, but she *knew* spirits existed. She wasn't going to take any chances with them. She wondered if the spirits were trying to take her child because she had somehow incurred their wrath. She knew the circumstance of her marriage with Winston was not normal and it went against social taboo. Sylvia would learn later that she should have sacrificed a chicken to apologize to the local spirits at Lila's birth. But she was at the mercy of what Patience told her or remembered. Patience never mentioned this chicken ritual, so the spirits reminded Sylvia of her spiritual debt by inflicting sickness and disease on her child.

Not fully understanding the spiritual origins of Lila's illness, there were so many things Sylvia could have done. Trying to understand, Sylvia consulted anthropology books about Patience's Beng culture many years later. She should have washed Lila after birth with the traditional black soap and lemon, used by Patience's people only for newborns or corpses. The black soap, made by female elders, facilitated the transition between life and death. But Patience overlooked this detail, perhaps the black soap was too hard to make or find. Whatever the reason, Sylvia did not follow all of these rituals and Lila's crossing from the afterlife to the earthly life was troubled from the start.

The blood test confirmed Lila had contracted malaria, and the nurse added chloroquine to her IV. She cried from the fever, and the nurse shook her head.

"I won't let you take my baby away," Sylvia said out loud to the spirits, to God, to whoever would listen. Her defiant voice reverberated across the bare tiles and white walls of the compound clinic. It was Sylvia's affirmation, her oath as a mother. She needed to hear it herself.

When evening came, the nurse made up the bed next to Lila's plastic cot for Sylvia. Patience lay a blanket on the floor and went to sleep, but Sylvia couldn't sleep. Lila barely stirred, and Sylvia put her hand on Lila's chest throughout the night to make sure she was still breathing.

Eventually, Sylvia drifted off to sleep. When she woke up, it was light, and the nurse was in the room, checking Lila's vital signs. It was seven in the morning, and Patience was already sitting by Lila's cot. Sylvia's breasts felt hard, and her blouse was soaked with milk.

"Is she alright?" Sylvia said.

"Yes, she's doing betta. Her fever is down," the nurse said. "De medicine is working."

Sylvia went over to Lila's cot. Her baby started to cry as soon as she smelled the milk on her blouse.

"She go feed her de milk. It will be good for her. Can you take dis thing off?" Patience said, pointing at the IV.

The nurse ignored her, pretending she was not even in the room.

"Woman, I go speak to you, eh," Patience repeated. "You go be deaf?"

"Can you ask the doctor?" Sylvia said, desperately. Lila was crying for her now, and her breasts were leaking.

"I go ask him," the nurse said and quickly left the room.

The English doctor appeared and took Lila off the IV. The nurse was nowhere in sight.

"Looks like we've got a hungry baby. That's a good sign, love," the English doctor said, smiling at Sylvia.

Lila nursed hungrily. It was the first time in her young life that she had eaten so well.

The next day, Lila's umbilical cord fell off, and her daughter began the difficult journey from the spirit to the earthly world. According to Patience, this process usually took a child seven years. But would Lila even make it to seven years?

Chapter 3

The black plantain birds feasted on the ripe bananas rotting in the late afternoon sun. Winston returned home that afternoon, after four weeks away.

"The baby was ill while you were gone," Sylvia said.

"How is she?" Winston asked, flatly. The lack of emotion in his voice bothered her.

"She's fine now, but it's hard...you're away so much."

They sat at their dining table on the screened porch. Outside, the breeze scattered fragile, white frangipani blossoms, a deceptive beauty with poisonous white blood leaking from its stems.

"I'm sorry. I know I've been travelling quite a bit," he acknowledged. "I have no choice." But he didn't look directly at her when he spoke. They had been married now for over a year, and he still couldn't look in her eyes. Sylvia felt lonely even when her husband was sitting right next to her.

"I understand. You have important work to do. I don't want to get in the way," she said, but she felt something akin to resentment even though she admired him for his work.

"You should sign up for that nursing program at the university.

Like you planned," he said. "It will keep you busy. Give you something to do while I'm gone."

"I can't right now. I can't leave Lila, it's too dangerous. She needs me."

"I think Patience can manage."

"I can't leave her right now. You don't understand. The spirits are after her."

"Spirits? You believe this nonsense?"

"It's not nonsense, and you know it."

"Why don't you go to the wives' coffee mornings? Richard's wife, Elizabeth, goes to these things." He spoke to her as if she were a child, making her feel their ten-year age difference. He was trying to help, but somehow he made her feel worse.

She ate her dinner in silence. Winston went over to the small altar with a framed photograph of his deceased mother in the corner of the living room. Patience put a bowl of fresh fruit on the altar every day at his request. He bowed three times, a daily ritual he performed without fail when he was home. Then he retreated to his study.

• • •

She had met Winston at a Chinese Student Association party at the University of Reading. She had just left her English boyfriend, even though she was pregnant. Sylvia hadn't told anyone, not even her lover, who she knew would only propose marriage. She had spent the week in despair, twisting her hair into complicated knots that she had to trim with her nail scissors. Pregnancy had ruined her plans. She didn't want to live an ordinary life; in fact, she craved the extraordinary, even though she knew it was silly of her. But now here she was, like any other girl, on the precipice of marriage and children. She feared being trapped in a tiny English village unfriendly to foreigners—an isolated, uneventful life. So instead, she spent the morning standing outside the abortion clinic in the rain. She stood there for hours until she was damp and cold, but still she couldn't go in. Her hands shook with the memory of her cousin hemorrhaging from a botched abortion in Hong Kong.

That evening, she didn't know why, but she let her roommate talk her into attending the Chinese Student Association party. Sylvia walked into the crumbling common room with tall, drafty windows and an ornate carpet patterned with downtrodden violet roses. It was the usual crowd of Hong Kong students, a tight-knit circle she had avoided because they reminded her too much of home, of her parents. The men talked only of how to make money or how to save it. The women, dressed in neat little Chanel or Dior suits, reeked of designer perfume. It made her feel nauseous, dizzy, and full of doubt about coming. Then she noticed Winston standing taller than most of the men around him.

"I just got a job in Africa," Winston said in English. Most likely a Northerner, she assumed he didn't speak Cantonese like the rest of the party. She moved in closer to listen.

"Why go backwards to somewhere worse off than where we just came from?" One Chinese student mocked him.

"You think *here* is better than where we came from?" Winston said.

"I think England is horrible," Sylvia said suddenly. Everyone turned to stare at her, including Winston. She wasn't sure why she spoke, but something compelled her, perhaps Winston himself, standing there awkwardly, the others not appreciating his uniqueness.

"Well, why don't you go with him? He'll be lonely out there

without his people," the same student joked. Then he turned to Winston. "Isn't that the reason you've graced us with your presence at these parties. Looking for a wife?"

Everyone laughed, and Winston looked down at the floor.

An hour later, the party was in full swing, but she noticed Winston heading toward the door. She followed him. She didn't know why, except that somehow she didn't want to lose him. He intrigued her.

"You're leaving too?" She called after him.

"I don't like parties much," he said, not looking up. The two of them walked down the campus path in the cold night. Around them were tall stone buildings with stained glass windows. The bare, thorny rose bushes cast dark shadows on the path.

"I hate those parties too. All their talk about the latest designer handbag or Rolex watch bores me," she said, her breath blowing like smoke in the winter air.

He glanced at her. "Can I walk you home?"

She nodded.

"So I assume you didn't study business or finance," she said.

"Got a PhD in Soil Science. I'm going to work on an agricultural aid project in Africa. With new hybrid seeds, we can double harvests. No one should be starving anymore."

"Why Africa?"

"Because I can't go back to China. Where our own people are starving."

She had never met anyone pursuing something so lofty. "I wanted to study nursing, but my father said no."

In fact, her father had refused to let her see or touch naked, bloody bodies. In her father's eyes, women were ornaments. It was obvious in the way he treated her mother, dressed in silk and jewels, his arm possessively around her. Her parents had attended endless parties in Hong Kong with her brothers in tow, but Sylvia had been left at home with the amah.

"My father forced me to study Home Economics," she continued, embarrassed. Everyone knew it was the "get-married" degree.

"You should do nursing," Winston said. "My father wanted me to study Chinese literature. I ignored him."

"You did?" She laughed at the thought of doing something so rebellious. But he was right. She should have studied nursing and she hoped he wouldn't think less of her. They stood awkwardly in the doorway of her dormitory now.

"You know you can still do nursing in Africa," he said, suddenly.

"Even without a degree?"

"I'm sure they'll take any volunteers they can get."

She didn't know if he was asking her to go with him or just giving her advice.

"Really?" she said, in disbelief that it could be that easy. She felt as if her conversation with him was already resetting her path or at least its possibilities. They were silent for a few minutes.

"I have…I have tickets," he stumbled over his words. "To the Royal Albert Hall. In London next weekend. Do you want to go?" He seemed shy and looked to the side when he asked her.

"I'd love to."

She smiled up at him in the dim light. She guessed he was in his early thirties. She was only twenty-one. He had a kind face, even though he seemed a bit distant. It was the first time in days she had felt something other than despair. She recognized it as hope.

That next weekend, he came to the women's hall to pick her up. He was oddly dressed in a mismatched blazer and pair of trousers, probably borrowed, but she found it endearing, especially after the slick, tailored suits of her Hong Kong friends. They caught an afternoon train to London. As the lush, green English countryside glided by their window, they talked of their war-torn childhood.

"When did you leave China?" she said.

"During the war with the Japanese. Before the Communists." He spoke reluctantly, staring out the window. "We fled our estate. Left everything behind. Some vases and paintings worth a fortune."

"At least you got out alive."

Suddenly, he looked as if he were in pain.

She should have been more careful with her words; she bit her lip for talking too much. After that, he clammed up, and they both stared out the window in silence. She wanted to tell him about her predicament. Winston seemed unconventional to her, not like a typical Chinese man, but would he understand? In her mind, she was ready to go to Africa with him. But was he ready to go with her?

During the symphony performance, Winston seemed captured by the music, and afterward, his mood lightened. They took the underground to Leicester Square and walked to London's Soho Chinatown. With five-floors and greasy plastic seats, Wong Kei was famous for its noodles and *won ton* soup. The waiter put them at a large round table with a family full of noisy children. Like most Cantonese restaurants, Wong Kei was not known for its customer service or romantic ambience.

Surrounded by the clatter of chopsticks, slurping of soup and barking waiters, Sylvia looked sideways at her date. Winston was not conventionally handsome, but when he walked into a room, people noticed. He had the solid build and height that characterized the northern Chinese and their diet of steamed *mantou* buns and thick, wide noodles.

"When are you going to Africa?" she said.

"In a month."

"Are you really looking for a wife to go with you?" she mustered up the courage to ask.

"Yes, but no Chinese girl wants to go to Africa. They all want to stay here. Or go to America."

"I would go...except I have problems—" she said, looking down.

"You would go?" Winston interrupted. "You would marry me?"

"You don't want to hear what my problem is?"

"I can guess," he said, but he didn't look at her.

• • •

Winston and Sylvia were married by the end of the month before any sign of her belly showed. It was a small wedding with a borrowed wedding dress, dry cake, and cheap champagne, nothing at all like a Chinese wedding with its twelve-course banquet, red envelopes, and multiple silk gowns worn by the bride throughout the evening. None of their parents travelled from Hong Kong or Taiwan for the wedding. That night Winston touched her, fumbling with her bra. Afterward, she held him like a child, stroking his hair. The next day, they boarded a flight to Nigeria.

Chapter 4

After her baby's birth, three months went by with Winston travelling to countries Sylvia had never heard of—Ghana, Benin, Sierra Leone, and Cameroun. She felt the distance he was putting between them.

She found the nights in Africa were not silent. They were filled with the shrill chorus of nocturnal insects and the constant undertone of drumming coming from town. Alone in her white-tiled house in the middle of a vast garden, she felt the isolation of this place—a solitary figure in the savannah, invisible villages hiding in the darkness. She had grown up in crowded, garishly-lit, urban Asia, constantly jostled by sweating people. She missed that cramped life, people in small places.

While Winston was away, Sylvia woke up at all hours of the night, responding to Lila's every whim. She was discovering that the soft, pastel love of her baby had a dark, hushed-up, twilight kind of underside. Lila was colicky and had bouts of unexplained crying, especially at night. Sylvia knew it was the spirits' doing.

One night, when Lila was three months old, her crying suddenly drove Sylvia to the edge of what felt like madness.

Sylvia got out of bed, picked up Lila's wicker bassinet, and walked quickly down the hallway. She placed the bassinet on the floor of the car and started the ignition. She found the repetitive hum and vibration of the car was the only way to calm her baby.

Fenced in from the real Africa, she circled around the identical houses and smooth lawns of the expatriate compound built to mimic an American suburb with its own swimming pool, clubhouse, and golf course. She never left the confines of the compound except to buy food and supplies at the local market. But tonight, as she drove the smooth concrete streets, doing her usual loop to lull Lila to sleep, she could only think of fleeing. She heard the music coming from the town, a muted rhythm and voice over the static of an old amplifier. She had to leave this place and take her baby somewhere safe. At the fork in the road, instead of turning to go home, she swerved up the hill lined with royal palms, toward the gatehouse.

The night watchman stopped her car at the tall, white gates flanked by a cement wall lined with shards of broken glass, separating them from the town outside.

"Madam, where are you going at dis time of night?" The night watchmen were Hausa, a northern warrior tribe known for their black, carved arc-shaped swords. They were hired because they held a natural suspicion and disdain for the local Yoruba tribe, making them immune to bribes from the local population.

"I have to leave this place," Sylvia said with determination, even though she had no idea where she was going.

The night watchman looked Sylvia over. She was dressed only in a white silk robe and slippers.

He said, shaking his head, "Sorry madam, but I cannot let you out of dese gates. It is not safe dis time of night, you hear?"

Bands of robbers prowled the deserted road at night, ready

to pounce on imported Peugeots or Mercedes—cars of affluent Nigerians and expatriates. Sylvia knew this, but she didn't care about the dangers of night driving. Suddenly, she craved the chaos, stench, and teeming crowds of the town beyond the compound walls. It reminded her more of home than the quiet, clean American suburban feel of the compound. She had never lived in an American suburb; she didn't know what kind of life they were trying to recreate in the middle of Africa.

"But I have to go. I have to leave," she said. Sand flies feasted on her exposed arms, but in her state, she did not notice.

On the other side of the gate, a Peugeot pulled up, entering the compound. The security guard went over and murmured something to the car's driver. Sylvia noticed it was the young doctor, Ayo Ogunlesi, coming back from his clinic in town. It was one o'clock in the morning. The doctor parked his car and strode over to her. Suddenly, Sylvia felt embarrassed. She knew there was no logic to her impulsive plan. How would she explain this to the young doctor? She wanted to turn around and speed home, but her hands seemed stuck to the wheel, and she couldn't move.

She had seen Ayo a couple of times at the clubhouse and pool on the compound. It was hard not to notice him. He was of African-English descent; his mother was English and his father Nigerian, a taboo marriage against all odds during colonial times. His unique looks—skin, the color of terra cotta, hazel-tinted eyes, a face where cultures collided. It was a sort of talent, these extraordinary good looks, these far-flung genes that had produced this novelty.

"It's Sylvia, right?" he said, coming up to her car window. "It's a bit late for you to be driving around outside. But you know that, I presume." As he spoke, he dug his hands into his pockets.

28

When she didn't respond, he said, "Right, let me take you home."

Sylvia let him help her out of the car. He put his arm around her and coaxed her into the passenger seat. Then he got into her car and drove her back to her house. She felt him glance over at her bare legs. She tried to pull her short silk robe toward her knees. She felt even more agitated, her nerves complicated now by this man sitting next to her. Her long black hair fell over her face, and she kept brushing it back nervously. She felt his attractiveness, and it put her on guard. She kept her face averted, staring out the window, turned away from him. The night air rushed in through the open windows—a faint scent of the thorny bougainvillea blossoms and the smoke of slowly dying cooking fires and burning garbage.

He parked the car in her garage, but she didn't move. He reached across her to open the door, his arm lightly brushing her body. That sent her scrambling out of the car, her heart pounding from the adrenalin of fleeing and the closeness of this man. He carried the bassinet into her house with Lila screaming. She needed to nurse her to calm her down. She leaned down to pick up her baby, inadvertently revealing her full breasts. He looked away, saying, "I'll get your housegirl."

He went to the servants' quarters built behind each house, the one architectural feature on the compound that was unique to colonial Africa. When he came back with Patience, Sylvia was sitting on the sofa, half-naked, nursing her baby in her silk white robe. She felt dazed and not quite herself. She only thought of calming Lila. With his eyes averted, Ayo took his leave.

Her eyes followed the outline of his broad shoulders as he walked out the door. In the distance, she could hear the harmony of voices and electric guitar matched by a rhythm of talking drums. It was nothing like the music of her culture—the dissonant falsetto voice of Chinese opera or the melancholy wail of the Chinese violin. She thought the music of Africa was filled with joy.

• • •

A few days later at Patience's insistence, Sylvia ventured out to the compound wives' coffee hosted by her neighbor, an Indian woman named Meghal. As she walked out of the house without her baby, Sylvia felt empty-handed, as if she were missing an appendage. She wanted to return home, but she instead she kept walking. A part of her was trying to please her husband, just as she worked to please her father. She was trying to do the right thing, even though inside, it felt all wrong.

She thought of Baba, a Latin-handsome playboy from Shanghai, an accomplished swimmer and businessman. Every year her father swam the Hong Kong Harbor race, gulping the grimy water and sweeping the trophies. After the race, he would throw a huge party at their Hong Kong penthouse overlooking the harbor, serving delicacies like sea cucumber, illegally harvested from the sea. Her father always smelled of cigarettes and chlorine from swimming pools. He had a foul temper and often slapped Sylvia for something as trivial as dropping bits of sticky rice on the floor as they ate dinner. As a child, she had walked on eggshells in his company. She worked hard to please him, to do as he said, or risk the wrath of his erratic temper. Sometimes at night he would fall asleep, sitting up in his bed with a cigarette dangling from his mouth. She feared one day he would burn them all to death. She was glad Winston didn't chain smoke.

Sylvia knocked on her neighbor's door, and the maid let her in. Meghal's house was identical to Sylvia's with the same standard-issue Danish furniture, except it was adorned with objects from Meghal's homeland—Indian silk woven carpets, a tiger's skin, and paintings of the blue god, Shiva. In contrast, Sylvia had noticed the Europeans filled their houses with souvenirs from their travels throughout Africa—Kenyan soapstone sculptures, Nigerian thorn carvings, and Fulani tapestries.

Richard's wife, Elizabeth, waved to Sylvia. Elizabeth was a tall, robust, blonde Englishwoman, raised in Kenya. To her, Africa was home.

"Do join us, dear," she said cheerfully, although Sylvia felt it was forced. Elizabeth was simply being kind because their husbands were colleagues.

Sylvia sat down with the mostly British crowd that surrounded the glass coffee table full of dainty Indian desserts. Not knowing what else to do, she reached out and tried a creamy white square. It was full of cardamom and pistachio nuts, and she liked its vaguely perfumed taste.

The English women continued to chat.

"You really should work on your backhand dear," Elizabeth said.

"You know who could teach you," another English woman said.

"Oh him, he's too busy being a doctor, saving the poor brown children. I doubt he even notices me," a young, redhead said.

"It was just a suggestion. You know, to pass the time."

They all giggled like schoolgirls. Sylvia immediately felt left out of the conversation, and no one made any attempt to include her. It reminded her of her British school in Hong Kong. Sylvia had been one of the few Chinese girls at the school, constantly left out of the English girls' games and chatter. Dressed in the same green uniform as the blonde girls, her black hair stood out. She had hated that school, but her father insisted that all his children should be educated in English, and he refused to send them to the local Chinese school. She knew he had been thinking about their future. She and her siblings went to the UK for university, presumably to a better life. But when she thought about her life so far, she wasn't sure if that school had been worth it.

Sylvia glanced over at the small group of Indian women, they were speaking Hindi. Meghal, her host, noticed Sylvia was uncomfortable, and she came over to sit by her.

"Did you like the sweets?" Meghal said. She was a pretty woman with long, thick eyelashes and a gorgeous blue sari. "Please, take more."

Sylvia helped herself to a cake-like ball covered in syrup.

"My favorite," Meghal said. "It's called Gulab Janeem."

But then another Indian woman spoke in Hindi, and Meghal went to talk to her.

The wives on the compound were polite enough, but finding themselves trapped in a backwater West African town, they naturally gravitated to the company of their own kind. Sylvia felt they kept her, the only Chinese wife, at arm's length.

• • •

The next morning, Sylvia skipped the wives' coffee. Her driver, Ige, took her to the town market instead. Sylvia preferred the town to the compound, and she used shopping as an excuse to escape.

Outside her car window, a man lay down his colorful, woven plastic mat beside the road and knelt toward Mecca. *Suya* kebabs stuck out of a circular mound of mud, roasted by the flames in the center. Half-dressed children with protruding bellies crammed *Made in China* combs, Bic razors, and synthetic shirts through the open window of her car. Yellow, blue, and pink cement or mud houses with tin roofs lined the road. The skeleton of an unfinished tall building lay abandoned. The builder had run out of money. They travelled on a paved tarmac road, but in parts, the rain had already drilled deep holes, letting the road revert back to its original orange dirt identity. The charred remains of an oil tanker that had crashed into a mud hut and palm tree lay strewn on the side of the road.

A mustard-brown *mammy wagon* stopped in front of her car at the wave of a hand by the roadside. Faces, arms, baskets, and chicken feathers stuck out of the wooden bars that sufficed as windows. On the back of the bus, someone had painted the words: *Are you Ready? Jesus is Coming.*

When they reached the market next to the University of Ibadan, Ige parked the car under a large, shady acacia tree in the dirt lot. Sylvia wandered around the market by herself, browsing the stalls made of scraps of wood, cardboard, corrugated iron and rusty nails. Tins of Nido powdered milk, Elephant Power washing powder, mangos, and pineapples crammed the tiny stalls. Sellers squatted behind mats lined with neat piles of red chili peppers and tomatoes while other vendors, toting large baskets of eggs and fruit on their heads, wove their way through the vibrant crowd. A little boy pushed a deflated bicycle tire with a stick. Chickens and goats wandered through the decrepit stalls, colorful fruit, rotting meat, flies, and throngs of people. She found comfort in the cacophony. It reminded her of home, of the crowded night markets in Hong Kong full of fresh fish, headless frogs, and caged dogs.

She stopped at one stall to buy some stiff, deep blue, *adiera* batik cloth that she used as tablecloths. Out of the corner of her eye, she thought she saw the African-English doctor. When she looked again, Ayo was buying fruit at a stall across the market. He was busy bargaining with the vendor and didn't notice her.

She continued to shop, wondering if he would see her. She was not hard to spot, the only Chinese woman in the market.

"How much?" Sylvia asked.

"Twenty naira, madam, good price for you," the vendor said, a plump woman dressed in a yellow and green wrap with an alligator print.

"This cloth is no good," Sylvia said, shaking her head. "You try to charge me too much! Ten naira."

"Eh, you try to rob me? Fifteen, dat is my last price."

She started to walk off. The vendor called after her sulkily, "Okay, ten naira. Take it."

Suddenly, Ayo was standing next to her.

"Not bad, really. Looks like you've got yourself a real bargain," Ayo said, smiling. "You're more of an expert at this than I am."

"Um…thank you." She felt wary and embarrassed, remembering her last encounter and her state of mind. He must think she was a wreck. She looked up at him and noticed, in the bright African sunshine, his brown curly hair had hints of blond.

"It's bloody hot, isn't it? How about we go inside get a drink?" Ayo said.

She couldn't help feeling drawn to him—his towering height and athletic physique, the jaunty, masculine way he moved, the deep brown of his skin. She followed him even though she knew she shouldn't.

They walked into the cool, air-conditioned supermarket across the street. Its large sign, *Kingsway*, seemed to boast of its superiority. The one Western supermarket chain in town, owned by a Lebanese family, it flaunted an interior lined with chrome shelves, metal carts, and German-made freezers. Perched on those pedestals were imports from the UK—jars of marmite, bottles of blackcurrant Ribena juice, cans of Spam, butter cookies as well as chocolate and champagne. In 1973, the shelves were stocked full of imported items. Nigeria, drunk on its newly discovered oil, embarked on a shopping spree. Still, Sylvia rarely found anything to buy at the supermarket. It was mostly coveted Western food, nothing she found appetizing. She rarely came into the supermarket, preferring the far more "superior" market outside.

They walked up to the lunch bar located at the back of the store. Sylvia sat down on one of the torn plastic yellow stools at the Formica bar. She felt uncomfortable, wondering what she was doing here with this man. She unfolded a sandalwood fan that she kept in her purse and fanned herself nervously.

"Two cokes and some chin-chin, eh? Bring it fast fast de lady is hot and thirsty," Ayo said to the barman in the local pidgin English. Born in two different worlds, he could easily switch between the local pidgin to perfect BBC English.

"Most of the other wives are bloody frightened of coming out of the compound," he said with a laugh. "That lot can't handle the dirt, bits of rotting garbage, throngs of people. But you, you don't seem to mind."

"It's not that different from where I'm from. We've got markets just like this in Hong Kong."

The barman brought their drinks and chin-chin. She wiped the top of the coke bottle with a napkin from her purse and took a long sip.

"So I take it, you're surviving here then?" Ayo ate the crunchy sweet squares known as chin-chin, a popular local snack made from fried dough.

"I suppose…"

"Suppose it must be hard for you with your husband gone all

the time," he said.

She pushed stray strands of hair away from her face, embarrassed that she was such an open book to him.

"Look, is everything alright?" Ayo asked. "Pardon my prying, but I'm a doctor, and I must ask."

"Oh no, I mean yes. My husband's a good man." She realized as a doctor, Ayo probably had protocols for dealing with wives running away in the middle of the night.

"Right, I'm glad to hear that. But honestly, if you need anything, anything at all, even just someone to chat with, please do call." He took out a worn business card from his wallet and handed it to her.

"You don't need to worry about me. You probably have other lives to save."

He suddenly looked as if he were in pain. "I might save one or two, but the rest I fail," he muttered, looking down, the muscles in his arm clenching the sides of his chair. "It's the novice doctor in me I suppose, still unused to the inevitable deaths on my watch." She guessed he was probably in his late twenties, and this was his first assignment out of medical school.

"I always wanted to be a nurse," Sylvia said, her voice resigned as if the dream was in the past and would stay that way.

"You should come to the clinic some time and volunteer. We're always short-handed and could use an extra pair of hands." He looked straight into her eyes.

"I don't know…I can't…I can't leave my baby just yet," she said, but he had stirred something in her long forgotten.

"Of course. Whenever you're ready, we're always here."

"I have to go, but I wanted to thank you…for everything." She suddenly got up from her stool. She held his business card tightly in her hand, the paper getting damp from her sweat.

"No need." He touched her bare arm.

Hours later, as she bathed, she would remember the brief touch of his hand, the spicy aromatic scent of the sandalwood soap reminiscent of her fan, and the promise of something.

WINSTON

Chapter 5

Winston drove down a nameless dirt road through the jungle, the vines and branches striking the sides of his Landrover. He glanced into the forest, the shapeless trees covered in thick vine seemed dark and claustrophobic to him. As he made his way deeper into the forest, the foliage closed in on him, an invisible army camouflaged in leaves. He felt a nagging sense of fear that the road was leading him to a dead-end, a trap from which he would never escape. He pushed this thought from his mind.

Behind him, a small pickup truck followed, carrying bags of hybrid maize seeds. The bags were printed with the insignia of a maize plant, the iconic logo of Cole Agribusiness, an American multinational. As the truck drove over deep potholes, its contents were thrown around. A bag toppled off the truck, yellow seeds spilling onto the dirt road.

He came to a painted house in the middle of the forest. Its mud walls were decorated with red, black, and white geometric patterns. The design had a dizzying effect as if it were an illusion.

Winston wondered if it was a symbol or if it was meant to ward off something. The decorated house, perhaps belonging to the chief, was surrounded by a cluster of plain mud huts. Winston and his colleagues approached the house. Children with flies clustered around their eyes shouted out *O'Ebo*. Their screams served as a warning, and other villagers started to appear. Women, with babies wrapped on their backs, stopped pounding yam and stood by their large, mahogany mortars and pestles, staring at the newcomers.

A rag-tag group of villagers dressed in torn t-shirts and batik wrappers started to congregate. A woman with a baby on her back tripped on a small stone. Winston tried to steady her, but the woman regarded him with suspicion.

Winston thought of his own wife and baby. He knew he had fled them, feeling confused and helpless. He had married Sylvia because he thought she had understood his work, its significance to the world and to him. But since the baby's arrival, he felt she had changed. All her focus went to the baby. She had lost interest in his work, in her dream of nursing, and only seemed resentful of his travelling.

He felt betrayed in some small way, making him retreat. Everything he had learned in his life programmed him to protect himself. He thought of his mother, those dark days hiding in the broken building, the terrible way he had lost her. He had vowed he would never feel that way again. It had become his mantra, a mantra-building wall, monastic-like, holing his heart up in a small, six-by-six foot cell.

Winston's Nigerian colleague, Tunde, explained to the villagers, "Dese men are here with an international NGO. The Agriculture Development Agency, the ADA 2000 project. Dey are working to improve farming in Nigeria. Dey have new solutions. Can we meet with you and your chief?" Tunde was a local agricultural extension worker, a position newly created by the national government to support the project. But Winston noticed the villagers seemed to regard him with caution.

The ADA 2000 project in West Africa was funded by a major philanthropic foundation in New York and donor governments like the United States and the United Kingdom. By distributing free "Starter Packs" with bags of seed, fertilizer, and pesticides to small rural farmers in Nigeria, the project leaders hoped to jumpstart high-yielding hybrid maize production. The goal was to find an initial group to cultivate their land as a demonstration plot and then scale up throughout Nigeria and West Africa. As a partner in the ADA 2000 project, Cole Agribusiness supplied the hybrid maize seeds while the ADA was tasked with distribution, outreach, and training among local farmers.

Winston and his colleague Richard, a thin, sunburned Englishman, sat down with the male villagers, even though he would later learn, it was the women in Nigeria and West Africa who did the bulk of the farming—tending to the crops every day, planting, and harvesting. The men helped seasonally with the hard labor such as clearing new land or making the mounds of dirt to plant new yams. But the women were not called to the meeting, and Winston, not fully understanding the roles of women in farming, did not request their attendance.

Winston and his colleagues sat on a bench on the side of the painted house, their backs leaning against the geometric patterns. In front of the house, a man sat in a pile of wood shavings, holding a large knife. He wielded the knife adeptly, carving a stool from a single piece of wood. They sat waiting for the chief. The villagers assembled around them, staring at the *O'Ebos* or foreigners, and Winston didn't feel entirely welcome. But he noticed one man, wearing a Nigerian All Stars soccer T-shirt, grinning widely at him, seemingly eager to talk.

"My name is Simeon Balewa. I'm de chief Balewa's son," he said, pointing at himself. He was a stout man with a round face, friendly eyes, and like his fellow villagers, three scars engraved into each cheek, the identity marks of his tribe.

"Where are you from?" Simeon looked directly at Winston. "I know de English, but neva seen a man like you." He seemed more educated than your average villager.

"China," Winston responded.

"China? What it look like in China?"

"Much like this but rice paddies," Winston said.

"Like dis?" Simeon said, seeming curious and surprised.

Finally, the chief came out of the painted house. He wore a flowing *agbada*, and Winston felt somewhat intimidated. The chief sat down on a wooden stool held up by ornately carved elephants. A woman poured palm wine from a bright yellow plastic container into an enamel tin cup. Winston winced when he saw the old label for engine oil on the side of the yellow plastic container.

"Please," the chief said as the woman held out another cup to him. The chief wore a fake gold Rolex watch, but Winston noticed the hands of the watch were frozen in time, either broken or the battery needed to be replaced.

Winston took a polite sip of the thick, milky drink. "We're doctors of the soil and plants," he explained.

"Is that so?" the chief retorted, and his eyes narrowed in disbelief. His attitude reflected his thoughts; no doubt he had met many a white man coming to his village promising magic— first it was their God, then their doctors, and now doctors of the dirt.

"These are improved seeds, hybrid seeds. We crossed two different breeds to produce a new, stronger, and healthier plant. You'll get two or even four times more harvest with this improved seed," Richard explained, waving the seeds in his hand with a flourish. It all sounded like a modern Jack and the Beanstalk.

"Eh, what is dis? Dis I neva heard before. You white people, always coming wit something. Promising miracles." The chief let out a loud, raucous laugh.

"We're part of the Green Revolution. Scientists in America made these seeds. They were successful in Asia, where I come from. Before, people were starving. Now, everyone's belly is full," Winston said, patting his own stomach for effect.

"Ha! Da Green Revolution, eh! Dis is new; I haven't heard of dis one. Who is it going to make rich dis time?" The chief clapped his hands loudly and rubbed them together, but Winston noticed Simeon listening intently.

"This Starter Pack we will give each of you for free," Winston continued. "It should be enough to plant a one hectare plot." He showed them the contents of the Starter Pack—a ten-kilogram bag of hybrid maize seeds, a fifty-kilo bag of nitrogen fertilizer, and a small pesticide backpack containing a hand-pumped sprayer. The ADA 2000 Starter Pack program was part of the American aid package to West Africa, millions of dollars pledged, then used to purchase the seeds and inputs from Cole Agribusiness.

"Free, eh?" the chief looked even more suspicious. "What you tink I am? I am not stupid. Noting is for free in dis world."

"Can we look at your farms?" Winston changed the subject. He could see they weren't making progress with the chief. He thought they might fare better talking to the individual villagers, and he wanted to talk to Simeon directly.

The chief waved his hand dismissively. He said to Simeon,

"Son, show dem de fields."

The "fields" were small, random, slash and burn clearings in the forest, each one full of tomato, cassava, cowpeas, and okra. In between the plants were piles of dirt, some three feet tall. Simeon dug into one of these mounds with his machete, producing a large, gray-brown tuber.

Without the chief, the men were more talkative.

"Don't listen to my fatha. He is of de old way. But not me. I practice de new way. I go to missionary school. Ma wife and I, we practice family planning. You know dis? Family planning? We only have four children," Simeon said.

"He only has four children because he has problems...you know da kind I'm talking about," another villager laughed.

"How was your last harvest?" Winston asked the villagers.

"No good, sah. We had small small rain last year," Simeon said.

Winston opened a bag of the high-yielding maize seeds. He scooped up a handful and showed the villagers. These were the seeds of plenty, manufactured from the good intentions of Western science. Winston, the bearer of these seeds to Africa, on that first sunny day, was himself bewitched by their promises.

• • •

After several months of peddling the seeds, Winston's truck of seeds was still just that—full of seeds. Of the small number of Starter Packs that had actually been distributed, half had been left unused and pecked by chickens while industrious wives had sold the other half at the market. These same wives poured out the pesticide and used the empty metal canisters and backpacks for carrying water. Winston estimated that some of the buyers at these industrious wives' stalls might have planted some seeds.

But without the fertilizers and pesticides, he didn't know if the laboratory-bred seeds would work their magic.

All in all, Winston knew, the last few months had not been particularly successful. But he told himself, it was only the beginning, although he had envisioned a different kind of beginning altogether. He dreamed of being a hero of sorts, saving the world from hunger and all that. But was he really after saving lives or was he trying to salvage his own life? The question waged a quiet tug of war in the back of his mind.

Winston and Richard drove to the same painted house in the forest outside the town of Ife, about fifty miles east of their compound in Ibadan. Simeon greeted them, smiling, "My fatha is at a funeral in anotha village. But please, please, welcome to my village."

Without the chief around, Winston hoped they would have success with Simeon and the younger generation of the village.

Simeon showed Winston and Richard his home and introduced them to his wife, Abike. Winston squinted as he entered the dark, smoky mud hut. As his eyes adjusted, he could make out a small fire in the middle of the hut and some straw sleeping mats in the corner. Simeon seemed somewhat embarrassed by his living quarters.

"Your hut is nice and cool," Winston complimented Simeon. "The palm leaf roof creates a breeze unlike the tin roof bungalows the British built. It's so hot in those."

"You tink so?" Simeon said, confused. "I like de British house betta."

"Well, then you'll have to get air condition," Winston said, and Simeon grinned.

Winston stepped out of the hut and stood in the middle of the village. Flies buzzed around his shoes, attracted by the animal dung from the cattle and goats kept inside the village walls at night. Women with babies strapped to their backs crouched on the ground crushing alligator pepper to flavor their stews— reddish brown seeds from the pods of trumpet-shaped purple flowers, a cardamom-like peppery spice known by Portuguese traders as the grains of paradise. Children with protruding navels, the telltale sign of malnutrition, clustered around him. Although the Western media concentrated on famine in their stories, Winston knew the lack of protein in growing children was the more insidious killer on the continent.

Simeon led them to the fields bordering the village.

"Can we take some samples of your soil?" Winston asked. "We need to test its nutrient levels in order to decide how much fertilizer you will need."

"Yes, yes of course," Simeon said.

Winston set to work with a group of villagers watching. He put on rubber gloves to avoid contaminating the soil sample with the calcium chloride in his own sweat. He first scraped leaves and manure from the surface of the soil. Then he pushed a long metal probe into the ground about a foot deep. The probe pulled up a core of soil in its tube, which he emptied into a clean, plastic bucket. He did this several more times, then carefully put the soil samples into plastic bags, which he placed in a cooler full of ice for transporting back to the lab. The ice kept the soil cold to avoid mineralization caused by the heat.

After he was done, they walked back to the shade of a thatched canopy made of dried palm leaves, built at the center of the village. A group of villagers followed them and sat down, the group quickly increasing in size.

"I will bring stools to sit on," Simeon said to Winston and Richard, embarrassed that his countrymen sat on straw mats on the ground. Simeon returned with intricately carved wooden stools for them.

"I don't think your father will notice we took the samples, the cores were very small," Winston said.

"No problem, no problem. My fatha is backward. If we follow him, we no move to de future."

"My father was like that too. He didn't want me to study science and come to the West," Winston said.

"We can't listen to dem. Dey are of de old ways." Winston recognized that impatient, dissatisfied tone of youth in Simeon's voice. "I want to be like de English wit lights and TV and air con."

Winston understood what that glimpse into the modern Western world could do, how it made you look at your own people, how it drove you to want something more. He had felt that same longing when he first saw a visiting American professor's house in Taipei. In the professor's house on campus, there was a flush toilet with a seat. It was so clean, Winston was impressed; he was obsessively hygienic. After that, he couldn't use the Chinese latrine, that reeking hole in the ground. He was embarrassed at how backward his people were. They used to be the Chinese Empire and they had fallen to this.

"Listen, plant our seeds. You'll get two or three times more harvest," Winston explained. "Sell the surplus at the market. Eventually, you'll make enough money to buy a TV and an electricity generator. You can have lights and air condition in your house too."

"Is that so?" Simeon said. "De whole village will go envy me, eh?"

"Not me, brotha," said a tall, well-built man with a permanent scowl on his face. Simeon introduced him as Oluwa, his brother-in-law, married to his eldest sister.

"Oluwa, you're as backward as my fatha. No wonder my sister married you. You not smart enough to study at de missionary school. Dey send you home," Simeon said, laughing at him.

"I don't want your T.V. or whateva," Oluwa said, angry now. "I grow enough to feed my family. We take de left over, and my wife sells at de market. Enough we can buy all de tings we need."

"Tst Simeon, you de one stupid," Oluwa continued, pointing to Simeon. "Dey go be robbing you blind, eh."

"If you grow more maize, you can also use the extra cash to hire someone to help you on the farm," Winston said, trying another approach.

"But, why would I want to do dat?" Oluwa said, appearing ready for a good fight.

"So you can relax, sit under this tree, and enjoy the lovely view," Richard said, grinning. "Like so." He sat down, crossed his legs, and pretended to enjoy the view of the towering jungle beyond the village.

"But dat is what I do now." Oluwa's wide eyes looked indignant, and he looked around at his fellow villagers, his eyes bulging and his mouth stretched in an expression of ridicule. The other men laughed, but Simeon did not join in the laughter.

Winston didn't know what to say. In one sentence, the man had questioned the core of capitalism—the grow more, want more, get rich mentality. Winston felt uncomfortable and suddenly out of place as if he and Richard had been accidently dropped in the jungle, bundled haphazardly in some sort of aid care package. He imagined the villagers staring in awe but then quickly casting it (and them) aside. He didn't like the way Oluwa had laughed at their expense as if hinting at some superior knowledge of the way things would turn out in the end. There was some truth to what Oluwa was saying. Perhaps Oluwa could see right through him, see him for the charlatan he might be, nothing more than a man with a bag of tricks. Winston stood up abruptly and took his leave. Only Simeon took a Starter Pack and agreed to plant the hybrid maize seeds as a demonstration plot on his small farm. Winston and Richard drove off in silence; the orange dirt swirled in front of their jeep, caking the windshield with a layer of dust.

SYLVIA

Chapter 6

Sylvia had married Winston as an escape, but in reality, she found herself in a prison full of large rooms, high fences, and the solitary company of herself. She kept the young doctor's card in her pocket for a few days, touching it occasionally before eventually placing it underneath a dusty stack of canned Chinese food in her kitchen pantry. She didn't know why she hid it there or why she had to hide it at all. But she knew Winston wouldn't have any reason to enter the pantry and the servants could not read.

While she was in the pantry, Sylvia stood staring at the rows of canned Chinese food around her. She had forced the essence of her culture into the boundaries of a suitcase, cramming her bags with bottles of soy sauce, sweet lychees, fermented black bean sauce, and dried *ro sung* pork purchased in London's Chinatown. Since Lila's birth, these bottles and tins had sat on the shelves of her pantry, collecting dust. Suddenly, her mouth watered for her forgotten food. She took a tin of sweet lychees off the shelf and walked into the kitchen she had seldom used, looking for a can opener.

In an effort to make something of her marriage and life, she turned to the food of her culture. It required great improvisation to cook Chinese food in Africa. With her steward Energy's help, she planted dark, leafy green Chinese vegetables in the back garden. She found a local supply of soybeans on the compound, an experimental plot grown by the scientists.

She made the tofu from scratch. It was a labor-intensive process that involved soaking the beans for several days until they were soft. Then she strained the creamy mixture through a cheese cloth to produce the liquid soymilk which she poured into a plastic Tupperware container. She placed several of Winston's heavy books on top to harden the tofu. It was a labor of love, an effort to please her husband, all of her loneliness and longing went into this process.

Sylvia cut pieces of her fresh, white tofu and cooked it together with chili peppers and ground pork, making Winston's favorite spicy tofu dish. She fried up the tough beef from the "meat man," who came door-to-door with bloody shanks hanging on a metal rod across his shoulder. The West African cow was a skinny creature with a large bony bump protruding from its back.

She served the spicy tofu, beef and broccoli, steaming garlic noodles, and fried shrimp to her husband. Like a dutiful Chinese wife, she kept replenishing his plate throughout the meal, making sure it was never empty. This was the first meal she had prepared for him since their marriage and arrival in Nigeria. It was a small, unspoken way to show some kind of affection toward him, a substitute for the physical embrace she so craved. She watched him eat, shoveling the food into his mouth as if he had been starving the past few months. She realized he missed their food just as much as she.

"You're a good cook," Winston said, his mouth full of her homemade tofu. He smiled at her, it was a crooked smile, a half-smile, his eyes still did not meet hers, but she held onto this little sign of love. She was starved for any kind of affection and wanted to be close to him.

That night, she offered herself to Winston in bed. But the roles were reversed. He was like an ancient Chinese bride, face hidden behind an opaque red veil, a distant stranger in her arms. Long after he was sound asleep, she lay awake in the dark, listening to the West African highlife music and drumming coming from the town.

Chapter 7

The spirits, particularly the snake spirits, began to assault Sylvia's house. From the dense bamboo bush in the garden, the snakes found their way into the house, slithering through the open pipes that let out condensation from the air conditioner. The first snake to enter the house—a poisonous green mamba—came into Lila's room. She was seven months old, sitting up, playing with her toys on the floor, but not crawling yet. Sylvia stepped out of the room for just a second, assuming since Lila wasn't mobile yet, she couldn't get into any trouble. But the spirits knew her daughter was alone, helpless, and dangerously trapped. The snake came out from under the air conditioner and slithered toward Lila. She stared at it, mesmerized by the moving, bright green scales glittering in the sunlight. As it moved closer, she reached her arms out for it.

• • •

Sylvia heard her baby scream. She and Patience rushed into the room, only to see a flash of green, a snake slithering away. Sylvia grabbed Lila off the floor. Had the snake bitten her? She frantically searched the baby's arms and legs. The bite marks of a green mamba were small and difficult to see, but she was almost sure there were faint red marks on Lila's right arm.

"Sometimes de snake bite, but it no spread poison," Patience said, looking at Lila's arm. "We have go to doctor now now. Dey can fix it." It was a Saturday just after five o'clock and the compound clinic was closed for the weekend. They kept the antivenom for snake bites there. But how much time did they have before the venom spread all over her body and took her?

Sylvia let out a bizarre, animal-like wail, even she didn't realize she could make such a sound. She ran down the hall, her eerie wail carrying beyond the walls of their house. But her neighbors didn't recognize it as human, and no one came to help. Winston was away as usual. Where was he when she needed him? She ran into the kitchen pantry, still holding her crying baby in one arm. She knocked down the tins of Chinese food, looking for Ayo's card.

• • •

Ayo arrived in ten minutes. He kept vials of poly antivenom in the fridge at his apartment, a combination of antivenom concocted for the multitude of snakes in West Africa. The green mamba was a common poisonous snake in the region, not as a fatal as the black mamba, Sylvia had read, but still, death could happen any time between thirty minutes to four hours. Thirty minutes. This random fact terrorized her.

Ayo quickly placed Lila on the couch and examined her arm.

"There's some swelling and bruising round the bite marks, which means the snake injected some venom. But I don't know how much yet," Ayo said as he wrapped Lila's arm in a crepe bandage and splint from his doctor's bag.

53

Then he took out four vials of antivenom and emptied the contents into a syringe.

"I'm going to give her the first dose now. Then, we need to get her to my clinic. Help me hold her down."

Sylvia held her squirming and crying baby down on the couch even though it went against her natural instinct as a mother. All she wanted to do was pick Lila up and comfort her, but instead she had to forcefully hold her down. Lila could not understand, her eyes pleading to be held and comforted. What kind of mother was she? She had left her child alone and vulnerable. She thought of her sister Mei Mei's death. Sylvia felt cold and hot at the same time, and suddenly she was drenched in sweat.

Ayo injected the first dose of the anti-venom, and Lila screamed. Afterward, he picked her up and carefully placed her in Sylvia's arms.

"Keep her arm hanging down, it needs to be lower than her heart. With the bandages and splint, this should slow the spread of the venom," he said as he adjusted Lila in her arms. He spoke calmly and with so much confidence. If she could just anchor herself to him, maybe she would be alright.

He helped Sylvia and her baby into his car. They turned outside the compound walls toward town, driving through the faded, painted cement houses and blackened mounds of burning garbage that lined the road. People, vendors, goats and chickens, mopeds, and buses cluttered the road, stopping all traffic. They were stuck in the usual go-slow, now of all times. Thirty minutes, the random thought came back to her. Death could happen in thirty minutes. How much time had passed? She kept glancing down at Lila, fearing the venom was taking over her little body. Couldn't they somehow bypass the traffic considering this was an emergency? But she knew there were no ambulances in Nigeria, and even if they had existed, no one would pay any attention to its sirens. She had heard of another child from the compound dying on the way to hospital because of injuries from a terrible fall. Trapped in the usual grinding traffic, the girl just didn't make it to the hospital in time. She tried to push this thought away.

But Ayo seemed to read her mind. The traffic in the opposite direction was relatively sparse. He suddenly drove over the dirt, garbage, and overgrown grass that divided the road into the lane of oncoming traffic. Others followed, suddenly reversing the direction of the third lane. The road could be three lanes one way and one lane the opposite way, depending on the flow of traffic and the whims of the drivers.

Ayo drove like a maniac, weaving between the other cars, breaking all the rules like a local driver. She thought of his words, *I might save one or two, but the rest I fail.* She pulled Lila closer, holding her breath, looking at her child's arm, the arm full of venom.

• • •

At Ayo's clinic, Lila was burning with fever now. To prevent a massive release of the venom trapped in her arm, Ayo un-wrapped the bandages extremely slowly. The bruising and swelling seemed worse, even Sylvia could see this. She looked up at Ayo, something in his eyes seemed less confident.

He rewrapped the bandages, then pulled up a chair next to Sylvia.

"The blood and urine analysis show there's more venom in her bloodstream than I originally thought. She's going to need another dose of antivenom."

"More venom?" Suddenly, Sylvia struggled to breathe as if the poison were attacking her own body.

"Don't worry," he said softly, placing his hand on her shoulder. "We've got this under control."

He turned to the nurse in the room. "Monitor her vital signs frequently. Check for any neurological or respiratory symptoms. And keep the fluids going through the IV."

"What symptoms? What are you monitoring her for?"

"Don't worry, the antivenom should do the trick."

"I want to know. What symptoms?"

"The venom from snakes is neuro-toxic," he spoke slowly so she would understand. "What this means is that it can interfere with the body's nervous system and could result in tissue or organ damage or, very rarely, paralysis. The odds are very low. I'm monitoring these symptoms more out of routine protocol, not because I think it's likely."

She nodded, trusting him was all she had now.

Ayo got up. "I'll get the nurse to bring you some dinner."

The warmth of his hand on her shoulder had steadied her. She wanted him to stay with her, but it was now eight o'clock at night. Of course, he had other patients, other lives to save. He left the room and went on his rounds. She watched the IV flood more antivenom into her baby's system trying to stop the toxin from doing its deadly deed.

They were given a private room, but she stepped out into the hallway overflowing with patients. Some of the children were naked, dressed only in torn T-shirts. A dirty mosaic of brown fingerprints covered the lower half of the clinic's walls. These same walls absorbed the sound of children in pain.

When she returned to the room, she noticed Lila was drooling. The nurse kept suctioning the excessive saliva, so Lila didn't choke. But what did this mean? Didn't paralyzed people drool? Sylvia was frightened. Where was Winston? Was this the way it was going to be, him absent when she needed him the most? She wished Ayo would come back into the room; his presence alone was somehow reassuring.

• • •

She watched Lila's heart rate pulse rapidly on the machine. Ayo had explained that this rapid heart rate was to be expected. Her body was fighting an attack. It was one o'clock in the morning. On the table next to Sylvia was a half-finished plate of food—gari and a spicy stew of muddy river fish.

The nurse came in and began her periodic vital signs test, testing for paralysis by jabbing Lila's legs hard enough to see if she would react or cry. Luckily for all of them, she cried.

Ayo came in, looking concerned.

"How are you holding up? You should get some sleep."

"I can't," Sylvia said. Sleep was the last thing on her mind. She wanted to be by Lila's bedside every waking minute.

"I'll get a cot for you."

He returned carrying the kind of cot the military used, made of dark green material and wooden legs that could be easily disassembled into a bag. He gave her a pillow, sheet, and blanket. She sat on the cot and started to cry. He hesitated at first, but then he sat down next to her and put his arm around her. She pressed her face into him, craving that warm feeling of being held by someone. She could smell him—sweet yet bitter, yesterday's fading cologne, his sweat, the pungent smell of life. She felt his heartbeat and hers, both were beating fast.

• • •

In the morning, she found herself lying in the cot. She must have fallen asleep in his arms. She felt disorientated, her hair tangled. She got up and checked on Lila. She felt the regular rise and fall of her little chest and was somewhat reassured. She peered out of the room, hoping to see the nurse or him. Ayo was standing in the hallway full of sick children, looking ragged, unshaven. Their eyes met and he said softly, "How are you doing?"

Had she cried in his arms? She couldn't remember, but she had probably fallen apart. No one had just held her like that in long time. Winston rarely hugged or kissed her.

"Lila…" Sylvia began.

He came over to her, put his arm over her shoulders. "Her vital signs are improving a little. That's the direction we want things to go. So that's good. But I'll be honest, we're not out of the woods yet."

A part of her wanted to collapse in his arms again, he had that effect on people, women of course. It wasn't just his looks—it was his confidence, openness, a kind of vulnerability, all of it drew her in—but she tried to be strong and stepped away from him.

"Thank you," she said, formally and awkwardly. "Thank you for…your kindness." She wanted to say thank you for holding me, but how could she say something like that, even though her heart ached to tell him how good it had felt in his arms.

"Come," he said cheerfully, this time careful not to touch her. "Let's go and get some breakfast. I'm famished."

"But Lila…"

"The nurse will be with her the whole time. I promise." He spoke in Yoruba to a nurse in the hallway instructing her to check on Lila.

They went down to the cafeteria on the first floor. His clinic was just two floors, funded by a combination of nonprofits including the Red Cross and Oxfam. The cafeteria was busy, full of children—some dressed in hospital gowns but most barefoot, clad in torn t-shirts.

"We feed a lot of hungry street children here," Ayo explained. "Basically, anyone who comes in our doors, especially a child, is given a free, hot meal. It wasn't our original intention for the cafeteria, it was just supposed to feed the patients, but that's what it has evolved into."

It was hard for Sylvia to think about all these other children when her own child was struggling upstairs, but she tried to concentrate on what Ayo was saying.

"How do you manage, I mean funding wise?" Sylvia said, searching her brain for some way to make conversation. She desperately wanted to connect with him. He was so noble, handsome, the modern-day hero, she felt herself falling for him.

"We manage. We get bits and bobs here and there. I do a big fundraiser gala every year back in London with Oxfam to raise money specifically for my clinic. I simply have to show up in black tie and tails and give a speech about the place."

She thought he probably cleaned up nicely. The wealthy ladies in London would have no problem reaching into their pocketbooks on his behalf.

They ate toast, eggs, fresh pineapple, and tea. Sylvia couldn't help looking at all the hungry faces around her, dark-eyed children with swollen bellies. The place, the children, the man—suddenly she felt like dedicating a part of her life to his cause. To him.

"When Lila's better," she said. "I want to come back here. To help you."

"I would love that," he said, looking directly into her eyes. She thought she saw something else there too—desire, longing, loneliness, the same things she felt. But then he stood up abruptly and said, "Right, we should get back to Lila."

When they returned, the nurse looked slightly panicked. Ayo spoke in Yoruba as if to deliberately exclude Sylvia.

"What is it?" she asked, rushing to her child.

"She's developing a slight fever. I'm not sure what from exactly. Perhaps from fighting the venom or even from the anti-venom itself. I'm going to add aspirin to her IV to bring the fever down and then we'll watch her closely."

"I shouldn't have left her, I shouldn't have…." She sat down on the chair next to Lila's cot. She shouldn't have been thinking of him.

He sat down next to her. "Don't fret. It will be alright. Trust me."

She felt his breath on her face. "Stay with me," she said. He let her rest her head on his shoulder for a few brief minutes before leaving for his rounds.

• • •

A few hours later, he returned to the room.

"Good news, her fever is abating," he said, examining Lila's charts.

She sat next to Lila's cot, staring out at the window. Beyond the clinic walls, she could see the town, clusters of rusty tin roofs and spirals of smoke in the sky.

"She was an accident," she said, still looking out the window. "I didn't want her at first. That's why the spirits are punishing me." She wanted to say more, but she didn't.

"No one is punishing you. Least of all the spirits," he said, sitting down next to her.

"You don't believe in them then, the spirits?"

"Oh I believe in them all right. But I don't think they're punishing you."

"Then how do you explain all that's happening to Lila?"

"Sickness happens. Things happen. I'm in the business of fighting off these evil things however they come about. Science can explain it in terms of germs or dirty water. But I suppose we humans believe in spirits to fulfill this psychological need…this need to feel like we have some control in all of this."

"And do we? Have control?"

He put his arm around her. "There's a myth we have in Nigeria. It's about bush-souls. We believe a person has four souls—the soul that survives death, the shadow on the path, the dream-soul, and the bush-soul."

"That's beautiful," she said, her head next to his chest, breathing him in.

"But the bush-soul is special. It's external to the body and takes on the form of an animal in the forest—a leopard, turtle, elephant, or hippo. Everyone has one. In the Calabar region of Nigeria, there's this sacred lake where the fish are carefully preserved because the people believe their own souls reside in the fish. There was a chief in a village whose bush-soul lived in an old crocodile. When a hunter tried to kill it, the chief's leg was mysteriously injured."

He paused, and she looked up at him, willing him to go on. She felt the warmth of his chest next to her face. She could stay like this forever, listening to him talk, the melody of his voice lulling her into believing the world was a safe place, when it clearly wasn't.

"If someone falls sick," he continued. "It's because the bush-soul is being neglected and an offering should be made to one's animal. I want you to go home and pick an animal for your daughter, one that makes sense, and then make a little shrine, a little dwarf-sized hut in the forest and offer fruit to her animal.

I'm not saying she will not fall sick ever again, but at least you'll know there's a bush-soul out there protecting her. It will help ease your mind."

Later that afternoon, Sylvia went home for a few hours, leaving Lila in the clinic with Ayo. Energy and Patience helped her build a little shrine for Lila out of bamboo and banana leaves. Since Lila was born in the year of the boar according to Chinese astrology, Sylvia decided her bush-soul resided in the wild boar found foraging in the local forest. Wild boars sometimes came from the forest that bordered their garden. She placed an offering of fruit, as Ayo suggested, at the edge of this forest where the wild boar had last been seen.

A few days later, the antivenom eventually succeeded in neutralizing the poison in Lila's blood, much to the spirits' chagrin. Ayo smiled when he signed the medical release forms. Her daughter had been in his clinic for four days. Sylvia impulsively hugged him to thank him, holding him near for a little too long. The nurses probably wondered or maybe they had seen everything that had happened the last four days. Four days, a small slice of her life really, but to her, it felt like a seismic shift. The ground had moved and she would need to find her bearings again.

When she got home, she religiously changed the offering at her daughter's shrine to her bush-soul. She believed in what Ayo said about the bush-souls because they were his words and his beliefs. She realized it was a psychological need for her, a ritual she performed every morning because she needed it as much as she believed it, just as he had said. Every day, when she placed fruit at the shrine at the edge of her garden, she thought of Ayo and the wild boar, watching over her daughter. She imagined the wild boar and her daughter would become intimately bound, invisible blood exchanged. The animal would protect Lila, and she, in turn, could not kill any of its species. The wild boar with its comical face, gray coat, and stunted tusks, capable of spearing snakes in the neck, would become Lila's protection against the snake spirits.

After the snake attack, Sylvia also got Energy to tie up all the open air-conditioner pipes with cloth to keep the snakes out. But Patience and others still whispered that there was a snake spirit assaulting their house, and it would come back.

WINSTON

Chapter 8

His wife was in the garden when Winston returned. Energy crouched on the ground harvesting Chinese cabbage and dark greens from the vegetable patch under the kitchen window. Sylvia stood next to the leafy mango trees at the edge of the garden, her long, dark hair lit up by the late afternoon sun. She was beautiful, but Winston saw her beauty as a liability. Her looks intimidated him, repelled him in some shy, awkward way and left him fumbling with his words in her presence.

"Patience told me about the..." Winston began. "I should've been there."

"We managed," she said, but she felt very far away to him. He sensed the first stones being laid out between them. He suddenly felt a small sadness growing inside of him, but he kept it contained, isolated before it had a chance to thrive.

"No, I should've been here," he said stiffly, staring off into space. He didn't have the words in English or even in his native Chinese to repair the damage that had been somehow done by his absence. He wasn't the kind of man who understood how to pry open a women's emotions, so he just stood there, his arms hanging limply by his sides.

She turned and walked quickly to the kitchen, clutching the basket of dark Chinese greens. Something about the way she abruptly turned her back on him made him reluctant to follow. He didn't know what had happened while the baby was in the clinic, but he sensed something in her had changed.

• • •

The next week, he left for the bush again. He told himself he preferred to be away. It was easier that way. He didn't have to deal with the messy emotions of marriage. Winston also had to be on the road more than ever now, peddling the miracle seeds. The ADA headquarters in New York and its international donors had set a timetable. If the seeds had not been adopted by a decent percentage of farmers in two years, the project's funding would be up for review. He didn't want to go back to Taiwan and face his father as a failure, not with everything that had happened between them. He had to redouble his efforts to evangelize the seeds. A part of him wanted his praises sung loudly and widely so that his estranged, disapproving father could hear.

He thought of his childhood, bitterly cold Northern winters in Shandong, when his maid would put coals under his *kang* brick bed to keep him warm at night. He wanted to curl up in his mother's bed like he usually did on cold nights. But that night, his father was home, visiting from Beijing where he was studying at Beijing University. Even though he was only six years old, he felt that he and his father were somehow rivals for his mother's love. His mother adored him and his father knew this, detested it even. "Don't coddle him," his father would say sternly. As a boy,

Winston was glad that his Baba was never around, spending most of the months in Beijing, studying classical Chinese poetry.

His mother let Winston do as he pleased in their huge courtyard mansion with multiple gardens and a small pond. He liked climbing his favorite gingko tree. He loved this tree with its fan-shaped yellow leaves because his favorite Uncle Han-ru claimed that the tree was over a thousand years old. Gingko trees were resilient and naturally disease-resistant, and because of this, some lived for two thousand years. Uncle Han-ru told him about the gingko trees in Hiroshima that were still standing. They had been only slightly charred by the American nuclear bomb and later had regained healthy leaves. Winston admired this characteristic, the resiliency, the ability to survive war and the worst calamities, and still rejuvenate. Secretly, when everything in his life fell apart later on, he tried to mimic the characteristics of his favorite tree.

His Uncle Han-ru had also been in Beijing with his father, studying at the university, but Winston wished Uncle Han-ru was his father instead. Uncle Han-ru was full of fun, laughter, always tickling him and telling stories. In contrast, his father rarely interacted with him, acting as if Winston had a contagious disease.

But after his mother's death and their escape to Taiwan, he and his father had been left alone in a tiny Japanese paper house bordering the rice paddies. Politics and war had forced them to face each other, all the space that kept them at a distance collapsed, leaving them trapped in a thirteen hundred square foot house with paper walls.

The worst part of it, Winston knew, was that he and only he witnessed the effect of this dramatic social change on his father. Born and bred an aristocrat, his father had never worked a day in his life. He was an intellectual, trained in the classical sense as a Chinese poet-scholar. Outside of his aristocratic world, he was useless, and Winston saw this. That was what broke their relationship, Winston knew. Instead of getting a job, his father continued hanging out at teahouses in Taiwan, reciting poetry with other aristocrat exiles from China as they slid further into poverty.

• • •

Winston returned to Simeon's village. If he could just get Simeon to adopt the seeds, all the others would follow once they saw the bounty of his harvest. He peered into Simeon's hut. Bare of furniture, he only saw some woven mats, cooking pots, and the bag of Cole Agribusiness seeds—still unopened. Simeon welcomed them warmly, inviting them to stay for dinner. But it made Winston question Simeon's friendliness and enthusiasm. He wondered whether he had misunderstood Simeon's intentions. The man may have just wanted to be friends out of curiosity rather than because of any real interest in the seeds. Winston felt a kind of desperation. He knew time was running out, and Simeon was his only "lead" so far. They had been coming here for over six months now, and neither Simeon nor anyone else had adopted the seeds.

Winston noticed Simeon and his family sitting on plain wooden stools under the tree while the rest of the village crouched on cane mats. Next to them, over a fire, a blackened clay pot simmered with a pepper chicken stew. Simeon's wife served the stew and *gari* on enamel plates. Richard refrained from eating and advised Winston, "As a rule, never eat the food the locals serve. It will upset your stomach. Trust me." But the stew smelled appetizing to Winston, sick of eating Spam and tuna fish out of tins on these trips. He accepted the food, rolling the starchy *gari* into a ball and dipping it into the red sauce of the stew, relishing the spicy and flavorful taste.

"You like it?" Simeon watched as Winston gnawed on a chicken head from the stew.

"Yes, very good, much better than English food. In China, we eat chicken heads too, and feet. Considered delicacies."

"Is dat right?" Simeon said. "One day, I want to visit your country."

After dinner, Winston washed his hands, stained orange from the palm oil sauce, in a small bowl of water. As the sun began to set, the women washed the plates in large basins of water on the ground while the children played with the chickens and goats in the twilight, and the men talked.

"Sorry I no find time dis week to clear de bush to plant your seeds," Simeon said. The chief was sitting on the front porch of his house next door, pretending not to pay attention but listening all the same.

"He go be scared of de bush-souls," the chief suddenly yelled from his porch. "De forest dere is sacred, you hear? Our bush-souls go live dere."

"Sacred? I didn't realize," Winston said.

"Our village has been guarding de forest for many generations. No one can cut a tree dere. We use de forest for offerings to de spirits," Simeon explained.

"But is there a way around it?" Winston knew from his own experience with Chinese superstitions, there was always a way around it, a visit to a shaman or something. He also wondered if this was just an excuse put up for the foreigner. He knew the locals practiced slash and burn agriculture, cutting and burning new forest for farming while letting the jungle takeover the old farm land.

"Maybe, but why should we do what you tell us, eh?" the chief said.

"I want to tell you a story," Winston said. "My people, the Chinese, are poor. We used to be the richest, most powerful in the world when the English were still running around in animal skins."

Simeon and the villagers laughed at this comment.

"But you know why we fell behind?" Winston continued. "Because we fell behind in technology. We invented gunpowder, only we didn't know it. We used it in firecrackers. The English took it and made it into guns and shot us with it."

"Dat is crazy crazy," Simeon said. "Dey steal your tricks, eh."

"You shouldn't fall behind either. You can't let the white man rule. You need to take his tricks and make yourselves strong too."

Winston didn't know if his argument would have any effect on the chief or Simeon. But he was appealing to that side of Simeon that was in himself too. It wasn't simply a desire to be like them, it was a competitive motivation to one up them, to be better than the white man. Just then, a black snake, the most widely feared and dangerous black mamba, slithered from a tree. The venom from a black mamba was usually fatal, resulting in immediate cardiac arrest. Simeon moved quickly, slicing its head off with his machete.

• • •

That night, Winston and Richard drove to a hotel in the nearby shantytown several miles away from Simeon's village. The hotel had peeling pink paint, dark green shutters, and West African highlife music blaring from the bar downstairs. It was dirty, noisy, and full of heavily made up girls standing around in hallways garishly lit by red and blue light bulbs. Winston, Richard, and their local guide sat down at the bar-restaurant for dinner. The menu was "whatever caught in the bush today." Tonight it was snake meat.

After dinner, Winston walked down the hallway of his hotel-brothel, and the girls followed him to his room, yelling "*O'Ebo*, I give you pleasure! Please take me!" He threw some *naira* bills toward the girls and then pushed them out with his door. His room was poorly furnished—a cast-iron bed, a thin, bug-infested mattress, stained walls, gray cement floor, and a lone exposed light bulb hanging from the ceiling. Winston noticed a small window up high, covered with a screen full of holes. There was no glass. He took out a dark green mosquito coil and lit it on the floor. The sharp, incense-like smell of the burning coils suddenly brought back a feeling of his childhood.

He recalled his mother the way all men remember their mothers—sweet-smelling, soft-spoken, warm. His mother was holding him in her arms. They were in his room, one of the many rooms on their estate. It was dark and windy outside. He could hear the tree limbs hitting the wall of his room. But when he tried to bring up his mother in his mind, he couldn't remember her face exactly, only the idea of it.

He staggered to the bed and sat down. He could hear the sound of sex and scurrying cockroaches. Suddenly, here in this dingy brothel room, he felt the isolation of his own life. Since the loss of his mother, he hadn't been close to anyone. He had long suppressed the terrible events of her death and his guilt in the dark recesses of his memory.

He recalled his mother's body lying inert and cold in the corner of the broken building. He and his mother had been on the run. They were supposed to have met his father at the port in Shandong and to have sailed to safety in Taiwan. But they hadn't fled fast enough. With Japanese troops everywhere and Communists not far behind, they hid in an abandoned farmhouse, its roof caved in by a bomb.

He thought of the abandoned farmhouse with the broken tiled roof, a gaping hole in the ceiling, so that he could see the stars at night. They only had a few steamed buns and some cold tea. His mother rationed their food each day, but now he realized she had only given it to him. His mother didn't drink or eat anything for several days. He woke one morning and found her body so still, lifeless like an inanimate object. As an eleven-year old child, he assumed she had died of hunger, although in reality it was dehydration that had killed her. He had been so hungry and thirsty that he had devoured whatever they had, not even thinking of sharing.

This guilt propelled him, drove everything he did. It was the reason for his personal crusade against hunger and famine, the reason he had come to Africa. Deep down, he also knew it was the reason he found himself in a dirty brothel feeling this thing called loneliness. Since Lila's snake bite, his wife had retreated into the far corner of their tepid marriage. He had put himself in this desolate corner, and he knew there was no one else to blame. He lay down on the creaky bed and closed his eyes. As he heard the moans of pleasure through the thin walls, he half-wished it was him.

• • •

In the spring of 1974, after over a year of Winston trying to convince him, Simeon finally cleared his land. Winston stood on the burned, charred ground being readied for planting. He could smell the lingering scent of ashes. His feet crunched on the blackened wood and plant debris. The sun was hot that day, and Winston knew he should be feeling hope. This was the first milestone in his project, but the heat and the acrid smell of the smoke made him feel dizzy.

Winston sat down on a large granite boulder in the shade. Parts of the rock had rounded, indented holes, left from grinding corn. He picked up a small rock and examined its slightly greenish hue in the light. His mother would have liked this rock, he thought, remembering their shared hobby of collecting interesting rocks. He put the rock in his pocket, running his fingers over its smooth edges every once in a while. In the distance at the edge of the village, several girls braided each other's hair into elaborate patterns, each one unique. Other girls helped shell palm nuts. A group of boys threw stones at each other. He could hear alternating cries of laughter and pain. He closed his eyes for a second in the shade.

He told himself he would help Simeon, and together they would show the rest of the village what could be done. He hoped if they saw the miracle of the seeds, the bounty of Simeon's harvest, they would follow in his footsteps. His mind raced ahead, dreaming of taking Simeon around the region, as a sort of poster-farmer. He just needed one success and then all others would follow.

Early the next morning, Winston and the agricultural extension worker demonstrated how to plant the hybrid maize seeds. It was May, the beginning of the rainy season, the perfect time to plant. The maize growing period mirrored the local seasonal shift between rainy and dry seasons. The maize could be planted at the start of the rainy season in May and then harvested at the onset of the dry season in October.

Simeon's wife, Abike, and several village women crouched

down, using hoes to break up the soil, taking out any roots, stones, or plant debris. Afterward, Winston helped Abike distribute the fertilizer as they planted the maize seeds in rows. The amount of fertilizer had been carefully calculated in Winston's lab. He had analyzed the soil samples himself, determining the levels of nitrate, potassium, and phosphorus, critical minerals that would be absorbed by the roots. He knew the soil was a deeply weathered, loamy sandy soil with clay subsoil, a *kaolinitic* soil common throughout the humid tropics of West Africa. It had moderate agricultural potential and had to be enriched if they were to have any success with the hybrid maize.

After they were done planting, Winston and Simeon walked through the forest several miles to a nearby plantation. The large farm was owned by a government official, a green tractor from America ploughed vast tracts of cleared and flattened land. Bags of seeds stamped with the Cole Agribusiness logo were waiting to be planted, stored inside a red barn, an exact replica of an American farm. Jeeps and American consultants, wearing green Cole Agribusiness caps with the maize insignia, swarmed about the farm. The ADA was collaborating on this project as well, hoping that once small rural farmers saw the successes of a "modern" large-scale farm, they too would follow suit.

The red barn felt out of place and bothered Winston, sticking out in his mind like a bad omen. Winston and Simeon stood at the fence of the plantation, watching the tractors driving around, the metal glinting in the slanting sun.

"Dis farm is impressive," Simeon said.

Winston understood the envy, the longing in Simeon's voice. When he had first arrived in England, he was impressed by how neat and tidy the streets were. It was unlike Taiwan, where everyone threw trash everywhere, and he had to watch where he stepped.

"You'll get mountains of maize, and your farm will look like this too one day," Winston promised.

SYLVIA

Chapter 9

A few days after Sylvia returned from Ayo's clinic, Ayo came by the house to check on how Lila was recovering from the snake bite.

"How's my patient?" he said. Sylvia felt her heart doing cartwheels inside her rib cage. "And how are you?" he added more softly.

She felt her cheeks redden as if being a doctor gave him the ability to measure heartbeats, even without the stethoscope hanging around his neck. So much had happened between them over the last four days at his clinic, she felt they were no longer strangers. What were they exactly? Friends? She would have to settle for friends, even though she knew her feelings were clearly not in the friend camp.

"She's doing well, thanks to you," Sylvia said, leading Ayo to the living room flanked by screened porches on each side. It was early in the morning, and the glass sliding doors were still open, letting the morning breeze in.

Patience brought Lila out and handed her to Ayo.

"Doctor," Patience said, respectfully. "Tank you for saving her. Tank you, sah." Her deferential behavior wasn't in keeping with Patience's usual brash style. Patience was in awe of Ayo, Sylvia thought, a half-African English doctor, like her in many ways and not like her in others.

Ayo examined Lila, checking her temperature and pulse. "Everything is going as I hoped," Ayo said, smiling both at Sylvia and Patience. He handed Lila back to her mother.

"Would you like some tea, sah?" Patience said.

"I ..." Ayo said.

"Sit down, sah, please. I will get some tea for both you and madam," Patience interrupted, her bossy manner coming back.

It didn't take much convincing for Ayo to linger. He sat down on the couch. Sylvia put Lila in the playpen where she could sit up safely and play with her toys. Patience disappeared into the kitchen, and they were left alone.

"How are you doing?" he asked her again, perhaps not knowing what to say.

"Me? Oh I'm fine," she said, fidgeting with her long, black hair.

Her hair seemed to distract him for a moment, and she felt him watching her. She wanted to lay her head against his chest again.

"How's Lila doing otherwise, I mean developmentally?" he said as if trying to pull himself together.

"Actually, I'm worried about that. She's getting close to eight months old, and she still has no desire to crawl," she said.

Just then Patience came in with their tea.

"I told you, madam, dis is because she not want to move away from de spirit world, dat's why she not walk yet," Patience said as

76

she set the tea tray down on the coffee table. "We have to watch for de snake spirits."

They both turned to look at Ayo, waiting for his authoritative response.

"As a pediatrician, I'll say this. Every child is different. Every child learns to sit up, crawl, walk, talk at different speeds. Although there are general parameters. So I wouldn't worry if at eight months, she's still not crawling yet, she might skip the crawling stage and go straight to walking."

Sylvia felt relieved, but she still asked in a small voice, "What about the spirits Patience mentioned?"

"That's a different matter. One I'm not an expert in, but I nonetheless respect and obey," he said. "As for the snake spirits, always be cautious. Patience's right about that."

Patience nodded, as if to affirm she was correct and then left the room.

"So people here believe in these snake spirits too?" Sylvia said.

"The worship of snakes in Africa is the oldest form of religion known to mankind," Ayo said. "Local priests in Nigeria used to keep pythons in temples, feeding them often so the snakes slept all the time."

"How do you know all this? It's fascinating." Sylvia found the local lore and his interpretation of it intriguing. She wanted to keep him here, sitting on the couch talking to her, as if it were the most natural thing for him to do.

"I pick up the odd cultural anthropology book from time to time. Light reading."

"Light?" She laughed.

"Compared to medical journals, yes. I didn't know you were so interested. Most of the folks on the compound find it all nonsense."

"They have no idea, I think. I mean, they didn't grow up with it."

"And you?"

"We Chinese have our own beliefs about spirits or hungry ghosts, as we call them."

"That's what they are, hungry ghosts. I fight them every day in my clinic." He sighed as if burdened or fatigued by these endless battles.

Lila began to cry. Patience rushed in to grab her and whisked her out of the room before Sylvia had a chance.

"Patience is quite the model of efficiency," Ayo said, his mood returning to its usual cheerfulness again.

"Yes," Sylvia said, but there was ambiguity in her voice.

"You don't like it?"

"No, I mean, what would I do without her? She's...she's just like an annoying mother at times."

He laughed. "Well, I'm glad you've got one. A surrogate mother and grandmother, when it comes to caring for babies, one needs all the help one can get. At least I know I can leave you here in good hands." He stood up to go. She felt her heart slouch, the walls caving in. She didn't want him to leave but could think of no other reason to make him stay.

"I'm definitely in good hands," she said with resignation.

"Thank you for the tea. And thank Patience too," he said, standing at the front door on the side of the screened porch.

He moved as if he were going to give her a hug but then seemed to decide otherwise. Instead, he put his hand on her shoulder and said softly, "Take care."

She nodded, his hand a poor substitute for being in his arms. She watched him drive away in his Peugeot, the sunlight reflecting on the windshield, obscuring his face.

• • •

After Ayo had gone, Sylvia sat back down on the couch, and Patience brought Lila for her to nurse. Although Patience fed Lila bottles of formula, Lila still liked to nurse herself to sleep. Sylvia knew she was nothing more than a human pacifier, but it was the one thing left she had with Lila, and she held onto it.

"You see, de doctor told you about de spirits," Patience said.

"Why is Lila so stubborn? I mean, why doesn't she want to move away from the spirit world? Why doesn't she want to walk?"

"I told you before, madam. You no listen. You have to work to keep her in dis world. Everyting has to be good, very very good for her in dis world, you hear, eh? Otherwise, she will want to go back. She is holding onto de spirit world, comprend?"

"Do most babies do this?" Sylvia asked out of fear and curiosity. "Or is this just her?"

"Yes, most babies do dis. Dey don't want to leave de spirit world, why would you want to leave heaven and come back to earth which is not dat much betta than hell, eh? But after awhile, if dey feel de love from their motha and fatha and their family, then dey want to stay here."

Sylvia looked outside the screened porch and into the garden. The grass was still wet with morning dew. She imagined the snake spirits hidden in the long grass, waiting to turn Lila into her snake-spirit form. Deep down, she knew partly why her baby girl still held onto her spirit lifeline.

Winston came home that evening, and Lila suddenly crawled for the first time, it was a hybrid crawl, a kind of hop on all fours. She reached Winston's legs, her arms climbing up his legs. But he brushed her off, like she was pest of some sort. "My pants are too dirty, pick her up Sylvia," he said. Sylvia felt Lila's pain like it was her own.

It reminded her of the overt way her own father had preferred her brothers while her mother pined for her dead sister. Sylvia was the forgotten daughter. She remembered feeling jealous when her father began taking her brothers swimming, coaching them after school. They all came home smelling of chlorine just like her father. At her father's request, their cook served the largest pieces of beef to her brothers, stuffing them so they would grow strong. At the dinner table, she was often neglected as the conversation revolved around swim races that didn't involve her. She looked to her mother for camaraderie, but after her sister's death, her mother never quite recovered mentally or emotionally. Her mother spent most evenings in her room with a migraine and rarely joined them for dinner.

Sylvia didn't want Lila to be stunted by this lack of parental love. She knew that Winston's interaction or rather non-interaction with Lila had something to do with her holding onto the spirit world. Her daughter could sense this rejection, even though she was only a baby. She hugged her daughter tightly and kissed her cheek to compensate. As Sylvia held her child, she worried, but would her love be enough? Would it be enough to anchor her child to this world?

• • •

Later that evening, she knocked on her husband's study door. "Come in," he said.

She opened the door, but he did not look up. He was sitting at his desk, poring over tiny rocks full of purple, sandy brown, and green hues. The glass case of his rock collection was open. He was gluing the new rocks into the case, classifying each one and writing its name neatly on the labels under the rocks. The labels had words like *Kalsilitic leucite*, not names of rocks she recognized.

"Dinner's ready," she said, feeling like she was intruding somehow. She wanted to say something about Lila, but she didn't know how to begin. He was not her real father and he had generously taken her on. Could she really expect more?

He came out of his study and went into the kitchen. She watched him soap and scrub his hands thoroughly as if his rocks had been full of germs. He was a neat man, almost too hygienic. He was always washing his hands.

As they ate dinner, she felt him glance at her, almost furtively. That night, after dinner, Sylvia undid her silk robe. Winston was already in bed with his back turned to her. Most nights, Lila's crying bothered Winston, so he got up and moved to the spare bedroom, leaving Sylvia alone even when he was home. Sylvia climbed into bed and pressed her naked body against Winston's back, trying to keep him near. He turned to her and lay on top of her, pushing into her. He was certainly eager, and this gave her hope at first. But after he was done, he simply rolled off and fell asleep, snoring in matter of minutes. Sex to Winston was like eating or drinking, he needed it to nourish himself like the next man, but he was not a romantic. He did not whisper tender words in her ear or hold her close afterward, and this made her feel more desolate.

Chapter 10

She recognized the tightening at the center of her abdomen as the fertilized egg settled into her uterus. This time, she didn't feel despair but instead a kind of hope. She would give Winston a baby that was all his, a son to cement their relationship. It was her chance to make her marriage and family life work. She pushed thoughts of Ayo to the far corner of her mind.

As she had hoped, news of the baby changed Winston in subtle ways.

"You should get to bed. It's late," he said one night. "Need to make sure you get enough sleep. It's important for our baby."

Our baby, she held onto his words. He sounded concerned, maybe even a little proud. She let herself feel a small sort of happiness. She wanted to give him this baby, *our baby* as he said. Their family seemed to be loose pieces in a bag, banging around, and she wanted wholeness. That night in bed, she reached out for his hand. He didn't move away. He let her hold his hand until sleep loosened her grip.

In the morning, when she woke up, he was already awake. Lila was crying in her crib. She nursed Lila and then dressed herself.

She found Winston in the kitchen, stirring a pot of *shefan* rice porridge over the stove. It was Sunday, Patience's one day off.

"You sit," he said.

"I didn't know you knew how to cook," she said, surprised.

"I don't, not in the way you do. But I can prepare a few basic things. I cooked for my father and me sometimes. When it was just the two of us in Taiwan."

In another pot, it looked like he was boiling some eggs.

She put Lila down in the plastic playpen in the adjacent living room. Then she went over to the cabinet, reaching up to get some large, Chinese porcelain bowls for the *shefan*.

He came running over. "Let me do it. You shouldn't strain yourself. It won't be good for our baby."

She looked up at him appreciatively, warmed by his sudden attentiveness. She felt more optimistic about the future.

They sat down to breakfast. Winston put two tea-leaf eggs on her plate—hard-boiled eggs with cracked shells steeped in soy sauce and tea leaves.

"Thank you," she said, putting her hand on top of his.

They still ate in their usual silence. Winston was a man of few words, but this time, the silence didn't bother her.

Winston finally made arrangements to move Lila to her own room, and he asked Patience to sleep with her, so Sylvia wouldn't worry about the snakes. It also meant if Lila woke up at night, Patience could attend to her needs, and Sylvia could sleep. She saw Ayo again at a clubhouse event and noticed he was with a young, blonde, Swedish translator, hired to translate the ADA reports into the five languages of the donor countries. It hurt to see him with this woman, but Sylvia was not entitled to feel jealous, he was not hers and never would be. He waved at her, but Sylvia turned away. She was pregnant now with her husband's son, as she should be. She didn't have time to entertain such thoughts anymore.

•••

When it was time to have the baby in the summer of 1975, Winston made arrangements for them to travel to America. They went to Minnesota where Sylvia's brother, John, and his wife now lived. Winston wanted to make sure his baby was born in a proper hospital with the best doctors.

Everything was different at this birth. Winston paced the ammonia-scented hallways of the hospital, waiting eagerly for the arrival of his child. Sylvia did not get to hold her son covered in amniotic fluid, fresh from the birth canal like she did with Lila. Instead, he was whisked off, scrubbed clean by nurses in rubber gloves and then left in a plastic crib in a nursery lined with rows of crib-trolleys, each identified by a typed label on the front with the mother's name. Winston was the first to hold his baby boy dressed in the hospital-issue blue hat with *Mt. Sinai* written across it. When Sylvia finally saw her son, it was through the glass window of the nursery.

At the hospital, she watched Winston hold his son. He was in awe of the miracle of it all. She knew that feeling. It was how she had felt when Lila was born. He simply stared into his son's eyes, and the baby did the same, taking in this man who was his father.

"He's beautiful, isn't he?" Sylvia said, proud of the gift she had given her husband.

Winston looked up at her, his eyes full of tears.

WINSTON

Chapter 11

The birth of Winston's son coincided with Simeon's record harvest in October 1975, the second harvest a year after planting the original hybrid seeds. Winston sat with Simeon and a group of villagers under the thatched canopy. He looked around at the smiling villagers, the mood noticeably changed since the first day he had met with them. A woman poured palm wine out of the old engine oil canister into enamel cups. Winston saw a few red ants floating in his milky palm wine, but he downed it anyway. The chief sulked on his front porch, not participating in the celebration. But the villagers didn't seem to notice the chief's silence. They passed around the gourd of palm wine, congratulating Simeon on his record harvest.

Simeon boasted, "I have four times more maize den before, you can see wit your own eyes, eh?"

"You a big man now, eh?" a villager said.

"I have dis big man to thank," Simeon said, turning to

Winston. Winston felt the palm wine going to his head.

"I take your seeds," the same villager said, nodding at Winston. Other villagers also chimed in, requesting Winston's bag of seeds. Luckily, Winston had anticipated this and brought a full truck.

Winston stood up, raising his chipped enamel cup, "*Ganbei,* it's a Chinese toast. You have to down your cup in one drink."

He felt buoyed by the good things happening in his life—his son and now this harvest. He made toast after toast. Most of the villagers shared one large gourd of palm wine, so it was mostly Winston that kept downing all of the liquid in his enamel mug, getting drunk on the milky, fermented alcohol. But it felt good to him. His body was warm, his mind hazy and unfocused, and for a moment in his life, he let himself enjoy this sensation, what others called happiness.

• • •

The next day, Winston helped Simeon's wife Abike transport the maize in his jeep to the market in the nearest town of Ife. As they got closer, suddenly the road was full of potholes, and Winston slowed his jeep. In front of him, he noticed a massive circular pothole, its diameter covering the road. Cars and mammy wagon buses slowed to a crawl to negotiate the cracks and crevices of this large crater. Winston pressed on his brakes and drove carefully through it. Vendors took advantage of the halted traffic in the pothole and shoved bananas and Bic biro pens through his open window. He noticed stalls clustered around the pothole on both sides of the road.

"We are here, sah. De market," Abike announced.

"I see the pothole *is* the market," Winston said. The giant crater had created the market organically with vendors strategically placing themselves near stalled traffic.

"I noticed the road just before the market was in perfect condition, newly paved. Why hasn't this part of the road been repaired?" he asked Abike out of curiosity.

"De government dey try to fix dis big hole, but we don't want it. A smooth, fast road would be bad for business, eh? De market vendors stood in de way of de construction machines. So de road neva got fixed. It's good, eh?"

"Yes, you're right, it's good." Winston smiled.

Winston pulled his jeep to the side of the road, parking beside the massive crater. A crowd started to surround his jeep, the unusual arrival of Abike had caught their attention. Most vendors balanced their wares on their heads and walked to the market. Others pushed wheelbarrows of chili peppers, the wheelbarrow serving as transport and stall. Another vendor rode on a bicycle with a stick of live chickens across the handlebars, the row of chickens dangling upside down, tied by their legs onto the stick.

Winston helped Abike carry the bags of maize, ground into a fine powder for the corn porridge that was a staple in this part of the world. She poured some of the bags into colorful enamel basins on the roughly-built wooden table of her stall, creating large mounds of yellow powder. Several women, dressed in their finest attire, batik wraps, and headdresses, came by Abike's stall to gawk at the piles of maize.

"Ooooh, look at dis, you been busy busy woman, eh?" one woman said.

Abike and the woman fell into their usual gossip, catching up on the latest news of so and so. The market belonged to these women, dressed in their finest wrappers and headscarves, all vibrant pattern and lace—they were the backbone of the market economy. Winston realized the women in West Africa played a role as wife, mother, and most importantly, trader.

Winston took this opportunity to slip away and lose himself in the labyrinth of the alleyways that stretched back from the road. The market was a lot larger than it appeared from the road.

By the end of the day, the latest gossip was Abike's mountain of maize. "She rich woman, eh?" the other women vendors said, laughing. "What is your secret, eh?"

"You go get dem seeds," Abike explained, pointing at Winston. "Dey grow betta, plenty plenty."

"You go give us some?" A woman asked Winston.

"Where is your village? I'll come and show you."

The woman explained she was only a few villages up the same nameless dirt road in the forest as Abike.

"I'll come," Winston said. "Next planting season."

"Yes, you come. We go wait for you."

He didn't mention he had probably come before to her village, but no one had shown any interest in the seeds. Then again, he realized, they had talked to the men only. They needed to work on reaching out to the women, particularly since he now realized the women did the bulk of the farming and selling. He knew word of Abike's mountain of grain would travel quickly, gossiping market women being the best form of advertising.

Winston helped Abike load what little maize was left into the jeep.

"Dere is not much to carry," she said, grinning. "Only all dat cash here." She patted the wads of naira bills hidden in the folds of her wrapper dress.

"You did well," Winston said. Success felt close now, just around the corner, the steepest slope behind them now.

When they returned to the village, Simeon put Abike's cash in an old pesticide canister in his hut until the next planting season when he would purchase the seeds and fertilizers from

Cole Agribusiness. This was the way the aid project had been structured. The first bag of seeds was free and then the farmers were expected to use their increased revenues to purchase the next rounds of seeds. It all made perfect sense.

Winston asked a villager to take a photograph with his camera. Simeon and Winston posed next to the mud-walled granary used to store the rest of the harvest, the thatched roof made with a hole so that the maize could be poured in from the top. Simeon grinned, his arms hanging by his sides. Winston pressed his lips tightly together—the usual stiff pose he gave for photographs, but inside he was smiling ear to ear.

• • •

That weekend when Winston returned home, he was in a celebratory mood. Holding his four-month old son in his arms, his precious *baobei*, he suggested they go to a new Chinese restaurant that had recently opened in town. On the drive, Sylvia seemed excited about the prospect of some good Chinese food, and he hoped it was good.

When they walked into the restaurant, Winston felt oddly comforted by the gaudy, mismatched colors. The place was decorated with blue, imitation Ming dynasty vases and scrolls of Chinese paintings of birds and flowers—its thin paper already yellowing in the tropical humidity. There were also the usual fish tanks—big fat goldfish swimming in the front for prosperity and ugly catfish crammed in the back tanks for eating. The walls were painted a cheap coat of mint green, clashing with the red tasseled lamps and Imperial yellow cushions.

"*Huanying huanying,*" the Chinese manager welcomed them. He introduced himself as Mr. Lee from Shanghai.

"My wife is from Shanghai," Winston said in Mandarin. "I'm

from Shandong province."

Sylvia and Mr. Lee exchanged greetings in their Shanghainese dialect.

"My fellow countrymen, I will order something special for you. It's not on the menu. Sit, sit." He pointed at the rosewood chairs huddled around large round tables. "Your son is so fat," Mr. Lee said, pinching Thomas' cheeks before he left for the kitchen.

Winston sat down, holding his son. He looked down at Thomas. He was the perfect baby, chubby-cheeked and almost always smiling. Holding his son's small, warm body close to him, Winston felt choked up inside. It hurt so much when he thought much he loved him.

Mr. Lee brought out haizibi or crunchy jellyfish as an appetizer.

"Haizibi? In Nigeria?" Winston said, surprised.

Sylvia dived into the haizibi jellyfish, serving it to Winston. She gave a few pieces of the jellyfish to Lila, now two and half years old. Lila's face wrinkled up, not wanting to try the unusual food. She was a moody, difficult girl, Winston thought. He still didn't know quite how to interact with her.

Mr. Lee brought out more dishes. "*Xiao long bao*," he said, uncovering the bamboo steamers.

"Shanghai soup dumplings? How I've missed these," Sylvia said, smiling.

"Please join us," Winston said to Mr. Lee.

"I will for a moment. Then I must get back to the kitchen," Mr. Lee said.

"Do you have family here?" Sylvia asked.

"Unfortunately, my wife and daughter are in China."

Winston knew Communist China kept families behind as collateral for overseas Chinese workers, preventing them from defecting.

"I'm sorry to hear that," Winston said.

Winston didn't mention that his own family had fled to Taiwan before China had fallen to the Communists. It was understood, of course. But at the end of the day, they were all Chinese, especially here in this far-flung West African town. It didn't matter that Mr. Lee was from Communist China, and Winston and Sylvia were from the other side of the political straits in Taiwan and Hong Kong. They shared a culture and language that superseded Cold War politics.

"What's your business here?" Mr. Lee asked, as his waiters brought more food out. The last dish was a whole fish steamed in ginger, soy, and sesame oil.

"I'm with the Agricultural Development Agency or ADA's Starter Pack 2000 project. It's an international NGO. We have hybrid maize seeds," Winston explained.

"Interesting," Mr. Lee said.

"He's just had his first round of record harvests," Sylvia added, complimenting him.

"It was all uphill at first. But the project is taking off now. More farmers are signing up now that a few demonstration farmers had a record harvest. They see now what our seeds can do," Winston said, enjoying this moment of happiness with his son on his lap, his wife by his side, and some excellent Chinese food. Who would have thought he would be eating *xiao long bao* here in Ibadan?

"And it's due a lot to Winston's hard work," his wife said, genuinely happy for him. He turned to her, and she smiled. Mr. Lee returned to the kitchen, leaving them alone.

He looked at his wife across the table, she was a good wife, he thought. He knew he was fortunate, and he should count his blessings, but yet he couldn't let himself enjoy this small happiness. He didn't want to gloat because he feared what was around the corner. Anything could happen, he knew. He had learned that, it was the lesson of his childhood. The sweetness could sour like milk in a matter of hours. He didn't want to savor the sweetness, instead, he did the opposite—he blocked it out, guarded himself from its sugary taste. Mr. Lee returned with a sweet red bean soup, a Chinese dessert, but Winston declined.

• • •

A week later, Winston received a message delivered by a fellow villager of Simeon's. The news was not good. He immediately jumped into his jeep and was gone.

The previous night, a gang of armed robbers from the nearby town of Ife had descended on Simeon's hut. They pulled Simeon up from his sleeping mat. They thrust a blinding flashlight into his stunned face and pointed a gun at his head.

"Where is de money? All dat cash you made at de market, eh? Where is it?"

A man punched Simeon in the face. His wife and four children cowered together in the corner.

"Where is it? Go now get it you," the leader of the gang yelled harshly, waving his gun in front of Simeon's family.

Fearing for his family's safety, Simeon got up and with his hands shaking, pulled the wads of naira bills out of the old pesticide canister. A neighbor heard the noise and, knowing the armed robbers would pillage the rest of the village, rode his moped into Ife to get the police.

The men kicked Simeon as he lay on the floor. "Dat will teach you a lesson. Tinking you are betta than us. You are nothing but a white man's monkey, eh. Dat's right, eh." The gang members laughed as Simeon curled up in pain.

92

Then the gang ran out of Simeon's hut and paid a visit to every other hut in the village, including the chief's house. They took whatever they found of interest—a pair of Levi jeans, a wireless radio, a grandmother's life savings, which didn't amount to much, but they took it anyway. When the police drove down the dirt road to the village, they moved slowly over the potholes and through the mud. The robbers, hearing the police sirens blaring in the distance, fled into the forest.

By the time Winston arrived, the men sat congregated under the thatched canopy, talking about the incident. Several had black eyes or bruised ribs. Most had lost something of value.

Simeon recounted the robbery, joking almost. "Tell me why do de police come wit their sirens so loud if dey want to catch dem? Of course, de robbers heard de sirens and ran away into the bush. If de police really want to catch dem, dey would come quiet quiet. Dat's because dey don't want to catch dem. De police and robbers are one and de same, eh?"

Other villagers agreed, laughing at Simeon's comment despite their anger. Winston looked around for Oluwa but didn't see him.

Winston was quiet. He suddenly felt nauseous, and the heat only made him feel worse. This whole business made him feel nervous. With no money, how was Simeon supposed to buy the next round of seeds from Cole Agribusiness? He feared what little progress they had made would be erased if Simeon could not replant. They had come so far and yet, they were still nowhere. A few successful harvests were hardly widespread success.

• • •

Winston drove up to the Cole Agribusiness offices on the plantation farm next to Simeon's village. The offices were in a narrow, low-slung building with doors that opened onto a front porch. Each office had its own box air conditioner hanging from the window, dripping water and staining the cement floor of the porch. The area around the office had been cleared of any natural plants or flowers, so it had a barren, almost forlorn look.

Winston knocked on the door of Jim McCormack, the lead Cole representative in the region. He had met him briefly at a meeting between Cole Agribusiness and ADA. Jim opened the door, smiling, and invited Winston to sit down. Jim seemed nice enough, and he had a wholesome smiling face like a boy's, Winston thought. He had seen many Americans with this face. He knew it was a face that had not known hardship.

"Coffee?" Jim offered. Winston accepted the offer, mainly because the room was freezing. Winston shivered as he sat down. It was a shock to his system, coming in from the balmy, tropical heat outside. He noticed the man was dressed in a short-sleeved shirt despite the temperature of his office.

"Well, nice to see you. What can I do for you today?" Jim asked. A secretary came and poured instant Nescafe coffees for them.

"I noticed when I visited last time, the work you're doing out here on the plantation," Winston said.

"Yeah, it's going to be the biggest harvest these guys have ever seen. I'm amazed at how backwards they are. I mean, I feel sorry for them picking at the dirt with one rusty hoe. We've brought in tractors here. We're really showing them how it can be done. If they had all this technology like we have, no one would be starving in Africa. We're going to make this happen."

The man spoke with a zeal that made Winston nervous. He sounded more like a sports commentator before a big game.

"We've had a small success with a rural farmer nearby. He had a good harvest. Through him, we were able to convince more farmers to adopt the new seeds," Winston continued.

"That's great to hear. These poor rural farmers really need to modernize their way of farming. It's such an inefficient way to produce food, a patchwork of random little village plots. There are no economies of scale."

Winston took this as a good opportunity to explain Simeon's situation and ask for a possible second round of seeds, fertilizers, and pesticides for free. He couldn't just give one of the many bags of seeds in the truck to Simeon. He had to ask for Cole's sign off first. When each bag had been handed out during the "free" first round, they had recorded the names of the farmers.

Jim paused when he heard of Simeon's trouble and said, "I would if I could. But I'm not authorized to do that. Problem is, Cole Agribusiness can't keep giving out bags of seeds and stuff for free, we have to make money eventually, down the road, if you see what I mean."

"I see," Winston said, even though he knew in actuality, the US government aid money had been used to pay for the first round of seeds from Cole Agribusiness. Cole hadn't given anyone anything for free although it may have appeared that way.

"There's a rationale behind the way the aid agreement was structured. Give out the first bag free to get them hooked as paying customers. We're trying to break into new markets here. We're not a charity."

"Of course," Winston got up abruptly. He felt the coldness of the room invade his senses, putting him suddenly on edge. He would have to find another solution to Simeon's predicament. Winston bid farewell politely and walked out into the African sunshine, the humid warmth for once felt inviting to him.

• • •

A month later in December, Winston returned to the village and met with Simeon under the palm-leaf roof of the village center. They ate lunch, moi-moi made from cowpeas, soaked until the skins had fallen off and then pounded and mixed with palm oil, red pepper, and salt. Winston opened the moi-moi, steamed in banana leaves.

"I think I have a solution to your problem," Winston began, eating the moi-moi with his fingers. "A micro-loan program. The government just started it as part of the ADA 2000 program."

In the distance, Winston could hear school children reciting their lessons in the cement block schoolhouse with its shiny, corrugated tin roof, recently installed to replace the usual thatched roof. On a sunny day like today, the so-called "modern" roof made the school unbearably hot. During heavy rains, the loud noise of the rain hitting the tin roof drowned out the teacher's voice. Winston thought of Simeon's sons inside, sweating and staring at the "blackboard," the front cement wall of the classroom painted black in a rectangular shape. He wondered how Simeon could still afford the school fees.

"What's dis loan ting?" Simeon asked.

"It's a new program. Established by the government. They'll lend you small amounts of cash, enough to buy the seeds and things. You pay them back, with interest, of course, after the harvest."

"Ma friend, we're back in business, eh," Simeon said, clapping his hands together.

"De government? I don't like de sound of it," the chief interjected. "I neva heard de government give away money. Heh! Dey full of tricks. Dey go be jealousing your success, dey will come and take your money just as easy easy as dey give it."

"Dat's right. Listen to your fatha," Oluwa said. "He knows

what he's talking about."

Winston noticed the chief looked older, more stooped, his voice slower. He had begun to suffer from dementia, repeating his words and forgetting things. His rants seemed more like madness. As the chief aged, Winston realized there was a power struggle brewing in the village between Simeon and Oluwa as to who would take the old man's place.

Winston took Simeon to Ife to fill out the loan paperwork at the local government office. They were confronted by bizarre bureaucratic rituals, the legacy of the British colonial era seasoned with plenty of fiery, local flavor. Four times they had to circle around to various officials, each pointing to the other, until by the fourth time, they came back to the broad-faced and smiling official they had started with who finally helped, motivated at last by the flash of *naira* bills. Simeon's paperwork changed hands many times, blackened each time by greasy fingerprints and the stench of greed. Winston began to wonder if they would ever see the money.

Chapter 12

Five months later in May 1976, after the rains had come, Winston and his driver followed the nameless dirt road toward Simeon's village. It had become a muddy swamp during the rainy season, and the jeep got stuck in the mud. Winston and Ige stood knee-deep in the sticky mud, trying to push the jeep out. Winston cursed the viscous river of a road, annoyed at being held back. He wanted to reach Simeon's village to find out if Simeon had received the loan yet, the ADA 2000 Starter Pack program hinged on this. Five months had gone by, and the new planting season had just begun, but still no word from the government loan agency.

Winston climbed out of the mud. "I will walk to town for help," he said. He knew most villagers walked this road to town, so it was not an impossible feat. He estimated it would probably take him half a day.

"No Masta, let me walk to town. It's too far. You stay wit the jeep," Ige argued.

"I would prefer to go," Winston said. He didn't want to be trapped in the jeep, waiting for hours on end. Waiting, he had learned, made one feel powerless.

Winston started walking back in the direction of the town. With any luck, he hoped he might run into a bush taxi, a Japanese-made minibus crammed full of bodies, bundles, and the odd chicken, the necks and backs of people contorted and bent to fit in the tight space.

He walked in the hot sun for about two hours, but there was no sign of anyone. He reached for his water bottle, but it was empty. His shirt was soaked through with sweat. Monkeys called out to him in the trees, jumping from branch to branch above him. Suddenly, an old man appeared, seemingly out of nowhere.

"Who are you?" the man called after him from the edge of the forest. The man had yellowed eyes, but his face was clear and unwrinkled, despite the gray hair and stooped demeanor of someone much older. There was something about the tone of his voice that seemed menacing, almost threatening to Winston.

"I'm a friend of Simeon Balewa, son of the chief in the next village." Winston introduced himself, trying to sound calm and unafraid.

"You, eh? De one causing trouble!" The old man moved closer and grabbed Winston's arm, rubbing leaves of some sort on his skin. Winston struggled to break free. The man mumbled something. He couldn't understand what the man had said, but he sensed it was a spell of some sort.

"I go give Simeon juju. Dis is why he had de robbers come to his hut," the old man said.

Winston had heard of the power of juju magic or witchcraft. In Nigeria, death and misfortune were often attributed to spells cast by enemies through juju doctors or witches. Witchcraft and the supernatural explained these random events. Why had misfortune fallen on one and not another? The answer was simple: a spell had been cast.

"We've come to…help Simeon," Winston said, struggling to speak.

"Help? You people help?" the old man said, gesturing at him as if he were mad. "You help, you will die. Stay away from de village. Or I will give you juju too. You hear me, eh?"

The old man let go of his arm, and Winston started running down the dirt road toward the town.

"Bad tings going to happen," the old man called after him.

What bad things? Suddenly, Winston felt his throat start to close up, and he couldn't breathe. He wondered if it was some kind of allergic reaction to the plant the man had rubbed on his skin. This was not good, he thought. He hoped it would pass. He had some antihistamine back in the jeep, but not with him. If it was more serious than that, he had nothing out here in the jungle. He had to get to town.

Winston didn't want to admit it, but deep down, he had an awful feeling about the old man. Throughout Winston's childhood, his mother had planted superstitious fears deep in his mind. No amount of Western rationality, PhD or otherwise, could stamp out this raw, intuitive fear. Suddenly, his breathing became more difficult. If he helped the villagers, death would be waiting for him. This is what the old man was trying to tell him. The choice was clearly his, if he wasn't already dying. This was his last thought before he passed out.

• • •

When he woke up, he was lying on a wooden slab fixed to the axel of two old truck wheels, some sort of a donkey cart driven by a boy.

"What happened? Where am I?" he asked the boy.

"Sah, I find you lying on de road."

Winston touched his throat. His breathing was back to normal, whatever had happened had passed. He still wondered if he should go to the doctor.

"Did you see…was anyone with me?" Winston said.

"No, sah. Just you."

"Did you see an old man in the forest?"

"No, sah. No old man."

Winston felt relief and confusion at the same time. Was the incident with the man just a hallucination, perhaps brought on by the heat and dehydration or had it really happened?

At Winston's request, the boy took him to a local car mechanic in town. The mechanic's shop was by the roadside—a graveyard of auto carcasses rusting on the oil-blackened dirt, many of the useful pieces already reused. A patchwork of corrugated iron and tree branches served as a covered working area for the mechanic. The hand painted green and white sign read "Good Health Mechanic." Winston wasn't sure what health had to do with fixing cars. Did the sign mean to imply healthy engines or was it an attempt to convey that the mechanic himself was a strapping lad and in good health, capable of fixing cars?

Winston and the mechanic returned to the forest in an old Datsun tow truck that looked like something pieced together with mismatched parts. Winston wasn't too sure if the truck could make it, but there wasn't much choice in the matter. He paid the boy with his donkey cart to follow them just in case. As they made their way slowly along the muddy dirt road, Winston scanned the forest, nervously expecting the man with the yellowed eyes to reappear. But he didn't see anything, and fortunately, they found Ige and the jeep intact.

Winston asked his driver to return with the jeep and tow truck to town to supervise its repair. He then jumped on the boy's donkey cart contraption, instructing him to take him to Simeon's village. He felt safer with a witness about him. It seemed the juju man or whoever he was wouldn't approach him with witnesses.

The robbery had been a serious setback. But what else lay in store? Winston felt anxious. Superstitions and prophecies had guided his mother's life. He remembered she had fretted about such things, consulting a Chinese fortune-teller for the most auspicious day before she scheduled anything important. Before their planned escape from China to the island of Taiwan, his mother had wanted to go into town to consult with her fortune-teller about the date of their leaving. But his father had laughed, ridiculed her even, saying there was no time for that sort of thing. And so she had not checked her calendar. The day they had fled had sealed their fate. She would die because his father had not abided by her superstitions.

As the donkey cart approached the village, Simeon's children waved him down. They were smiling. Winston wondered if this meant good news. But then again, children were perhaps more resilient than adults, always finding something to smile about.

The children were followed by their mother. She looked worried.

"Simeon he go to town," his wife Abike said. "He go see about da money. He come back tomorrow."

Winston knew it would be easy for him to just buy the bag of seeds for Simeon, but he didn't want to hurt the farmer's pride. He knew what it felt like when the white man gave you hand-outs. But still, as a last resort if the loan hadn't materialized, Winston knew he would have to consider this option.

Due to the condition of the road, Winston decided to stay the night in the village and wait for Simeon's return. Abike made up some sleeping mats on the floor of their guest hut. That night, Winston had a vivid nightmare—the menacing face of the yellow-eyed juju doctor in the background, his mother in the corner quietly dying, a boy crying, he couldn't tell if it was him or his son.

He woke up at dawn, feeling exhausted and unsettled. He hadn't dreamed of his mother and those last days in a long time. It felt so real to him, as if it had happened yesterday, not two decades ago. He heard the crowing of the roosters and the echo of the women pounding yam with the large wooden mortar and pestle. His body was stiff from lying on the straw sleeping mats on the dirt ground. He got up and came out of his hut but almost tripped on something at his feet. He looked down at some chicken feathers, drenched in what looked like blood, tied to a bone. He stepped away quickly, wondering if it was some sort of fetish. Simeon's wife Abike approached his hut balancing a bucket full of warm water for him on her head. When she saw the bloody feathers and bone in front of Winston's hut, she gasped, spilling some of the water. Suddenly, the village broke out in a commotion, and no one would touch the thing.

"What is it?" Winston said, fearing it was somehow related to the man he had encountered in the forest.

"It no good," Abike said.

"What does it mean?"

"It no good," Abike repeated, covering her mouth with her hand but refusing to explain.

Winston turned to a male villager standing next to him. "Please explain. What does it mean?" He sounded desperate now.

"Someone go give you juju," the man said. "It mean death."

Abike started screaming and hitting the man. Winston had not stayed away from the village as the old man, possibly a juju doctor, had advised. A spell on his life had been cast. The blood-soaked fetish was meant for him. Fear pumped throughout his body, each limb breaking out in sweat. A part of him wanted to flee, but he stood rooted to the spot.

Winston went to the enclosed bathhouse behind his hut. He used a pink plastic cup to pour the warm water over his body. He breathed in deeply, trying to calm himself. He poured the water carefully, trying not to waste it. He knew Abike had carried the water from the stream earlier this morning while he still sleeping. He had watched how people in the village washed their faces and hands, using the water with such frugal economy. There was no wasteful sloshing of water all over the place.

As the warm water ran down his face, he couldn't stop thinking about the disturbing offering outside his hut. What should he do? Run like his heart was telling him? But why? He was not afraid of death. After his mother's death, he had secretly coveted death. He had tried to jump off a tree once, but he had just broken his arm. He drank some soap, but that just meant a trip to the hospital. Life had stubbornly clung to him. And now, here was death offered up to him. So why was he so frightened? He thought of his son—sweet, innocent Thomas.

After breakfast, Winston followed the village men as they went to work in the fields. A few villagers had taken the free bags of Cole Agribusiness miracle seeds. But Oluwa, Simeon's brother-in-law had not, planting his fields with seeds leftover from last year's harvest as he had always done. He scowled at Winston as he walked by. It was him, he thought, he had cast the spell or whatever it was against them.

It was overcast, but the humidity was intense. Winston was

drenched in sweat from helping the men hoe the ground. The soil here was dry, sandy, and infertile, not at all like the rich, black volcanic soils in Asia and Latin America where the Green Revolution had been successful. The only solution to this soil, stripped bare of its nutrients, was to add more fertilizers, but Winston didn't know if that approach would work.

He saw Simeon approaching the fields, coming to find him. He was swinging his arms and walking with large strides. Winston noticed he carried a large envelope in his hand. They counted the money together. Some *nairas* had been shaved off here and there from what Simeon had originally requested, but Winston couldn't back out now. And it wasn't just because of Simeon. Despite his fear, Winston had his own battles to fight.

"Tomorrow we will go and buy the seeds. My jeep should be fixed," Winston said. He tried to exude confidence, making no mention of the juju spell, even though inside he felt hounded as if someone were pursuing him in the dark forest.

"But sah...de juju magic," Simeon said.

Winston looked up, fearing Simeon would back out.

But Simeon continued. "It's all mumbo jumbo. Dese people dey believe it. Dey backward. I don't believe in dis things. I Christian. I go to English school."

Winston didn't know if being Christian would ensure objectivity in the matter. He had seen Simeon's church, a one-room, tin house affair. The minister incited his congregation with fear of witches and the devil while exacting "fees" to be rid of such evils. Winston also had noticed the minister's nice, new Mercedes-Benz parked outside the tin-roof church, the only car in the area.

"You aren't afraid?" Winston asked, not sharing Simeon's indifference.

"No," Simeon looked sideways at him. "And you, sah?"

"Me neither. I agree, it's all mumbo jumbo," Winston said quickly, although he sounded less sure of himself than Simeon.

Winston and Simeon walked back to the village through black clouds of smoke rising above the circle of huts and the surrounding forest. A little way outside the village, the women were firing a mountain of pottery on top of a huge bed of branches, covered with straw and then lit. Winston imagined how easily the wind could blow this fire into the surrounding bush and the village itself. In the distance, he watched the people—small stick figures—walking around the village. He thought again of the juju doctor's words. *Bad things will happen.* Winston continued to walk back to the village with Simeon. The smoke from the fire stung his eyes.

SYLVIA

Chapter 13

A few months later in the summer of 1976, Sylvia went to the market to buy some fruit and eggs. A line of white and brown goats ate from a trough, fattened until the end. Customers dragged their purchased goats with leashes of rough string. Slabs of raw meat lay on a wooden table, the blood darkening the wood. She could smell the sour stench of the meat already spoiling in the hot sun.

The crowd pushed her, and Sylvia started to feel a kind of hostility. She stopped at one stall, picking through the pineapples and oranges. Suddenly, a man grabbed her by the arm. He pulled her roughly into the dark, makeshift wood, and blue tarp stall. He was an old man with yellowed eyes and clear skin.

"You Winston Soong's wife?" he said menacingly.

"Yes." She nodded. She wanted to scream, but who would hear her above the din of the crowded marketplace?

"Tell your husband to stay away, eh?" he said, still holding her arm tightly.

She didn't understand what this man was talking about.

"Tell your husband, he go stay away from Simeon's village," he repeated. "I go give him juju. It go kill him, you hear, eh?"

She nodded. She was too afraid to say anything. Did she hear the word juju? She knew spells were associated with juju magic. Was Winston's life at risk? She didn't understand, she thought he was helping Simeon and the villagers.

The old man shoved her out of the stall, and she fell onto the ground, the orange dirt staining her dress. She got up and pushed her way through the crowd. When she got back to her car, she noticed a small pickup truck parked next to her. It was crammed full of several brown bulls piled on top of each other, their horns jutting out. Were they still alive? They were hardly moving, but when she looked into their eyes, she saw a skittish fear. She knew what she really saw was her own fear reflected in the eyes of the cattle. Next to her, a man pushed a wheelbarrow of freshly slaughtered beef, large bones of bloody meat piled high.

As she drove out of the market, she saw the old man with yellowed eyes. He was shouting out to her, *I go give him spell. I go kill him.* He was standing under the baobab tree at the center of the market, a variety of animal skulls used as fetishes for juju spells were spread out on his mat. She had heard that witches placed offerings under this baobab tree at the Ibadan market because they believed it was a spirit tree.

Spirits were known to live inside the hollowed-out trunk of baobab trees, water spirits swam in its interior lake. She had heard of a dying baobab tree exploding from a cigarette stub, its rotting trunk full of methane.

As she drove off, she saw the haunting image of the man in her rearview mirror. She pressed on the accelerator. But along the road back to the compound, she got stuck in the usual traffic.

There was a loud bang on her window. She jumped and looked over. A small boy pressed his face to her window, offering drinking water tied up in clear plastic bags—fatal, unboiled water. A man walked by, balancing on his head, a large basin with the macabre, sun-bleached skull of a cow. The empty eye sockets stared at her.

When she reached the royal palms and white gatehouse, for once she felt relieved. Luckily, Winston was home. It was Saturday, and he was playing golf with his colleagues on the compound golf course. Winston had taken up golfing with surprising interest. It was the only sport he played. As with everything, he did it with obsessive perfectionism.

Sylvia didn't know if she could find him, but still in a panic, she went straight to the course and parked in front of the golf clubhouse. A few men were drinking beers on the terrace overlooking the green golf course and small lake. She found Winston at hole seventeen. Her husband saw her running towards him, and he looked worried.

"Sylvia, what is it? Is Thomas?" he said, running up to her.

"No…" She stopped, trying to catch her breath. Sweat dripped down the sides of her face, but she didn't notice.

They stood apart from his colleagues, and he signaled them to head back to the clubhouse without him. The palm leaves waved wildly in the wind. The skies had darkened, and she could feel the increasing humidity of the approaching thunderstorm.

"What is it then?" he said, impatiently.

"A man grabbed me at the market," she said, explaining everything the man had said to her.

"What did…what did he look like?" Winston said, his face clouding over.

"I don't know. Old man, clear skin, yellow eyes."

She thought she saw Winston shudder, but if he did, he didn't say anything about being afraid.

"Don't worry about this. It's all mumbo jumbo, nothing will come of it," Winston said. She couldn't believe he was trying to reassure her. Mumbo jumbo? That sounded like something his colleague Richard would say.

"You know what I'm talking about. I know you do," she said, knowing he had been raised on the same Chinese superstitions as her, no matter how modern he thought he was.

But he ignored her, turning to hand his golf club to his caddy.

"The black magic here, it's strong. Don't ignore it, Winston," she continued. "You can't go back to Simeon's village. It's not worth risking your life."

He whipped around. "My life? My life is worth nothing compared to the many lives I might save."

"What about us? If something happens to you? What about us?" A multitude of lightning bolts streaked across the sky behind them.

"We'd better head back," Winston said.

They walked quickly back to the clubhouse. His caddy followed, pulling Winston's heavy golf bag.

"Look, Sylvia, I'm not going to get all worried about this. And neither should you. I came here to do my work, and I'm going to do it."

When they reached the parking lot, the rain was coming down hard. She quickly got into her car. As he was about to close her door, he shouted to her above the crashing rain, "From now on, I don't want you going to the market by yourself. Have Ige drive you and accompany you, understand? And don't take the children."

It was then she realized he *did believe* the juju spell was real.

Of course he did. He just didn't seem to value his life. Somehow they—his family—didn't anchor him to this life. She felt a coldness descend on her. She started the ignition. Winston still stood there, the rain coming down hard on him. He didn't run to take cover with his colleagues at the clubhouse but simply stood rooted to the spot, his clothes and hair wet, watching her drive off.

• • •

When Winston returned home from the golf course, the rain had stopped, and a rainbow splashed its colors across the sky. The children were in the garden, chasing butterflies. Winston came into the garden, but this time, he stood back, not rushing to hold or carry Thomas like he usually did. He was drawing lines around his son too, she thought, becoming angry now at her husband.

Winston watched Thomas, now one and half year, chase thousands of turquoise butterflies swirling in the sky—blue-green wings shimmering in the sunlight. Thomas was so busy chasing the butterflies that he didn't notice his father standing there. Why did Winston do this? Was he trying to protect his son from the possibility of his death by distancing himself so Thomas would not miss him when he was gone? She felt the pain in advance, the pain that her son would feel one day from his father.

She walked over to her husband, full of words she didn't or couldn't say.

"You're home," she said instead, disapprovingly.

• • •

That evening, she didn't cook her usual elaborate Chinese meal. Instead, she let Energy cook his English menu of chicken pot pie and over-boiled broccoli.

Winston sat down to dinner, and Energy served the meal. Winston didn't say anything, but she knew he would not like it. The pot pie was too creamy for his taste.

"It's not all your responsibility," she said, digging into him. "You can leave. We can leave this place. Go somewhere safe.

"I'm not leaving."

"But you're leaving us, by doing this."

He didn't say anything but seemed genuinely conflicted.

"I have life insurance," he said.

"Life insurance?" How callous, she thought. "How's that going to help when Thomas wakes up and finds he has no father?"

He winced at her words, but then said, "We have to win. At all costs."

"Win?" She didn't realize this was a game or battle of some sort.

"Win, yes. Against famine, against hunger. No one should die of starvation in this day and age."

"Of course not, but why you? Why risk your life for this?"

"You don't understand."

"Then help me understand."

But he was upset now. His face had reddened, and his hands were shaking. She had never seen him this angry. He got up from the table, barely touching his chicken pot pie, and went to his study. Through the crack in the door, she saw him poring over his beloved rocks, rearranging them in their glass cases. She felt as if there were something larger, deeper that drove her husband, but he refused to let her in.

Chapter 14

A few months later in the fall of 1976, Sylvia sent Patience and Ige to buy some fruit and vegetables at the market in town. Then she took Lila, now three years old, and one-year old Thomas to the clubhouse and swimming pool after lunch for a swim. On the way home from the pool, both children fell asleep in the back seat of the car.

Relieved that both toddlers were asleep for once at the same time, she didn't dare transfer them. She got out of the car but left the ignition on so that the air conditioner could keep going. It was humid and ninety-five degrees outside. She lay down on the couch in the living room, but she left the door to the garage open.

When she woke up, she realized she had drifted into a deep sleep. How long had she been asleep? She looked at her watch. It was four o'clock now. A full hour had passed. There was no sound from the garage. She was surprised the children weren't screaming by now. The silence was deceptive and a sign of trouble. She got up and rushed to the garage. The Peugeot sedan was gone. She looked around in a panic. What had happened? She ran around the outside of the house, searching frantically.

Had someone stolen the car with the children in it? Was it the juju doctor with yellowed eyes? Suddenly, she couldn't breathe. The round-the-clock security guards on the compound gave the residents a false sense of security. Many local workers came in and out of the compound during the day to work on the experimental fields, cut the grass, or work at the clubhouse. Maintenance of the compound required hundreds of workers to keep it going. How could she leave a valuable car with keys in it? It was pure temptation, how stupid of her.

She fumbled with the phone, dialing the gatehouse. The robber would have driven out of the gatehouse, she reasoned, even though she was panicking. Surely the guards would have caught them? Each car and license plate was registered to its owner on the compound.

"My car...it was stolen...my children are asleep inside." She told the security guard over the phone.

"Mrs. Soong, your car. We not seen it. Dat means it's still inside the compound. Don't worry, we will find it, madam." The chief of security got on the phone to try to reassure her. "I will come over myself and drive you around de compound looking." But she didn't feel reassured.

Her mind and body were overtaken by a kind of paralysis. Everything had been against them from the start—the spirits' incursion on Lila's life and now the juju doctor's spell. It was more than she could handle.

The security officer drove her around the compound, searching for her children. Another hour had passed, and now, many of the compound residents also pitched in, including Ayo and his Scottish friend. It was five o'clock. They only had one more hour before dark. The compound was large, about a thousand hectares.

Aside from residential areas, it included farm land where the scientists of the ADA grew experimental crops, trying to breed hybrid "miracle" seeds with native crops like cassava. There was also a reservoir for water supply and at the far end of the compound, plenty of unused bush and forest.

By now, Sylvia had gone into a state of shock, and she sat in the security chief's jeep, looking frantic and wild-eyed. If the car had not left the compound through the gatehouse, the security staff was sure of that, then where was it? It had to be somewhere in the compound. Or maybe the robber had switched license plates and made it past the gatehouse?

Ayo walked over to her in the jeep. He came up to her and put his hand on her shoulder. She looked up at him. She hadn't talked to him much since her pregnancy and the birth of her son. It had been well over a year, and right now, she barely felt his hand on her shoulder. Her mind was full of the demons of maternal guilt.

"We'll find them, don't worry," he promised. "The robber only really wanted the car. I doubt he wants your children." She hoped he was right. He didn't know about the juju spell.

• • •

Just before dark, the security guards found a large hole that had been cut into the far northwest corner of the compound fence. The hole was big enough for a car to drive through. This corner of the compound was mostly forest and bush, and here the concrete wall gave way to a chain-link fence. They followed the tracks through the bush to a dirt road outside the compound. But eventually those tracks led to the main tarmac road and disappeared. The security guards asked random villagers along the quiet road if they had seen the car or if they had heard or seen any children. Several women had thought they had seen the car, but no one could be sure if there were children in it or not.

By the time they returned to the compound, it was dark, and they still had not found Lila or Thomas. Ayo drove Sylvia back to her house. They were both silent. She felt like she was sinking into the deep abyss at the bottom of the ocean, the midnight zone where there was no light, where the weight of water above her would be so intense it would crush her. Ayo saw her despair and put his arm around her as he drove. But she only felt a numbness descend on her.

As they turned into her driveway, Patience came running out. She was out of breath.

"Where were you, madam? I came home from de market and de children, dey were just left here sitting at the front door. Crying."

She got out of the car and rushed inside to hold her children. They were both clean and happy, with no trace of recently being kidnapped. Patience must have given them a bath. She hugged them tightly, feeling their small, warm bodies close to her. She breathed in deeply and closed her eyes. She just wanted to hold them and never let go.

"Someone must have quietly brought the children back to the house once it got dark. But where were they all this time?" She heard Ayo saying to the security chief.

"Maybe, sah, dey were hidden in a servants' quarter?" the security chief surmised. "We neva checked dat."

"There was someone on the inside," Ayo said.

"Someone on the inside?" Sylvia said, her voice shaking. She asked Patience to take her children to bed. She didn't like the fact that someone had so easily penetrated the gate and walled fortress of her compound.

"Is there something else going on?" Ayo said, sensing her fear.

116

"Someone put a juju spell on Winston's life. I was threatened at the market." Saying the words in plain English to Ayo made them sound real to her now.

"Someone go give him juju?" the security chief looked frightened now.

"Yes," she nodded, feeling on edge from the guard's reaction.

"Has your husband written a report on this?" Ayo asked.

"I don't know. He thinks it's all mumbo-jumbo."

"It no be mumbo-jumbo, it real. He betta be careful," the security chief said.

"Unfortunately, the juju magic is prevalent here. Everyone is afraid of it. I would not take it lightly. After this incident, your husband will probably change his mind," Ayo said.

Winston would be insane if he didn't, she thought. After all, his son was almost stolen.

"What did de man at de market look like?" The security chief asked.

She described the old man with the yellowed eyes and clear skin. The security chief seemed to be jotting down notes.

"Have you seen anyone like this?" Sylvia said.

"No, madam, but we will have an investigation of all de workers and servants on de compound," the security chief said, but she detected an uneasiness in his voice.

"Maybe our security can work with the local police to track the car and find out who did this?" Sylvia said, offering another approach.

"Unfortunately, dey can't. As we speak, madam, your car is being dismantled and sold in parts. Your car no longer exists," the security chief said. He didn't mention that the local police force was inept and corrupt.

"Why did they return them?" Sylvia said in a small voice.

"The children? To show you that they can. To threaten you. It's a warning possibly," Ayo said. "Where's Winston?"

"Out in the bush. He's due back in a few days."

Ayo looked worried. He spoke in Yoruba to the security chief. She couldn't understand what they were saying, but they seemed to be arguing.

Ayo then turned back to her. "I told the security chief to take precautions. Someone has threatened your husband's life with a juju spell, and now your car was stolen with your children. We have no way of proving the two incidents are related. It's possible it was still a random car theft. But I think we should proceed with caution. He's going to send an extra security guard to watch your house. I would avoid going into town, at least until Security sorts things out."

• • •

The next day, she felt trapped in her house—the compound walls seemed one-way to her, thick and impenetrable on her side and flimsy and porous on the other side. They kept her inside, yet failed to keep anyone out. She kept worrying she would see the man with the yellowed eyes peering through her window. The security guard assigned to their house didn't seem to be concerned. As far as she could tell, he mostly slept on the job. Anyone could get past him. The only thing that sustained her those few days was the certainty she felt that Winston would change his mind and realize the seriousness of the threat against him. After all, his precious son had almost been stolen.

Ayo came by the next evening after the children had gone to bed and Patience had returned to her own quarters behind the house. Sylvia heard him arguing outside with the security guard.

"I had to give that guard a prod with a stick. Utterly useless. I should be guarding you myself," Ayo said as she let him in.

They both suddenly looked at the sofa. He could sleep on the sofa, she thought. She wanted him here. She hadn't really talked to him for the past two years since her pregnancy, but nothing had changed between them. For a moment, they stood awkwardly in the middle of her living room, and she felt he wanted the same thing.

But he seemed to collect himself and said instead, "Right, I'm going down to the security office at the gatehouse to request another man. I'll be back."

She waited for him to return. A part of her, the part of her that shouldn't, wished he wasn't such a good man. Why couldn't he stray into her arms, slip up just once? He came back with a new guard. She was pretty sure he was going to snore as loudly as the other guard, but Ayo seemed assured.

"Apparently, this man's a bit of an insomniac."

Ayo didn't come inside this time but stood firmly planted on the other side of her door.

"Do you want me to get Patience? I think she should sleep here with you in the house," he said.

"That would be a great idea, yes, thanks." Sylvia perversely hoped Patience would ply Ayo with her tea and cake to keep him around.

But Patience, groggy-eyed herself, seemed slightly irritated to be woken up at night, even by her hero-doctor.

"We be okay. I sleep here. No juju doctor going to take de children while I go be here." She had a large, heavy stick in her hand.

"I think you're in good hands," Ayo said.

Too good, Sylvia thought to herself.

• • •

A few days later, Sylvia was in the garden cutting passion flowers for the table when Winston returned from his trip. She heard his jeep pull up quickly, brakes screeching on the driveway. She stood up, holding the large, starfish-like, purple and white passion flowers in her arms. She heard him on the screened porch talking to his son. Then he came out into the garden, looking for her. She watched him approach, shielding her eyes from the sun. She thought, now of all times, he would capitulate. Maybe they would pack their bags and leave tonight.

"You heard what happened?" she said as he walked over to her in the garden.

"The security chief gave me a report. Apparently, it was a bit of a witch hunt. They interrogated every worker and servant on the compound. Fired several dozen workers."

"Did they find the man with the yellowed eyes?"

"I don't know. The security chief said your description wasn't much to go on. But yes, they fired several old men with yellowed eyes."

"You speak as if the case were resolved. They fired *several* men with yellowed eyes, the more the better, so we're safe now? How do we know if it's the right one?"

"We don't. But the security chief has assigned round the clock guards to watch our house from now on."

"Aren't we leaving?" she asked, stunned that the incident wouldn't send Winston packing his bags.

"Leaving? Where to?"

"I thought…" She realized how stupid she was. Of course, he wouldn't care. Suddenly, she felt a kind of rage toward him. She hit him on the chest, the bouquet of purple passion blossoms in her arms falling to the ground.

"Your son was almost stolen? You get that? Because of you,"

she said hysterically as she hit him.

He stepped back from her, his shoes crushing the flowers meant for their dinner table. She let her arms fall limply beside her.

"They've assigned security guards to watch our house permanently," he repeated. "If you go into town, Ige will drive you from now on. You are not to go alone. And under no circumstances are you to bring the children. They stay here with Patience."

"The result of all of this is I'm a prisoner in my own home. And you? You plan to continue on as you like?"

"We've discussed this before. I have no choice. I have to do my job. I trust the security chief will do his job and protect you and the children."

Winston turned and walked back to the house. She wasn't so sure. The security chief seemed as frightened as she was. Why wasn't Winston frightened like the rest of them? She stood there among the passion fruit vines and their lush garden—full of bougainvillea and hibiscus blossoms. Her stomach churned. The scent of flowers was both sweet and sickening to her. She turned to cut some violet bougainvillea blossoms. The plant's sharp thorns pricked her fingers, but she didn't care, letting them bleed. The violet bougainvillea blossoms fell carelessly onto the grass below. She didn't bother to save any for their dining table.

Chapter 15

After a few weeks of avoiding each other, Winston left again for the bush. She had no idea if she would ever see him again. Suddenly, she didn't care. If he didn't care, then she would do the same.

But she felt her solitude acutely as the days passed slowly, the only sign of life in the room the sound of the ticking clock. She fidgeted with last year's issues of British Vogue from January and February, winter clothes that she would never wear or buy. She only had these two issues, and she flipped through them over and over again, imagining these girls living a glamorous life in Paris or Rome, places she had never been.

An unopened invitation sat on her coffee table. She usually ignored these polite dinner invitations from her compound neighbors. But that morning, she tore open the cream envelope and read the invitation written with blue fountain pen. It was from the Scottish couple, her neighbors. She knew they were Ayo's close friends. She picked up the phone and told the Scottish woman that she would be attending tomorrow night's dinner. The woman sounded surprised.

She spent all afternoon getting ready for the dinner party. She put her long, black hair in rollers, so it would cascade down in curls. She carefully laid out all her clothes on her bed, trying to decide which dress was the most flattering. She settled on a slim-fitting, purple batik dress she had sewn herself out of material from the market. She had heard the Swedish translator had returned to Europe, her contract work finished.

Sylvia gave her children a bath and wrapped them in their towels, giving them a hug. They smelled of Lux soap and that sweet, powdery scent of babies. They were so young, they wouldn't remember any of this.

"Mama's going out to dinner tonight," she said.

"Where you going, madam?" Patience said, coming into the bathroom and looking over Sylvia's tight-fitting dress.

"To the neighbors. The MacDonalds."

"Oh dey go be Ayo's friends."

"How do you know?"

"My friend Virginia works for them."

"Oh, right," Sylvia said, realizing the house staff knew more about the compound residents than the residents themselves. She realized she couldn't hide anything from Patience. They each knew the other had a crush on Ayo.

"You say hello to him from me, you hear?" Patience said, slightly jealous, as if she knew why Sylvia was so dressed up tonight. Sylvia and Winston, raised by servants, were used to conducting their entire relationship or non-relationship in front of the servants. Patience knew everything.

"I will," Sylvia said, knowing full well Patience would get a report on the evening from this friend Virginia who would likely be serving drinks at the party.

Sylvia walked into the MacDonald's house, the identical floor plan as hers. The living room was full of the mostly British crowd on the compound. But she didn't see Ayo among them. What if he doesn't come? She suddenly regretted coming. She panicked at the thought of having to endure an evening with people that didn't really care for her. The crowd stared as if surprised to see her at the party. She didn't know what else to do, so she studied the museum-like walls and shelves in the living room. They were full of Nigerian wood statues of mothers with large breasts holding children and large oil paintings of marketplaces or village scenes in oranges, yellows, and reds. A house girl, dressed in a white uniform, asked her if she wanted a drink.

"Are you Virginia?" Sylvia asked.

"Yes, madam."

"Patience says hello."

Virginia smiled. "What do you want to drink, madam?"

"Bitter lemon," Sylvia said. She stood waiting, pretending to study one of the paintings.

"I'm surprised to see you here," Ayo said, coming over to her.

She looked up at him. He smiled warmly at her. No one had smiled at her all day, at least not like that. But the smile was a warning to her because of the way it made her feel.

"I shouldn't have come," she said. "These people…" She trailed off with a nervous laugh, the kind that hung off the end of her sentences when she felt on edge.

"Don't mind them. Just a group of English blokes and their silly wives. How are your children?"

"Well, thanks to you. I'm indebted to you again."

"No debts. I didn't do anything."

She felt his hazel eyes speaking to her. She and Ayo exchanged polite niceties, but their eyes conversed on a more profound level. She felt this invisible conversation in her heart—a connection, an understanding acknowledged only by eye contact. She held onto this moment and all that it promised.

An English woman came over, breaking the spell between them. She was in her mid-thirties, blonde and attractive, but the edges of her eyes were beginning to show the aging effects of the African sun.

"Hello, darling," the English woman said to Ayo, her hand brushing his shoulder. "You need a drink. Here's your favorite." She handed him a scotch.

He smiled at her too, Sylvia noticed. Not as warmly, she thought, but then again there was a familiarity between the two of them that made her suddenly jealous. She didn't know why she should be jealous, he wasn't even hers to possess in that way.

Ayo sat down to dinner next to her. The two of them were the only non-white people in the room. But being half-English, he seemed to be at ease with the company. The Scottish wife had made a British colonial version of the local chicken peanut stew, laying the buffet table with many little bowls of toppings—coconut flakes, juicy fresh pineapple chunks, grated cucumber, slices of banana, diced tomatoes, freshly roasted peanuts.

Sylvia turned to Ayo. "I want to come...and volunteer at your clinic. I have no training in nursing except that I've always wanted to be one since I was a girl. I don't know if that counts for anything."

"Enthusiasm is all you need. But it'll be difficult, painful even at times. I'm not going to deceive you."

"I know. I need to do something. With my life." She didn't explain she needed to do something with him.

"When can you come?"

"Anytime. Next week." She hoped she didn't sound too desperate.

"Next week it is then." Then he added, "Make sure your driver brings you and come only in the daylight hours. To be safe."

"I'm glad you don't think I should be trapped in the compound."

"No, of course not. You have to live your life. But still, take precautions."

"I don't know if it matters. They were here inside. I'm about as safe out there as I am in here."

"There's some truth to that."

After dinner, the men poured scotch and port. Sylvia got up and thanked her host. It was still early, but since she had come alone, it didn't feel appropriate to stay too late.

"You walked here, dear?" said her host, the red-haired, freckled Scottish woman. "I can't have you walk home alone. No, that won't do at all. I'll find someone to…" She turned and scanned the room quickly, her eyes settling on Ayo.

Sylvia followed Ayo out the door, stepping into the humid night air. They strolled down the quiet streets of the compound. The air smelled like wet leaves decaying after the rain. They walked in between the shadows of the acacia trees and flattened, dead frogs lying on the road.

"Glad to get out of there. You saved me this time," Ayo said. She had dreamed of this moment, walking alone in the dark with him. She felt fireflies flitting around in her stomach, burning the edges, the glow of pain and anticipation.

He stopped for a moment in the road and looked up at the stars. "I love this sky. Only in Africa." He took a deep breath. "I missed it when my Mum and I moved to the UK after my parents got divorced."

"I've never seen a sky quite like this before," she admitted, having grown up in urban Asia.

She looked up and studied the night sky. The stars were crisp and bright. Looking up at the sky from the equator and away from city lights, a silent chorus of previously invisible stars took the stage, a visual orchestra. She felt the tension in her body ease slightly. She and the night had an uneasy relationship. She had spent most of her nights awake with crying babies since she had come to Africa.

They walked down the paved driveway to her house, past the dark silhouette of the bamboo bushes. She thought she heard the snakes rustle in the grass.

They came to her door, and she turned to him. He was standing so close to her. She had this sudden urge to touch the outline of his face. She didn't know what was going on between them, but she knew it had started on that very first day. She was afraid, but she was also grasping for it. Insects covered the dim lamp above them, blindly drawn to the light. Their corpses rained down on her, scorched from the heat. Ayo reached out and brushed them away, touching her hair. She looked up at him, his hand on her hair. Suddenly, an image flashed through her mind of Ayo and her lying naked on the white terrazzo tile floor of her house. The picture was sharp, life-like, as if it was about to happen or had already happened. Their bodies left a faint imprint of perspiration on the cold tile floor.

Shaking, she quickly turned to open her door. Her keys fell. She could hear the loud *clink* as they hit the ground. He picked up the keys, and as he gave them to her, their hands touched. Neither of them said anything. Then, she went inside and closed the door.

Chapter 16

In November 1976, Sylvia walked into Ayo's clinic, unprepared for the stench of disinfectant mixed with unwashed and perspiring bodies. She hadn't been to the clinic since Lila had been bitten by a snake three years before. The memory of the place brought a confusion of feelings. It was where her daughter had fought the onslaught of the snake spirits, yet it was also the place she had fallen for him.

Even though it was only nine in the morning, and the clinic had just opened, the reception overflowed with women and children waiting for the doctor. Sylvia was surprised how full it was. The triage nurse sat at a wooden reception desk writing away in a spiral notebook.

"I've come to volunteer. I'm a friend of Ayo's," Sylvia said to the nurse.

"Oh yes, madam, we've been expecting you." The nurse handed Sylvia a white nurse's uniform. "You can put this on in de bathroom."

Sylvia nodded. She wondered where Ayo was, but she could hardly expect him to greet her. She went down the hall to change into the starched white dress. She couldn't understand why nurse's uniforms were white when the job to be done entailed the deeply-staining colors of sickness and death. How did they keep their uniforms clean? She thought it must be a special challenge for nurses. Dress them in white to see how quickly they can mess up their uniforms. What was the point? Who had thought of this ridiculous idea? She pinned the hat on her head and went back out to the reception.

"There you are," Ayo called from down the hallway. "You look like you've been a nurse your whole life."

She turned around and half-smiled, feeling like an imposter in the uniform, in his clinic. She wasn't really here to save lives. She was here to save her own life, she knew that. Even he probably knew that.

"I see you've met the triage nurse," he said, walking up to her.

"Yes." She looked up at him. He reached out and adjusted the hat on her hair.

"Why these hats?" she asked with her nervous laugh as his hands touched her.

"God knows," he laughed. "My donors send the uniforms. I just make everyone wear them, so we look like the real thing." He finished pinning her hat on correctly. "Right, ready for your job?"

She nodded and followed him to the wooden reception desk.

"Sit here and write down the symptoms of the patients as the triage nurse examines them." He handed her the worn, spiral notebook.

"That sounds easy enough," she said, sitting down at the wooden table. She looked at the last entry recorded in the notebook. *Taiwo, 6 month old infant, fever of 102 F, diarrhea, possible dehydration. Other twin deceased.* Maybe it wasn't going to be that easy. She knew they were more than words on a page.

Ayo left to do his rounds. The morning passed quickly and she didn't see him again. She kept writing down what the triage nurse said. *Femi, five years old, vomiting, fever, signs of malnutrition.* The little boy had the telltale bloated belly.

Suddenly, a bleeding woman came in, carried by two other female relatives. "She just had baby, but de bleeding it no stop," one of the women said. The triage nurse grabbed Sylvia, "Stop writing. Come wit me."

The relatives carried the bleeding woman to the operating table.

"Help me undress her," the nurse said to Sylvia. "Quickly!"

Sylvia fumbled, trying to untie the women's wrapper dress, which was wound many times around her waist. The nurse turned to prepare an IV.

"Cut it, quick," the nurse handed her a pair of scissors.

The women's green wrapper was soaked in blood. "Get Ayo now," the nurse barked. "Tell him de woman is hemorrhaging."

Sylvia found Ayo in one of the patient rooms.

Ayo did not say anything when she told him, but his expression revealed his fear. He went quickly into the makeshift operating room and shut the door. Sylvia went to the bathroom to wash her hands. She looked down at the rusty red spots on her uniform and tried to wash the blood out with soap. It was hopeless and it was only the beginning of the day. She returned to writing down symptoms in the spiral notebook.

After several hours, Ayo emerged from the operating room. He looked exhausted. There was blood on his coat, his gloves, and even on his shoes. She didn't want to ask what had happened. She saw the answer on his face.

"Let me wash up," he said. "Let's get some lunch." It was two o'clock. Neither of them had eaten yet.

They sat down in his clinic's noisy cafeteria with plates of jollof rice, chicken, and plantain.

"She travelled over thirty kilometers to reach us, she almost died in a slow-moving canoe en route," Ayo said. He pressed his fingers between his eyes, closing them for a brief moment. "If she had come earlier, she would have lived."

"You did your best," Sylvia said, not knowing what else to say.

"My best isn't enough." He banged the table with his first. "These mothers need to come to the clinic for the birth and even before that. Babies and mothers are dying for reasons that could be easily solved medically, umbilical cords tangled around their necks or breech babies, things that a C-section would easily solve. Instead, they stay home and come here when it's already too late."

She felt his pain, this burden of his. All that he did sometimes amounted to nothing at the end of the day. She sensed the futility of it slowly eating away at him. Suddenly, she wanted to be here for him, cushion him from the hard realities of his work. She reached out and touched the side of his face.

• • •

Her life settled into a rhythm of sorts over the next six months. She went to volunteer at the clinic two or three times a week. Winston didn't object. After all, it was what he had always wanted her to do. He was probably glad she was keeping herself occupied and freeing him up to do his work in peace. Although she sometimes felt nervous leaving two-year-old Thomas and four-year-old Lila with Patience, she had to admit Patience was much more capable than she. After all, it was she that had left the children alone in the car, not Patience. She was still frightened of the man with yellowed eyes, fearing he would strike at any moment, and she was glad now of the round-the-clock security guards. Still, she refused to be a prisoner in her own house. It felt good to get out to town, to do something useful with her time at Ayo's clinic and to be near him.

The work at Ayo's clinic was grueling, she could not deny that, but it was better than sipping coffee with unfriendly ladies on the compound. For her, the benefits outweighed the costs. She could work side by side with Ayo, the cure for her own ailment. She thought of her own diagnosis in the triage notebook: Sylvia, age twenty-six, dizziness, insomnia, possible lovesickness.

As for Winston, he was gone more than ever before. He would be out in the bush for three weeks at a time, returning home for barely a week before he had to leave again. Ever since the juju doctor's spell, she felt a renewed coldness and distance in everything he did. One evening when he returned home from a trip, he brought back a small drum. The children were in their pajamas, getting ready for bed when Winston arrived. But seeing the gift he had brought, Sylvia let the children come out to the living room to see their father. She hoped the gift was a sign of some sort, a sign that he still loved his son.

Winston's normally taut jaw muscles relaxed a little when he saw little Thomas.

"Thomas, look what I bought you. It's a talking drum," he said.

"Talks?" Thomas said, wide-eyed.

Four-year old Lila sat slightly apart, watching. Winston hadn't bothered to bring anything for her. Sylvia sensed a darkness descend upon her daughter; the same inky blackness had shaded Sylvia's heart as a girl. She knew what it felt like to be the daughter who was shunned. She went over and sat next to Lila, putting her arm around her.

"The seller kept following me, halving the price several times, so eventually I had to buy it from the poor man," Winston said to his wife. Why would he tell her this, she wondered? That he only bought it because he pitied the vendor? What about pitying his poor son, she thought angrily?

Thomas tried to play the drum, making a loud, chaotic sound.

Winston frowned and abruptly said, "That's enough. Time to go bed, children. It's late."

Thomas looked dejected, craving a kind word or hug. When he had been a baby, Winston had been so affectionate toward his son. Sylvia knew Winston had deliberately pulled himself away from his son. Why did he have to do this? He was becoming an absentee father who was never around, and even when he was home, he hardly spent any time with his son, holing up in his study. She had given him a son as a gift, and it felt like he was returning it, regretting it.

Sylvia took the children down the hallway to their bedrooms.

"Thomas, you played the drum so well," she said, tucking him in bed. She hugged him tightly, showering his face with kisses to compensate for the lack of love from his father.

Then she went to Lila's room to say good night. Lila was waiting for her, still sitting up in her bed.

"Why is my hair brown and not black like Thomas?" Lila said, point blank. "Is that why Baba likes him better?"

Her daughter had already made the connection between her looks and her father. Lila was four years old now and precociously becoming self-aware of her different looks. Sylvia didn't know what to say. She was torn. She didn't want to keep secrets from her daughter. But then again, could Lila keep a secret? Children were known to blurt out things in public.

So she told her daughter a bedtime story instead. She sat down next to her on the bed and held her close. She told her that her mother's family had Portuguese blood, an ancestor on a long-forgotten line, some clandestine love between a Chinese concubine and a Portuguese sea-faring merchant. That's why she looked different because she was not entirely Chinese, which was the truth to some extent.

Lila sat there listening to Sylvia's story, hugging her favorite, yellow stuffed elephant. Her large brown eyes widened as she took in the information. Sylvia looked at her sweet face, her little girl. Why had she lied to her? She would find out the truth one day and hate her for it, wouldn't she?

Lila accepted Sylvia's explanation for now. She was at the age when children were blank slates, sponges soaking up whatever their parents said. Sylvia's explanation was further reinforced by the fact Lila was growing up in an international expat compound, surrounded by a shifting kaleidoscope of races. This helped blur the edges of her differences. Spicy Indian curries and *somosas* were served side by side with English roasts and potatoes; the lilting language of Hindi sang harmonies with the dissonant tones of German. People were different, she saw it all around her. She believed Sylvia's lie because it made sense given the diverse children around her.

• • •

In October 1977, after about nine months volunteering at Ayo's clinic, he invited her to a small birthday gathering at his father's house in town. They had become friends, colleagues now. It only seemed natural he would invite her. She didn't think twice about whether it was appropriate for her to go.

She drove to the old part of town where the wealthy used to

live during colonial times. Ayo's father's house had a wall around it lined with broken glass and a watchman asleep at the gate. It was a traditional cement house with a corrugated tin roof, intricate verandahs, and sun-bleached wooden shutters. The front door was made of ornately carved wood depicting scenes of fishermen and farmers. She walked through a small reception area that opened up onto a dirt courtyard with mango trees, scarlet bougainvillea, and an old African gray parrot. The house was rectangular, the rooms and verandahs overlooking a central courtyard. Ayo led her across to the main living room. She followed him, watching his broad shoulders, his arms swinging by his side. When he turned to look at her, she saw his profile, his long eyelashes, square jaw. She resisted the urge to reach out and touch the side of his face.

"Right, come sit in here. This is the only room that's air-conditioned, I'm afraid," he said awkwardly, running his hand through his short, curly hair. "Looks like the others haven't arrived yet."

She sat on the sofa, embarrassed. Even though they worked together at the clinic, somehow alone in his house, she felt oddly out of place like she shouldn't be here. She shifted her bare legs self-consciously, feeling Ayo watching her. An old male servant came in and brought a Bitter Lemon soda for her, a cold beer for Ayo, and a bowl of plantain chips on a worn silver tray, blackened and dull from lack of polishing.

"My present," she said, producing a bottle of scotch tied with red ribbon from her bag. As she handed him the bottle, their hands touched.

"Thanks," he choked and stood up abruptly. He went over to the liquor glass cabinet at the side of the room.

He stayed standing by the glass cabinet as if keeping his

distance for protection. "I wonder what the others are up to?" he said. "They should have been here by now."

The others were the Scottish couple and another single Englishman, his close friends on the compound. Did he include her as a "close friend" now, she wondered?

"I like your house...it's...like the traditional houses we used to have back in China," she said, trying to break the uncomfortable silence.

"I love this house. I grew up in it," Ayo paused, fidgeting as well. "My parents divorced when I was fifteen, and I had to move to the UK with my mum. I came back for the holidays, but I missed this place. The cold and gray of the UK was such a contrast with the heat and color here."

They sat in the sparsely furnished living room, simple chairs with velvet cushions still in their plastic, but not because they were new. The plastic was ripped in places. It had become part of the furniture over the years. She looked around the room, trying to find a distraction to slow her heart down. The floor was a dark green terrazzo tile. On the bare white wall hung the larger-than-life smile of the current president, General Obasanjo, the picture updated constantly due to the rapid succession of generals and presidents. This particular picture had been replaced after the assassination of General Murtala Mohammed the previous year. The room had the customary television set even though most nights the local station only broadcast multi-colored stripes to the tune of the national anthem. There was nothing particularly African in the room. It was not like the European houses on the compound, crammed full of Nigerian wood carvings, paintings, and tapestries.

Ayo seemed to study her, the way she kept flipping her long hair back. At his clinic, he didn't have that kind of luxury. He was always busy, running around saving lives. But here at his house, he allowed himself to observe her. Her bare legs stuck to the plastic on the sofa. With just the two of them together in this room, an image of him touching her on the sofa flashed through her mind. As if he sensed what she was thinking, he came closer to her, but he didn't sit next to her. He sat on another chair near her, still keeping his distance.

Then he continued, trying to dispel the tension between them. Without the medical machines, the white uniform, the smell of the sick and dying—their attraction seemed to escalate, isolated now from the white noise of the clinic.

"When I was child, I used to think this house was a bit old and decrepit. But now I hold on to it, I don't know, for sentimental reasons. When my Dad built his new house, he gave this one to me. He knew how much I loved it, I suppose."

"Do you come here often then?" She knew he lived most of the time on an apartment in the compound.

"Sometimes. To get away," he said, looking straight at her.

Looking into his eyes, she felt that connection again. Only this time, they were alone without witnesses. Where were the others, she wondered? Would they come and save them or did she not really want them to come?

As if he were thinking the same thing, he got up, frustrated. "I can't imagine why the others aren't here yet."

"Maybe their car broke down." She said this because she wanted that to be the case. She wanted to be alone with him in this house.

"Right, well…let's just start our lunch without them. You must be hungry." He leaned out of the room into the courtyard and shouted something in Yoruba to his servant.

"By the way, I hope you like the local fare."

"Love it. I was worried your steward was going to serve that bland English food to us instead."

He laughed, and the tension seemed to ease a little. They sat down at the formally set dining table in the room and the steward came to serve lunch. The table between them and the constant coming and going of the steward helped reset the mood in the room.

"Why did you come back to Africa?" Sylvia asked, attempting some semblance of a normal conversation. "I mean why didn't you just stay in England? The locals all seem anxious to get out of the country and move to the UK. You're doing the opposite."

"That's exactly it. If all of us educated people left for the comforts of the UK or America, who would be left to build our country? Nigeria needs people like me. That's why I studied medicine and why I came back."

"Another hero," she said, falling for him all over again. "I am surrounded by them. Everyone is here for some selfless reason."

"Not really heroic," he laughed. "There's some selfishness in it too. You see, in England, I never really felt like I fit in, me being brown and my mother blonde and white. We lived in a small flat in London. We were not well-off. I felt like I lived on the fringe of society. But here, in my father's large house, I always felt rich compared to everyone else. People here looked up to me, wanted to be me. Whereas in the UK, it was the opposite. So you see it's a bit of ego too." She could see the real person in him, not some façade put up to impress or, in Winston's case, to protect.

"Not ego. Self-esteem," she said, "Don't be so hard on yourself. A place you fit in better. Makes sense."

"I don't know if I fit in better, I suppose I sort of feel torn in half. I'm from two worlds. I can live in two different worlds. Do I prefer one over the other? Or do I feel odd in both?" Ayo shrugged. "Honestly, now that I'm actually living here, I can't say I fit in here either." His voice trailed off, and he just gazed at her face, taking her in.

Is that why he was drawn to her? Because she was neither black nor white? With her, he wouldn't have to choose alliances. He looked melancholy for a brief moment, but then said, "Do you want to see the house?"

He showed her the blackened walls of the kitchen with its kerosene stove, large wooden mortar and pestle for pounding yam. He showed her the multiple bedrooms that had belonged to his father's three wives and their children. Then he showed her his father's room. They stood next to the heavy, mahogany, four-poster colonial bed with a gauzy mosquito net twisted above it. The half-closed, green shutters cast thin lines of light across the neatly made up white bed. A trapped moth fluttered against the shutters, trying to get out. She saw all these things as if in slow motion. Then, he was so close to her. He leaned her against the bedpost and kissed her. It was a desperate kiss, both of them wanting to act out what had been playing in their minds the whole afternoon. She pressed her body closer to him, but he abruptly moved away. "I'm sorry. You'd better go."

• • •

The next week, Sylvia went to his clinic, but now everything was different—the smell no longer bothered her, the endless sick children, the nurses, what had been white noise, was now in the background, insignificant, as if someone had turned down the volume.

Ayo looked at her awkwardly in the hallway, but he spoke as if nothing had happened between them, his tone professional and urgent.

"Go quickly and help Nurse Agnes in there," he pointed at a room down the hall. "Some children were just brought in, badly injured. One girl had a nail hammered into her head."

"A nail? Who would do that to a child?"

"I'm trying to get to the bottom of that."

She went into the room where the nurse was dressing the children's wounds. The clinic's volume had been turned up again, and Sylvia was thrust into another crisis, forcing her to relegate thoughts of him to the back of her mind.

While Nurse Agnes attended to the girl with the nail in her head, Sylvia cleaned the raw wounds around the other girl's ankles. There was no skin around her ankles, just raw, bleeding flesh.

"What happened?" she asked the girl, who she guessed was roughly ten or eleven years old.

The girl stayed silent, staring off into space.

The man who had brought the girls spoke up. "I go found her like dis, tied to a tree with a rope. Left in de forest to die."

"Who would do this to her?" Sylvia asked as she put iodine on the open wounds. The girl grimaced in pain, jumping off the table as if trying to escape from more torture and abuse.

"Her parents," the man said.

"Why would they do something like this to their own child?" Sylvia was shocked. She brought the girl back to the examination table, speaking kind words to her, putting her arm around her. The girl shrunk from her touch.

"Dey tink she is witch."

Sylvia felt herself jump at the mention of the word. "Why would they think such a thing?"

"Everyone in our village go be afraid. De pastor he go tell de village, dese girls are witches. He go ask dem parents to pay him, and he will do deliverance to take de witch away. I tink he go speak rubbish. He just take de money to get rich. But dese parents have no money, dey go be afraid of dere girls, so dey try to hurt dem. Other villagers try to hurt dem, dey all go be afraid."

"The pastor said this? What church?"

"The Savior's Miracle Evangelical Church."

"Have you reported this to the police?"

"What de police going to do?"

"Arrest the parents. The pastor."

"De pastor is rich. He go be big man now. He make so much money from doing deliverances for dese parents. He pay de police."

"I can't take dese children back to de village," he continued. "Dey will be killed. Can you keep dem safe here?"

"Of course they can't go back. I will find them a safe place to go."

Sylvia finished dressing the girl's ankles and went to find Ayo. He was performing a brain scan of the girl with the nail in her head. Sylvia waited outside the x-ray room for him. When he came out, he saw Sylvia standing there. For a moment, he looked disoriented as if wondering what she was doing here.

"How is she?" Sylvia asked.

"Luckily, the scan shows that the nail just penetrated her skull, not her brain. It wasn't that long a nail. But I'll still need to take it out. Then there's the worry of fractured bone getting into her brain."

"I found out what happened to these girls. The village thinks they're witches. Apparently, a crazy pastor told them this. They can't go back to their village. It's not safe."

"I suspected something like this. There's a good orphanage in town. I'll have a nurse take them there once they can be released from the clinic."

"I can take them to the orphanage. I'd like to."

"Are you sure? This is more than you signed up for."

"I signed up to help."

"You'll soon discover there's no end to helping around here."

"Shouldn't we do something? I mean, about the pastor. There may be more children at risk."

Ayo paused. "You're learning that for every child that walks in these doors, there's a story with a problem that needs to be solved. You'll run yourself ragged trying to solve every problem."

"Still seems like we should report this."

"I'll talk to a NGO that focuses on children's welfare about looking into it."

Sylvia waited in the staff room as Ayo performed surgery on the girl with the nail in her head. It was late, night had fallen, and most of day shift staff had gone home. Sylvia sat at the table, waiting to find out the girl's fate, waiting for him. She sat alone in the dark staff room, not bothering to turn on the lights as night fell.

He came into the room, and she stood up. The light from the hallway fell across her face. She knew her expression revealed far too much. He closed the door, enveloping them in darkness. He pushed her body onto the table and kissed her, running his hands under her white nurse's dress.

Someone walked up the hallway and opened the door to the staff room. They quickly separated. A nurse came into the room to get her things. She looked startled to see them in the dark. Sylvia walked quickly out of the room, and Ayo followed.

In the dark parking lot, they stood under the feathery tamarind trees, the spreading branches providing shade during the daytime for the parked cars. The wailing sound of the nocturnal insects suddenly seemed like a warning to her.

"I have to go," she said even though she wanted to stay. She felt a confusion of emotions—worry about her children at home, wanting him in that dark staff room. She remembered his hands touching her under her dress.

"I know. Forgive me," he said quietly.

She said nothing because she didn't want to forgive him. What would have happened if the nurse hadn't shown up?

"You would have to be the one woman I fall for. One that I can't have," he muttered under his breath. But she heard it.

It felt good to hear those words even though they were not good words. But she sensed the frustration, resentment even, at the edge of his voice. A mosquito landed on her bare arm. Ayo hit her arm, killing the mosquito, the blood staining her skin.

WINSTON

Chapter 17

Two months later, as Winston was driving home, his jeep got mired in the usual go-slow just as he approached Ibadan. It was Christmas Eve 1977. He wanted to return home on time for the annual Christmas Eve party on the compound at the ADA Director's house. But the cars slowed to a complete halt. Winston turned off his engine, not wanting it to idle for hours on end in this heat. He rolled down his window. The usual crowd, mostly vendors, swarmed his jeep, shoving their wares through his window. He thought he saw the juju doctor with the yellowed eyes, his nemesis, approaching. But when he scanned the crowd again, he wasn't there.

The predominantly Christian town of Ibadan celebrated the Christmas season. Woven palm fronds decorated the cement and mud homes, small palm trees sported tinsel, cotton-wool snow, and bells. Christmas music blared out of roadside stalls, and slaughtered goats hung upside down at the market. A lurid red cross lit up the main church in town. Here it was a religious holiday about the baby Jesus, few toys were given, only gifts of soap, pencils, cotton cloth, or sweets were exchanged. A group of Nigerian dancers and drummers went from house to house chanting hymns and holding a brown baby doll, signifying Jesus as a gift to mankind. Crowds mobbed the dancers, trying to touch the baby Jesus.

Winston waited in the heat for almost an hour, his clothes completely drenched in sweat. It was close to six o'clock, and he knew his wife would already be getting ready for the party, wondering where he was. The sun was setting. Finally, the traffic started moving. He turned the key to start the engine, but it sputtered out and died. He tried several times but with no luck. Cars behind him started to honk, their drivers shouting obscenities at him. Was the juju doctor involved? He was sure now he saw him. Would he come for him? Winston looked around, scanning the crowd anxiously.

He thought through his options. He could try and find a mechanic to fix the problem, but he didn't know if that would be successful. Or he could abandon the jeep and flag down a minibus or taxi to take him back to the compound. He was only thirty minutes to an hour away. The second sounded more appealing, but he knew he would lose the jeep.

A man approached wearing mechanic overalls. "You having trouble with your car, sah?"

"Are you a mechanic?" Winston asked.

"Yes, sah."

"Will you take a look?"

"Yes, sah, no problem, I fix for you."

The man crawled under his jeep to take a look. After about ten minutes, he slid out. "It's fixed, sah. I make it betta for you."

"That quickly?" Winston felt somewhat suspicious. He started his engine, and sure enough, it worked. Had this same mechanic crawled under his car earlier during the traffic jam and fiddled with something underneath? He had heard of such scams happening. Now he started to think maybe it was not related to the witch doctor but was just some random, everyday occurrence in Nigeria. Whatever it was, he wanted to get home quickly. He paid the exorbitant fee, the mechanic taking advantage of Winston's desperate situation.

When he arrived, it was eight o'clock, and Sylvia was already at the party. Patience was at home with the children.

"Where you been, masta?" Patience said. "Madam go wait for you, but she left. She go be angry."

Winston valued Patience's expertise when it came to the children, but he didn't appreciate her scolding. She was clearly in Sylvia's camp, and that bothered him. He could do no right in her eyes.

Winston quickly showered and then dressed for the Christmas Eve party at the clubhouse. The expat compound made an attempt to celebrate Christmas where there was no snow. There was aerosol-sprayed snow on windows, and someone always dressed as Santa. Lacking a Chinese community to celebrate Chinese New Year, Winston and Sylvia had succumbed to this compound holiday as a substitute. His wife bought a plastic tree at a garage sale from a family moving back to the UK and placed a few token presents under the tree. Still, it was not a big occasion for them. Every Christmas Eve, most families on the compound congregated at the Director of the ADA's house. Winston walked into the party, scanning the crowd for his wife.

Many of the guests wore their home country's formal, traditional dress as well—silk saris, Yoruba *iro* wrappers and elaborate *gele* headdresses, or Scottish kilts. The American Director of the ADA had ordered frozen turkeys, cranberry sauce, and sweet potato casseroles from the US just for the party. Guests stood in line to taste this American delicacy. In the corner was a large, artificial Christmas tree, heavy with teddy bear ornaments. Outside, people ate on white plastic tables and chairs under colored Christmas lights strewn on trees. It was a warm, balmy evening, not at all like the dark snowy nights most of the revelers associated with Christmas.

He saw his wife dressed in a red silk *qipao*, the long slits revealing her bare legs. Red became her, he thought. It was the Chinese color of happiness, good fortune, of all good things. She was talking to the doctor, engrossed in an intense conversation it seemed. She had been volunteering at his clinic for the past year, and he was glad, despite everything, she had found her vocation. The doctor embraced her and kissed her on the cheek. He knew this casual intimacy was a European custom, but still, it suddenly bothered him.

He quickly walked over to them. The doctor nodded at him as he approached and took his leave. His wife couldn't help smiling at the doctor as he left.

"You're late," his wife said to him, her face clouding over.

He had been away for three weeks, and this was how she greeted him. He knew he deserved it, but it still hurt especially after the way she had smiled at the doctor.

"My jeep broke down," he said.

"Again?" she looked alarmed.

"It's not what you think. It was just a random mechanic scam."

"Nothing is random, you know that. It's the juju spell."

"You're starting to sound like Patience. You really believe all of this? I came out unhurt didn't I?"

She seemed offended by his slighting of Patience. He knew she regarded Patience as a friend, a relative of sorts.

"For now, you might have escaped. But next time you might not? Don't you get it?" she responded.

"Let's not go through this again." Winston walked off to join his colleagues, leaving his wife standing there alone. He didn't want to go down this path because in truth, it frightened him. He didn't want to be dragged down by his wife and her superstitious world. As far as he was concerned, it was better not to dwell on it.

• • •

That night, after the children had gone to bed, Sylvia was in the living room wrapping Christmas presents for the following morning.

Winston pulled out a large box of Duplo Legos for Thomas, something he had bought on a recent trip to New York. He flew twice a year to New York to give the ADA donors an update on his ADA 2000 Starter Pack program.

"You didn't get anything for Lila from New York, did you?" Sylvia said, sounding annoyed. He sensed another argument brewing.

"Uh…" he mumbled.

"You treat her differently," she accused.

"They can share." He tried to placate his wife.

"Share? Legos are clearly for a boy."

"He's my son."

"You regret her," she said slowly. "You regret marrying me, don't you?" Her voice was shaking now.

Winston was silent, neither disputing nor confirming her words. She ran down the hall into their bedroom. Winston did not follow. Did he regret marrying her? If he could rewrite his

148

life, yes, he would do it differently. Marrying her had brought baggage, emotional baggage; he preferred to travel more lightly.

He knew he was a self-sufficient man, an introvert, operating mostly on his own. He did not require much in the way of attention or displays of love, and as a result, he didn't seem to think others needed it either. His own parents' relationship had been formal and aristocratic. They had never exchanged hugs or words of affection and mostly lived apart as his father studied in Beijing. He knew his parents' behavior stood in contrast to his wife's parents. She had told him her father was a passionate man, possessive and jealous of her mother, not letting her venture out without him. Even when Sylvia's mother went out to purchase sanitary pads and other "women's supplies," Sylvia's father insisted on accompanying her. Winston sensed his wife's expectations of marriage were entirely different from his. He and Sylvia were both Chinese, but they did not speak the same language, not when it came to love.

SYLVIA

Chapter 18

On New Year's Eve 1977, Sylvia spent the day picking frangipani blossoms and threading leis with the other compound wives for the New Year's Eve Hawaiian Luau party. Winston feigned illness and bowed out of the party. She gladly went alone and for one reason. She wore a grass skirt with her bikini, a pink coral necklace, and a white frangipani blossom tucked in her long, flowing black hair, echoing Polynesian princesses returning to the sea.

When she reached the clubhouse, she sat in her car for a moment. She closed her eyes. The scent of the frangipani blossom in her hair made her nauseous. What was the point of trying when her husband didn't care about their marriage or his life and obviously regretted the whole thing? He had not said it, but he didn't need to. She knew he was a man of limited words. He would not speak in smooth, sugary words to hide anything. His silence meant the truth was better left unsaid. But it still hurt. She got out of her car and walked up to the New Year's Eve party at the clubhouse swimming pool.

The swimming pool was lit up and decorated with red flowers shaped into the word, "Aloha." Paper lanterns were strung from trees and circled the poolside. Ayo came to the party late. He wore a local batik print shirt and shorts. But this time, she sought him out.

"Dance?" she said as she studied his eyes, dark-green pools waiting for her to dive, water smothering her lungs.

He hesitated at first, glancing at her bare midriff.

Soon he held her arm and waist, and they were dancing to a scratchy record of someone's lilting Hawaiian hula music. The touch of his hand on her bare skin as they danced made her follow him later down the dark hill to the room full of pipes underneath the swimming pool. Or maybe it was the words left unsaid by her husband that chased her to these watery depths. In the dark mechanical room, Ayo pushed her against the wall, his hands moved over her bare stomach, her thighs under the grass skirt, and then he was inside her.

• • •

What followed was a kind of malaria-laced madness, papery snakeskin shells left on the grass, hundreds of dead frogs on the road. Sylvia swallowed bitter white malaria pills every Sunday to ward off the mosquito-love poisoning her blood. She lay in bed thinking she was delirious from malaria when what she was really suffering from was a spell of lust. There were secret rendezvous at his house in town, their bodies sticking together from the humidity as they made love. Or love for them could happen behind a wall while the party's sherry glasses clinked on the other side.

She met Ayo at his father's house in town in the afternoons.

They lay on the mahogany four-poster bed, the room felt hazy and unreal behind the white muslin mosquito net. The blue paint on the bare walls was swollen and cracked from the humidity, the only decoration a faded biblical calendar and a large, gilded mirror opposite the bed. In the corner, a rusty green electric fan on a stool threw air back and forth around the room, comforting and suffocating the lovers at its will.

The metal window bars outside had bled tears of rust down the yellow walls of his father's house. Even the scarlet bougainvillea could not cover it up. This house had already endured the forbidden love of his English mother and Nigerian father during Colonial times. These mud walls, once painted a vibrant yellow outside, had been built by this kind of love. Only now the pale stucco had cracked, revealing the dark mud walls underneath.

Sylvia was the ignored child, nobody's favorite, trapped in a loveless marriage. She had been starved of love. When she finally found it, she became an addict. But what was she to Ayo? Was it that kind of love, like his parents once felt, a passionate, rebellious kind of love that went against all odds? She didn't really know. But she did know this: he waited for her those afternoons at his rust-stained house in town. Sometimes she didn't come, wracked with guilt at that particular moment. But he still waited. And sometimes she did come. Her long black hair flung across his face in their mad embrace while thunderstorms blew palm trees sideways.

• • •

Sylvia remained fearful about her husband and her daughter, guarding them against the spell and the spirits. She continued to put fresh fruit as an offering on the little shrine at the edge of their garden for Lila's bush-soul, the wild boar. Since Winston had been born in the year of the Tiger, she decided his bush-soul was the lion. She had Energy build a shrine for him too, and she put out offerings for his bush-soul as well. She knew the lion would protect Winston. After all, wasn't he the strongest animal here in Africa? She knew Winston would have simply laughed at her for doing this, but as far as she knew, nothing had happened, so she concluded it must be working.

Sylvia continued to volunteer at the clinic even though she and Ayo were now lovers. He never touched her at the clinic anymore. He maintained a professional stance toward her now that they were seeing each other in private. A year went by, and Sylvia was becoming a proficient nurse, learning on the job. The Nigerian nurses were happy to teach her. She lived for working at the clinic, it had been her calling. Even though the days could be harrowing, she was working beside the man she loved and doing something she cared deeply about.

In the spring of 1978, Sylvia wrote in the spiral notebook as the triage nurse spoke: *Grace, three years old, seizures, cerebral malaria.* Fatal at this young age, the triage nurse explained. Sylvia carried the little girl with cerebral malaria to an examining room. The thin toddler had journeyed with her aunt from their rural village for more than a day by a combination of foot, bus, and moped. By the time they had reached Ayo's clinic, the malaria parasites had already latched onto the child's brain.

Sylvia shaved some of the hair off the child's head, and then, under the nurse's instruction, she inserted an IV to administer quinine. The child lay unconscious, contorted in pain. Ayo came into the room to examine her. He embodied both the heroic and the sordid, brandishing his stethoscope in a blood-stained white coat. The doctor on the edge of humanity, hopelessly trying to save lives in the tropics where bacteria thrived and the water ran brown or red, but never clear.

"Will she…be all right?" Sylvia remembered when Lila had been on the brink of life and death with malaria as a newborn.

"She's gone into a coma already. But let's hope so," Ayo said.

"You don't sound so hopeful," Sylvia said quietly.

"I've seen so many children die from cerebral malaria, semi-conscious as I pumped quinine and valium into the tiny veins in their skulls. And then the sudden rasping struggle of breath, followed by death and the total collapse of their little bodies."

He looked defeated as he said this. She felt for him, doing this kind of work. Wanting to save lives, but in reality, watching life violently choke, gasp, and then pass away. But somehow, she didn't share his sense of frustration yet. Maybe she still knew too little, her medical ignorance protecting her from this despair that Ayo sometimes felt.

The little girl, Grace, lay on the bed, still unconscious and rigid, frozen in pain. Sylvia looked at the shaved side of the child's head with the IV still inserted. She saw how frail Grace seemed. The spirits' grip on her was firm. She remembered the time she had spent by her daughter's bedside when Lila had struggled with malaria. Suddenly Grace started having seizures, and her previously still body flailed around violently. The nurse showed Sylvia how to administer pain suppositories for the girl.

"Can you do anything?" Sylvia asked Ayo, feeling afraid.

He shook his head as if he knew death was coming and the only thing he could do was ease the pain.

That night, he came to her house around midnight. Sylvia opened the door, and he stood there in his stained, white doctor's coat, his face unshaven. He looked like he had come directly from the clinic. They didn't speak. He kissed her roughly, pushing her against the kitchen counter. His hands undid her silk robe. Grace is dead, Sylvia thought, he came to tell me.

He made love to her on the white terrazzo tile of her kitchen floor as if it were his life dangling by a thin IV line. Afterward, they got up from the cold, hard floor. Naked, she walked towards the living room. Ayo followed. The dark house was full of the swaying shadows of the palm trees outside. They lay down on the couch holding each other.

"She's..." Sylvia began.

"She's the same."

For one more day, Grace was still with them, she thought.

"Thank you," he whispered.

"For Grace?"

"For keeping me sane. You keep me sane," he said.

She wanted to ease the pain of his toiling in a place of death and hopelessness; she wanted to be his nurse. She massaged his tight neck and shoulder muscles, the places where he held all his stress.

That morning, she set up a shrine for Grace too. She didn't know what her bush-soul might be, so she picked the monkey.

The next day when she went back to the clinic, she felt obligated to sit watch by Grace's bedside, not just for Ayo but also for herself. Grace's precarious hold on life mirrored Lila's struggle with malaria years before. Both girls were ravaged by spirits except this girl had no mother to protect her.

As Sylvia walked into the clinic, a nurse came up to her and grabbed her arm.

"Come and see dis," the nurse said. Was Grace gone? She tried to brace herself.

They walked into Grace's room. Sylvia almost fainted in

surprise. The little girl's eyes were wide open.

"She didn't die, she woke up instead," Sylvia said, rushing up to her bed.

Ayo came into the room.

"She's come out of her coma," Sylvia said. She held the little girl in her arms, feeling emboldened by her results. "I made a little shrine for her bush-soul, you know, like you told me to do for Lila. And it looks like it's working."

But Ayo said nothing. It was then that Sylvia noticed the child's eyes were still cerebral looking, death-like, open but fixed, not registering anything around her.

Gradually, Sylvia nursed Grace back to health. In a few days, she was eating. In a week, she was talking again. Finally, Grace was released from the clinic. The day Grace left the clinic Sylvia stood with Ayo at the front doors. She watched as an aunt carried Grace on her back. She saw her little face disappear around the corner. She had grown attached to the small, frail girl that had vanquished death.

"She's doing so well," Sylvia said proudly.

"But she will never walk again," Ayo said. "Despite holding on to life, like thousands of other children in Africa, she will suffer lasting neurological damage from the malaria."

Sylvia saw the despair return to Ayo's eyes. She thought about what this might mean for her own family. In the best case scenario, if they remained unscathed, she feared Lila and Winston might hold onto life like Grace, even as they suffered lasting damage from the spirits' and the spell's incursions on their physical and mental health. And what about her own mental health? All of this was taking a toll on Sylvia. She had told no one, not even Ayo, about her recent nightmares—horrible, frightening hallucinations. They were all about Lila. Her daughter was five years old. She still had two more years to go, and presumably her connection with the spirits would be severed. And Winston? Sylvia didn't know about him. He continued to return to Simeon's village despite the curse. Every time he drove off in his jeep, she wondered if it was the last time she would see him.

PART TWO

1980-1983

SYLVIA

Chapter 19 1980

When Lila turned seven, the snake spirits came for her again. It was the local Mama wata spirit, the beautiful water goddess, sometimes a mermaid or a serpent. Mama wata brought her victims to the bottom of lakes and fed them black mud, worms, and raw fish. Divers claimed they heard voices and saw light coming from the deep under the water. They also said it was warmer down at the bottom of lakes. They believed that there were underwater mermaid spirit villages.

Along with some other children, Lila wandered down to the lake and the dam on the compound. Some older boys dared Lila and a few other girls to climb down into the empty dam. As Lila climbed down the ladder, she saw dragonflies and pretty butterflies, and they made her forget the danger. But when Thomas and the other children saw the snake, Lila began scrambling back up. It was a long way out of the dam, and Lila's hands, sweaty from fear, slipped on the metal rungs, and she fell.

A security guard on his moped drove by, and the children

shouted for his help. He climbed down and carried Lila out of the dam.

He brought Lila and Thomas on his moped back to their house.

"My arm hurts, Mama," Lila cried.

Sylvia was beside herself. Had the snake bitten Lila again? She called Winston at his office and then immediately took the children to the small compound clinic. Sylvia knew she had grown lax about placing offerings at Lila's bush-soul shrine. Nothing had happened for a while, and she had grown complacent. How could she be so careless?

The elderly English doctor examined Lila for signs of a snake bite. Lila lay on the table, crying in pain.

"Looks like she's just broken her arm," the doctor said.

Sylvia was relieved to hear these words. Most mothers would have panicked, but she was relieved. She hoped Lila was growing out of her connection to the spirit world since she had just turned seven years old. According to Patience, this was the age most children shed their ties to the spirits.

Winston came into the room at the clinic. Thomas ran up to him.

"You alright?" Winston knelt down to examine his son.

"I'm okay, Baba," Thomas said. "But Lila's hurt."

Lila was lying on the examination table.

"She's broken her arm," Sylvia said.

Winston barely looked at Sylvia. They had reached a stalemate in their relationship. They had both given up trying and kept their distance. It wasn't hard to do since he was rarely at home. Two years had gone by since the juju doctor's threat, and Winston was still alive, living proof, he said, it was all nonsense. But she knew things happened to him out in the jungle, things he did not tell her.

Winston went to Lila, but he didn't offer her any words of sympathy.

"You're the oldest, Lila. I expect you to be responsible for you and your brother," he scolded. "You shouldn't have gone down into that dam. It's dangerous. You understand?"

Lila said nothing. She looked like she was about to cry. His words hurt more than the broken arm. Sylvia stood closer to her daughter, stroking her hair.

Winston returned to his office while Sylvia waited for Lila's cast to set. Afterward, Sylvia took the children to the clubhouse and bought them ice cream, served in soft swirls on a cone from a machine. They sat down at a table on the clubhouse patio. She watched as Lila ate.

"Feel better now?" Sylvia leaned over and touched her daughter's face.

Lila looked up at her and smiled. That beautiful smile, thought Sylvia, what she would do for that smile from her little girl.

Later that night, Lila had a nightmare. She had these dreams often, and Patience said it was a sign of her travelling to the spirit world at night. This time, Lila was sleepwalking, and Sylvia coaxed her back into bed. Lila's eyes were open, but she was not awake.

"I went to visit the mermaid in the lake," Lila said as if in a trance.

Sylvia tried to shake Lila out of this dream by waking her up, but Lila started screaming and flailing her body around. Sylvia worried her daughter would hurt her arm in the cast. It took all her strength to lay her child back down in bed. She held her down, stroking her face. Finally, Lila drifted into sleep. Sylvia went back to bed exhausted. But she couldn't fall back to sleep herself. She was filled with dread.

According to Patience, a child grows out of the spirit world once she can separate the dream world from the real world. If her dreams still merged with reality, the connection to the spirit world remained. Clearly, Lila was still making her nightly sojourns to the spirit world, continuing her double life. She was holding onto her lifeline to spirit world, and unlike normal children at this age, she would not let go.

• • •

Sylvia tried to escape it all—the spirits, the curse, her failed marriage. For over two years now, since that New Year's Eve in 1978, she had been leading a double life of her own. She met Ayo at his father's house in town at the end of her shift and during Ayo's afternoon break, the two of them leaving the clinic in separate cars at staggered times. Ayo gave Sylvia's driver, Ige, a small "dash" or tip to ask no questions. Sylvia knew Ige had just had triplet boys, and he could use the extra income from Ayo's weekly tips. Ige didn't seem to care either. He mostly parked his car in the shade outside Ayo's house and leaned the driver's seat way back for an afternoon nap. It was easy money.

Ayo and Sylvia lay in bed, hiding behind the white mosquito net in that hazy, make-believe world of theirs.

"Spend the night with me this weekend," Ayo said.

"I can't."

"Why not? Isn't Winston away for several weeks?"

"His schedule is random. He could just turn up."

Ayo was silent as if he resented being constrained by the existence of her husband.

"I can't leave the children anyway. I'm worried about Lila," she continued.

"Patience can handle that."

"I know she can...but if I weren't there...if something happened."

"You can't let the spirits dominate your life. You have to take care of yourself too. You need a break. You're a ball of nerves. Stay the weekend, and I'll take you somewhere special, a place I used to love as a boy."

"I want to but..." He put his fingers on her lips.

"Right, it's final then. Doctor's orders," he said.

Sylvia left Ayo's house in town feeling apprehensive. She twisted her hair nervously in the car. They had made a plan to meet on Friday after their shifts at the clinic. Although she had agreed in theory, she wasn't entirely sure she would actually go. She worried about what she would say to Patience. Would Patience approve? Would she be willing to keep her secret?

When she walked into her house, the kitchen smelled like fried plantain. Now that she volunteered at the clinic several times a week, her steward Energy had started cooking more. She had taught him how to cook all the basic Chinese dishes, but tonight he was cooking a local dish—pounded yam, fish stew, and fried plantain—which the kids loved. Patience had already set the dining table and was bringing the hot dishes to the table where the children waited obediently. Sylvia realized her house and her family functioned like clockwork without her.

"Madam, you're here just in time," Patience said, smiling.

Sylvia went and hugged her children. After a hard day's work at the clinic, she felt grateful for her own healthy children.

"Mama, we caught a frog today," Thomas said. He was five

years old now and full of mischief.

"You did?" Sylvia said.

"The frog's disgusting," Lila said, rolling the pounded yam into a ball and then dipping it in the flavorful sauce of the fish stew.

"You want to see it? Patience said I could keep him as a pet," Thomas said.

"Yes, I'd love to. After dinner," Sylvia said, kissing both children on the cheek.

After the children had gone to bed and before she let Patience return to her quarters behind the house, Sylvia broached the subject.

"I'm going on a trip this weekend," Sylvia said. "I need you to take care of the children."

"Of course, madam. Dey go be safe wit me, don't you worry. You go. Relax. Be happy. You go look so sad all de time here," Patience smiled, encouragingly.

Patience did not ask who she was going with or where she was going, but Sylvia felt it was understood between them. Her secret was safe with Patience. Patience was the mother and friend she had never really had. She could rely on her in a way she had never been able to rely on anyone in her life before, except Ayo. Patience and Ayo, these were her true friends now.

"I will be back by Saturday evening. You can still have Sunday off," Sylvia added, knowing Sunday was the one day Patience dressed up and went to church in town. Church was a social activity, and Patience usually stayed well into the evening, returning home late at night. She had heard rumors from some of the other house girls that Patience was popular with the older men because she couldn't get pregnant, making her a low-risk woman to have an affair with. She knew Patience had needs just like everyone else, and Sylvia wanted to be there for her too if she could.

On Saturday morning, Sylvia woke up for the first time in Ayo's arms listening to the song of the tropical birds at dawn—a chorus of soprano voices and the low, melancholy echo of her favorite bird. As a child, she had awoken to the rude noise of traffic and alley street vendors clattering in between the tall, narrow buildings of Hong Kong. It was calming to hear the sound of birds instead, the music of their mating call. But she still couldn't forget her fears. What if Winston suddenly returned home? It wasn't likely, but it could happen. Worse still, what if something happened to Lila? Ayo seemed to sense her anxiety and he pulled her closer to him.

After breakfast, she and Ayo drove several hours north into the dusty savannah. The green jungle gave way to the dull brown landscape of the grassland—dead yellowed grass and dry, withered shrubs. After several hours, they came to a bright turquoise spring, so much color, an indulgence in the surrounding gray-brown landscape.

Ayo stripped off his clothes and jumped naked into the aquamarine spring, and Sylvia followed. The blue-green water was lukewarm, a natural, warm spring bubbling from underground. She floated on her back, watching the monkeys leap from branch to branch above her. The trumpeting of elephants echoed in the distance. The tension in her body eased, and she let herself feel some kind of happiness.

She swam after him to the far end of the spring where there was a rock wall. She noticed he was holding a flashlight in an airtight plastic bag. He took her hand, and they dived underwater and swam underneath the wall. It wasn't very deep. They surfaced inside a cave and swam to a rock ledge where the water was shallow. He took his flashlight out of the plastic bag. As her eyes adjusted, she saw they were inside a small underground cavern.

"It's beautiful," she said.

"Spirits are said to reside here. Good spirits," he added.

"How did you find this place?" she said.

"As a boy, I would come and swim in this spring with my half-brothers. We could tell the water was coming out from under the rock wall. So one day, we dared each other to explore what was underneath. We wrapped a torch in plastic just like I did today and swam under the rock. We felt a bit like explorers when we discovered this cave."

"So it became your secret hide-out?"

"Yes, of course. And back then, no girls were allowed."

"Then later, it probably turned into the place to bring girls."

"No actually, it didn't…I haven't. You're the first. I'm breaking the rules." He pulled her closer in the water and kissed her.

In the darkness of the cave, they made love with their bodies half-submerged in the water, the sounds of their lovemaking echoing off the walls of the cave.

"I love you, you know that?" he said, holding her in the warm turquoise water.

"I know," she whispered. She should have felt happy to be loved by him, this was what she had craved. But she felt a foreboding that their love would soon become a mere memory, a scrapbook of photographs in her head, a lonely woman's dream. She traced her fingers over the place where he had etched his name on the cave wall as a boy. She wanted to add her name underneath as if engraving it next to his would somehow lend permanence to their love.

WINSTON

Chapter 20

Winston sat with the villagers in the spring of 1980, watching the *egungun* masked dancer perform in the middle of
the village. The ceremony marked the planting of the new crop.
Simeon spoke to his ancestors through the *egungun,* praying for a
good harvest and presumably extra protection against the curse.

The *egungun* dancer wore a heavy helmet mask made of wood
with elaborate carvings of a face with exaggerated features and a
fish tail. Winston was told the mask, passed from generation to
generation, was believed to possess supernatural powers. Special
rites had to be performed by the men who wore the masks,
and the masks were believed to be dangerous to women. As the
egungun danced, strips of leather and cloth on his costume swirled
out. The dancer lurched violently and moved toward Winston,
putting him on edge. He didn't like the eerie mask or the dance
for that matter. He stood up and walked away from the village
festivities toward the fields.

Winston stood alone on the freshly plowed field in the setting sun. He knelt down and took out a plastic vial from his leather satchel, filling it with a handful of the dusty, red earth, transient flyaway dirt. He planned to take the soil back to his laboratory for testing. In the distance, he thought he heard a voice from the thick forest at the edge of Simeon's fields. He stood up and heard the voice again, it sounded like someone was calling his name. He cautiously walked closer to the edge of the forest.

Winston stood at the edge of the jungle and looked through the dark layers of the canopy and undergrowth—thick, opaque, claustrophobic. He saw nothing and was about to turn around when he heard the voice call his name, loud and clear now.

He hesitantly walked into the forest toward the voice, his heart drumming a fast polyrhythm. The sun was setting, and it would be dark soon. He knew he shouldn't walk alone in the forest. He turned around, planning to head back, but suddenly an old man with yellowed eyes stood in front of him. Winston instantly recognized him as the juju doctor.

"I told you, eh? You should not come here. Go take your legs and run. Run before it's too late," the old man said to him in a menacing tone.

Winston stood immobile, his heart drumming wildly now.

"Run, I said, eh? You hear? You stupid *O'Ebo*?" the juju doctor shouted in his face.

Winston began to run out of the forest, but men camouflaged with leaves suddenly appeared out of nowhere and blocked him. He turned instinctively and ran the opposite direction into the forest. The men dressed in leaves chased him deeper and deeper into the forest. Winston dropped his leather satchel with the vial of soil and kept on running.

• • •

Night descended, and the men in leaves still hounded him. Winston couldn't see where he stepped, there was no path. He tried to run through the dense undergrowth, but he kept tripping on thick, knotted roots. His arms became entwined in vines, net-like, tentacles reaching out and grabbing him. Then suddenly, something sharp clamped around his leg and pierced his calf. He howled and stumbled onto the ground. The sharp metal teeth tightened around his leg, puncturing his calf and ankle, the pain was excruciating. Winston realized it was a hunter's trap of some sort, possibly to catch bush meat. The men in leaves seemed to have disappeared just as silently as they had appeared. Or were they watching him from the trees?

He tried to pry the trap open with his hands but without success. His mind rationally ran through all the dangers. It was dark, and he knew he was lost in a forest he didn't know. He couldn't walk properly, his leg was killing him, the best he could do was limp toward what he thought was the direction he came from. It was also the sacred part of the forest, which was rumored to be inhabited by all sorts of spirits. On top of that, he knew the trap was probably rusty, and he couldn't remember if his tetanus shot had been updated. If he was lucky enough to avoid coming upon a poisonous snake in the dark, he figured he was likely to perish either by spirits or the tetanus or worse still, an infection in his leg. He had no idea how long it would take him to get out of the forest or if anyone would ever find him. He grabbed a long stick and used it to limp toward the general direction he came from, dragging the leg with the trap. He started shouting for help and wished he hadn't dropped his leather satchel. It had a flashlight, which would have helped him avoid the snakes. He felt small, vulnerable, and completely at the mercy of nature, the spirits, and the witch doctor.

• • •

The night passed slowly. The loud drone of the insects seemed to drown out Winston's calls for help. Eventually, his leg bled so much, he grew tired and almost unconscious. Winston lay on the ground in the thick bush. He could feel ants and flies swarming his bloody wound. Would anyone ever find him? He realized he would not get out of the forest by himself, and he had no idea what the juju doctor had in store for him. Maybe the trap was all part of the plan, leaving him to the natural hazards of the forest, a foreigner who knew nothing about surviving in a tropical jungle. It would be so easy to let him just perish naturally. No curse was necessary. He was that helpless. He knew Simeon would have a rescue team out. They should have found his leather satchel by now, dropped near the entrance to the forest. But would the witch doctor and his men thwart them as well? Winston supposed the men in leaves were meant to be spirits and would probably scare Simeon's fellow villagers. The last image in his mind before losing consciousness was the playful, ringing laughter of his son.

• • •

When he woke up at dawn, he saw Simeon and other villagers peering down at him on the forest floor. They took Winston to the nearest hospital in Ife. His leg and ankle were bandaged and stitched up. His wife looked shocked when they brought him home. He must have looked pale and weak. The night in the jungle had frayed his nerves. But she went straight to work. She put him to bed and made him a clear ginger and chicken soup. She undid his bandages and cleaned his wound, a tangled mess of bloody lacerations. Even he couldn't look at his wound. The doctor had prescribed antibiotics to stave off the infection, but they didn't know how well his leg would heal. In the scale of things, this didn't worry him. He had his leg, it could have been much worse.

Sylvia spoon-fed him some of the soup. She seemed to be trying too hard as if…as if she were guilty of something. Of what, he wondered? When it came to their relationship, they were both guilty parties as far as he was concerned. He ate her soup like an obedient patient, saying nothing. He still felt unsettled. She put her hand on his cheek, but he flinched under her touch.

For several weeks, they were held captive by his injury. While he healed, she barely left the house, not even going to volunteer at the clinic. He assumed he was her patient now. A few times the phone rang and she answered, but Winston couldn't hear what she said.

"You're good at this," he said one afternoon, complimenting her ability as a nurse.

"I've learned a lot. He's taught me…" her voice trailed off at the mention of the young doctor. "I should go back and get my nursing degree," she continued.

"It would just be a piece of paper now," Winston said.

"It would give me something to fall back on," she said. He knew what she was implying, in case something happened to him.

"You're right, you should sign up." Then he added, "I requested an armed guard to come with me on my trips."

She was silent for a moment. He thought she was amassing her argument for him to quit his project and leave Africa. But to his surprise, she didn't say anything. Instead, she hesitantly reached out for his hand. He let her rest her hand on his for a brief moment. He thought maybe she had given up on arguing her case. He was relieved, but somehow he also felt hurt and he didn't know why. He didn't want to leave, but he couldn't help wondering why did she suddenly not care anymore?

"I'm glad, Winston," she said finally. "About the armed guard." She didn't mention his son, but he knew this was what she was thinking—that he was willing to risk dying and hurting his son.

He turned and faced the window, away from her. His son—he felt his heart constrict.

She put her hand on his shoulder. "I'll go make you some tea."

His wife left the room, and he gazed out at the forest beyond the garden. Innocuous-looking green vines and trees, but underneath he knew real dangers lurked, waiting to pounce.

Chapter 21

His leg healed, but the injury left him with a slight limp. It didn't bother him though; it was a necessary casualty, a small cost in his mission to drive hunger from the world. In the fall of 1980, a few months later, Winston followed the harvest procession as the villagers walked through the dense sacred forest. Simeon and the villagers danced as they made their way through the forest, celebrating their record harvest. Winston's armed guard followed him closely. Winston didn't like being back in the dark, brooding forest, it brought back memories of that terrible night. He looked down at every step, fearing a rusty trap hidden in the undergrowth.

The procession came to a shrine, an old mud palace in the middle of the sacred forest, once belonging to a great *oba* or king. A village elder, dressed in a white robe, offered a white kola nut and a white pigeon to the shrine along with a mountain of maize. Everyone could see the seeds worked miracles.

Suddenly Oluwa was beside him. "I take your seeds now," Oluwa said.

"Uh…good," Winston said, slightly taken aback. "You will

not regret it." He thought Oluwa was their sworn enemy. Did this mean he had joined their side? Did this nullify the juju doctor's spell, that is, if Oluwa was behind it?

"Dat is good news, ma brotha," Simeon said. "I myself have cleared more land. My farm is de biggest in de village. I also buy big American tractor."

Simeon left out that he had borrowed money to purchase the tractor. Simeon had also bought the village's first generator powered by diesel gasoline. He was building a new house, the first house in the village with electricity.

The village elder cleared his throat, and the procession turned to see him perform the divination rite of the harvest ritual. Winston watched, full of apprehension. Just six months ago, his life had been at risk in this same forest. The place felt haunted to him now. What would the future bring? As he looked around at the village men, he couldn't help wondering, which of these men had dressed up in leaves and chased him in the forest? He knew it had to be some of them. He felt a fear rise up in him, a tightening in his chest.

The village elder cut a yam in half and then cast the two parts on the ground, how these fell would determine the destiny of the community, predicting success or failure of the crops for the next year. Everyone assumed the yams would fall facing up, indicating continued success. But when the elder cast the yams, the two halves tumbled onto the ground, one landing face up and the other face down—the future was uncertain. Winston felt as if a stranger had moved into his mind, making himself at home, upsetting the careful placing of his things. He didn't like this uncertainty, this messy roommate. Too much of his life had been decided by the vagaries of chance. He wanted to have everything mapped out, a concrete plan, not this.

The procession returned to the village for a large meal, a goat slaughtered for the occasion, pounded yam. When night fell, Simeon invited everyone to come to the yard in front of his house.

"Ma friends," he said. "I present you a show."

In front of his half-built house, he positioned a medium-sized television screen. He pressed the switch with a flourish, and suddenly the latest Nigerian soap operas beamed right into Simeon's outdoor living room. The villagers laughed in delight and clapped. Everyone forgot about the ambiguous prophecy of the harvest rite. For now, life was good.

• • •

In the spring, the villagers planted again, hoping for the best. But by next summer in 1981, Winston met with Simeon and a group of worried villagers under the thatched canopy.

Simeon complained, "De fertilizer it cost too much dese days, eh. I try to buy it, but de man charge too much, eh. Who he tink he is?"

"How's that possible?" Winston asked. "The fertilizers are subsidized by the government."

"I dunno. De man come from de city. He in de suit, always walking around tinking he is some kind of god, tst. Just because he wear a suit. It's not even new, eh?"

"Who do you think these city slickers are?" Richard asked, turning to Winston.

"I don't know," Winston said, shaking his head. "But looks like they're buying the subsidized bags for cheap and then reselling them at a profit."

"Dat cockroach, because of him, I no buy de bag dis year, I no have de money," Simeon said.

Other farmers echoed Simeon's complaints.

"Bloody hell," Richard said. "Look, the seeds here are bred to respond to a very precise mix of inputs. It's like baking bread. You can't leave one ingredient out. It won't work."

The villagers looked at Richard, confused.

"They don't bake bread," Winston said. He looked over at Simeon, he seemed nervous.

High on the past several successful harvests, Simeon had borrowed money with the expectation of continued bounty. Winston knew Simeon needed a decent harvest to pay back his loan. He couldn't afford the seeds to fail to perform their magic. The juju doctor's spell was still present and doing its deed despite Oluwa's adoption of the seeds. Winston could feel the curse's undertow, pulling them down. Was Oluwa playing both sides or was he up to something, Winston wondered?

Simeon invited them to stay for dinner as usual. Winston protested, but Simeon insisted, and he didn't want to offend him. Richard took out his spam sandwich. Winston got up and walked over to watch the women, pounding the yam, tossing their long sticks up into air as they beat the yams. They took turns, singing and arguing in the process. Abike, Simeon's wife, dressed in a bright purple wrap and green rubber slippers, crouched on the ground, sifting the pounded yam over a red plastic tub. He knew this pounded yam was being prepared especially for him. If it were not for the guests, they would not bother with all that effort. They would have had gari instead, the substitute made from a bag of powder.

Abike served the steaming pounded yam with a spicy fish stew, but she did not look at Winston when she handed him his plate. She resented him, he realized. Of course she would. Even if Simeon didn't believe in the curse, Abike probably did, just like his wife.

"I will request an armed guard for you and your family," Winston said, speaking directly at Abike.

"Why we need dat?" Simeon said. "We okay. No one botha us."

"It won't do no good, de spell will take us when dey want," Abike said, quietly

"I still think it's a good idea," Winston said, but they both ignored him. He wondered if maybe they felt uncomfortable trusting their lives to a guard they didn't know, a stranger from another tribe.

Winston sat down and rolled the pounded yam into a ball, dipping it into the spicy fish stew. He felt Abike's hostility throughout the meal. He could feel her glaring at him when he wasn't looking. In the back of his mind, he knew she was right to doubt him.

• • •

A few months later in October, Winston drove his jeep along the cracked tarmac road, littered with moon-like craters. There was no life on either side of the deserted road, only the African bush, trees swamped by vines. The outline of the bush was irregular-shaped like the curve of Winston's own life, spiking in all sorts of random directions he hadn't planned on going.

Winston watched the women harvesting the meager ears of corn on Simeon's plots—baskets full of nothing when he had promised everything. The fields were full of withered, dry, brown maize stalks. Without the potent supply of fertilizers to feed the addiction of the man-made seeds, Simeon's maize had produced only a few shriveled ears of corn.

Winston walked back to the village. He heard a rustling of leaves in the corn fields and sensed someone following him. He turned around, but he only saw the dried corn husks swaying in the breeze. He started to walk as quickly as he could, the sweat running down his face, but his bad leg slowed him down. Suddenly, a man appeared out of the dry corn fields and stood in front of him. It was Oluwa, Simeon's brother-in-law. Winston noticed he held a machete in his hand.

"Come and see my fields, sah," he said mysteriously. "It grow and grow."

Winston didn't trust Oluwa, but he followed. They came to Oluwa's fields, and Winston saw the women harvesting the maize, their baskets full of corncobs.

"Did you buy the fertilizer?" Winston asked, dumbfounded at Oluwa's successful harvest while Simeon and all the other farmers had suffered.

"I don't need da fertilizer. I do what my fatha and grandfatha do," Oluwa bragged. "Those dat grows under de crown of de acacia tree is always de most plentiful. De roots, dey go deep deep and bring good things to de top."

Winston looked at the majestic acacia trees interspersed throughout Oluwa's field. Oluwa had taken the miracle seeds, but he hadn't cleared all the trees like Winston had told the villagers to do. His farm looked more like the traditional West African fields—the maize mixed with trees and other vegetables, creating a multi-layered effect. Oluwa's land stood in great contrast to Simeon's plots—the monotonous, flat, single-crop maize fields reminiscent of American farms. Winston knelt down to take a sample of Oluwa's soil.

"I show you dis to warn you," Oluwa's voice suddenly turned dark. His eyes bulged out and his lips curled. "We do betta without you. Stay away, you only bring trouble trouble to our village, eh."

Winston stood up and tried to say something, but Oluwa, shouted at him, waving his machete.

"Go away, you hear, eh? You go bring bad tings to our village. You hear, eh?"

Winston realized it was the same words the juju doctor had threatened him with— *you bring bad tings to de village.*

Winston turned and started walking as quickly as he could with his bad leg. He looked back, Oluwa did not follow. Instead, he just stood there staring. Winston kept walking away, but inside, his mind was in chaos. What if the juju doctor's prophecy was true? He was afraid of what might happen to the village in the end, he couldn't describe or understand this feeling, but he felt it nonetheless.

Back in the laboratory on the compound, Winston discovered Oluwa's soil was naturally rich in nitrogen. In the absence of fertilizers, the acacia trees were doing the same job. Winston was promoting the fantastic inventions of Western science, but was this at the cost of the knowledge passed on by generations toiling on that same orange dirt? He sat down in the dusk of his laboratory, the odor of the chemicals invading his lungs.

SYLVIA

Chapter 22

Black was the color of rain clouds, an auspicious color, a source of life. Rain nurtured the dry soil in which crops grew. Because of this, black was the color of fertility. Long ago, Yoruba brides wore black on their wedding days, not white like the Europeans and not red like the Chinese. Brides, wrapped in black, were creators of new life.

Sylvia paid good money for black cloth at the market due to the labor involved and the amount of indigo required to dye the cloth so dark. Young village women collected indigo leaves, pounded and dried them into balls. Older women crouched next to deep blue holes of dye in the ground, dipping the cotton cloth into the hole over and over again until it turned from light blue to black.

Sylvia pinned flimsy brown paper patterns onto the black material and cut it into pieces of a summer dress. She hummed one of her favorite romantic Cantonese pop songs while she sewed with her black Singer machine. As Winston recklessly risked his life, she felt like he was pulling further and further away from his family. She could understand him waging his cold war on Lila and her, but how could he do this to Thomas? Who was this man she had married? She spent more and more time with her lover, who was real and by her side.

She wore the black dress even though Winston and the children accompanied her to the clubhouse party. Ayo's eyes followed her across the room. It was the summer of 1982, and they had been seeing each other for over four years. Ayo had been engrossed in his work at the clinic and establishing himself as a doctor, so an affair, a relationship without commitment, seemed to have suited him.

Sylvia saw her lover go out of the clubhouse doors on to the dark patio. Before their affair, she and Ayo had always searched each other out in public. But now that they met in private, they avoided each other anywhere else. The expat compound was like a small town. Gossip mushroomed among bored wives trapped inside the compound walls. So she waited ten minutes and then followed. She found him waiting outside. He kissed her against the wall, his hands feeling her body through the black material.

Ayo led her to the changing rooms by the dark pool. They made love, sitting on the bench in the changing rooms, she on top of him, so he could see her silhouette in the black marriage cloth. He leaned on the screened window of the changing rooms with shuttered slats, the moonlight throwing white stripes across her dress and her face. No one could see in, but sounds carried. They made love as the party spilled out onto the poolside outside their window. They could hear the distant laughter and screams of children pushing each other into the pool.

"Marry me," he said.

But she didn't have time to respond. She heard a commotion

outside, a child was in trouble. Lila.

• • •

Lila must have followed her to the poolside. On the other side of the pool, some teenagers pushed each other in, fully clothed, laughing. The laughs echoed from the pool, and Sylvia realized later their shouting must have turned into the voice of the spirit children. Lila was nine years old but still fully connected to the spirit world.

Sylvia didn't know how it happened. All she knew was that Lila jumped into the dark pool, fully clothed, and swam down to the shining lights on the walls at the bottom. Perhaps it seemed like beyond the lights there was a spirit world full of masked dancers in raffia skirts, mermaids and water snakes. According to the teenagers, Lila was underwater for a long time. She looked like she was drowning. One of the teenagers swam to her and hauled her out of the water. She was kicking and screaming in his arms. The other teenagers went back inside the party to find her parents. They found Winston inside and brought him out.

"Where were you?" Winston said when he saw Sylvia, but he didn't wait for an answer. "She's soaking wet. We'd better get her home."

Sylvia anxiously fussed over Lila, borrowing a towel from someone and wrapping her in it. She hoped her anxiety would explain why her hands were shaking. She wanted to do everything for her children to keep them safe and happy. But she realized it was because of this sacrificial love that she was becoming so fatigued. The schizophrenic part of her wanted to flee her children, find solace in Ayo's arms, and live a different life.

• • •

A few days later, Sylvia went to see Ayo at his father's old house. The town was dark, lit only by the soft glow of kerosene lamps. The power had gone out. But the sound of drumming and music continued from the center of the town. The darkness only seemed to increase the humidity in the room. She could taste the salt in his sweat. In the dark, Ayo pushed her against the wall, ripping her dress. Through the wall, she felt the vibrations of the drums, her bare skin against the cracks in the plaster, tiny veins leading to her heart. After they made love, he stepped away from her.

"You haven't answered my question," he said. She couldn't see his face in the dark, but she sensed the hurt in his voice. She stood there in her ripped dress, still leaning against the wall. The constant drumbeat suddenly made her feel unsteady, and her head started to throb.

"I want to," she said, sliding down on the tile floor, her back against the wall. "But how? How can we be together?"

"I was raised on English fairy tales my mother used to tell me, you know, the kind where the frog kisses the princess, and everyone lives happily ever after," Ayo said, sitting down next to her on the floor in the dark. "I suppose this kind of optimism makes me somehow believe that our story could turn out otherwise. But you don't believe that, do you?"

"I was raised on Chinese folk tales where the maidens always died or pined for their lovers. There were never happy endings."

She had thought of multiple versions of their story, but there was never a clear ending in her mind. But she realized now that for him, there was only one ending.

"I want to be with you. I want to believe in happy endings," she said, turning to hold him as they sat on the floor together.

"Then believe in happy endings."

"But what is a happy ending? If I leave Winston, what will happen to my children?"

Ayo stood up and moved away from her in the darkness. She realized the clandestine nature of their affair, what had perhaps excited him in the beginning, had begun to irritate him. The casualness of an affair had suited him for the past four years, but now he was in his mid-thirties, of course he wanted more. His life was not static, it was moving forward at a pace she feared she could not keep up with. She saw glimpses of children in his arms, a family sitting down to dinner—of course he would want these things, he was entitled to them. She looked over at him standing by the window, but she couldn't see his face in the darkness, only his silhouette.

• • •

Winston traveled with a worn, dirty-yellow suitcase that no one bothered to steal. It looked like it had nothing of value inside, a poor man's suitcase. But when he went to conferences in Europe or America, no porter ever wanted to carry it either, so he pasted stickers of famous hotels all over it—Hilton, Oberoi, Inter-Continental. This was the suitcase of her husband.

That morning when Sylvia returned home after being with her lover, she saw Winston's suitcase in the hallway. She panicked, her dress was ripped. It was nine o'clock in the morning. Winston must have driven in the night, not caring about his safety.

"Masta is in de shower," Patience said as Sylvia walked into the kitchen. Patience was her accomplice in all of this.

"I say you go to town," Patience said. "But hurry madam, change. Before he comes out of de showa." She glanced at Sylvia's ripped dress but gave the impression she had seen it all before during her years serving expat families. Caring for the children and their neurotic, expat wives was part of her job description.

Sylvia ran into their bedroom and changed quickly. She noticed the sheets on her bed were rumpled up as if she had slept in them. Patience must have deliberately messed up the neatly tucked in sheets to cover for her. Sylvia went back out to the living room.

By the time Winston showered and appeared in the living room, she had collected herself.

She said in her most calm voice, "I just got back from town. A nurse was sick, so I had to do her shift at the clinic." Her voice was never calm, so the calmness, the forced steadiness was out of place. She usually spoke quickly with an agitated, anxious undertone.

Winston nodded. Did he suspect something? She didn't know if Winston would buy her excuse, she knew just by mentioning the clinic, she was indirectly implicating Ayo.

"I'll put on a pot of shefan for breakfast," Sylvia said, knowing that a good Chinese breakfast was all that her husband needed. She cooked the rice porridge and served it with tiny dishes of roasted peanuts, plain white tofu with soy sauce and Chinese parsley, dried pork *rosung*, pickles, and tea leaf eggs.

Winston ate in silence. He seemed preoccupied to her as if he were re-examining her whereabouts over the last few weeks. She crossed her legs under the table, swinging her leg nervously.

• • •

Sylvia understood the threat of water. Her mother used to forbid her to play on the beaches of Hong Kong during ghost-month in August when unhappy murdered or suicidal ancestor spirits were hungry for lives.

A month after Lila's drowning incident, Sylvia and Winston

went to the pool as a family. She sat watching her daughter's every move and, to her surprise, so did Winston. He kept his eyes trained on both children. Sylvia hadn't wanted to go, but Richard had invited them to have lunch with his family at the club's poolside restaurant, and Winston was too polite to decline. The Englishman reclined on a pool chair, sipping gin and tonic under the African sun. It seemed to be his natural habitat. Elizabeth lay on the lounge chair next to him, tanning her back.

The pool was populated mostly by the Europeans and Americans who lived on the compound. For them, this was mandatory relaxation time out in the tropics. Most were leftover from colonial days, trying to sustain a sense of adventure and luxury all rolled into one—the expat lifestyle. The other residents, mostly Asians and Africans, wisely stayed indoors during the heat of the day, enjoying the imported air conditioners, a mandatory perk of the job for them. For them, this was a stepping stone, a way to get out of their countries—India or Tanzania—and to get paid in US dollars. It was the next best thing to immigrating to America.

Winston looked uncomfortable, not having spent his childhood reclining by swimming pools. Sylvia knew he detested the thought of swimming in what amounted to nothing more than a communal bathtub. The swimming pool was a Western concept. He sat under an umbrella, the only one by the pool fully clothed. He didn't understand why Westerners liked to roast themselves in the sun, turning candy-cane red and white striped. Winston turned to his three month-old Herald Tribune, the paper had been brought from London and shared among the expats until the black ink became smudged.

Sylvia lay with Elizabeth, staying mostly in the shade of the umbrella. She kept her eyes trained on Lila. It looked different in daylight, the blue ripples full of sunny smiles, nothing like the mysterious color it was at night.

"Is she alright in the water?" Elizabeth said, referring to Lila. By now, everyone had heard about her incident.

"I don't know," Sylvia said, unable to hide her anxiety.

"I told Richard it was a bit daft inviting you to the pool for lunch. I was going to have you come round for a roast instead. But Richard said Winston said it was alright to do the pool. I knew I should have spoken with you. These men can't organize anything at all."

"It's alright, honestly," Sylvia said. She knew Elizabeth was offering friendship of some sort, and she might have taken her up on that offer several years ago, before Ayo. Now she felt she didn't have the time or the need for friends anymore. Between volunteering at the clinic, her children, and her lover, her life felt more than complete, frantically so.

Sylvia noticed Ayo walk up to the clubhouse pool from the tennis courts toward the changing rooms. While she watched Lila, she also kept an eye trained on the door of the changing rooms, waiting for him to reappear. When Ayo emerged, he was in his swim trunks. Seeing his bare chest, she had to look away. Ayo walked by them, but before he dived into the pool, he glanced back at Sylvia, and their eyes met for a brief moment. It was not just a simple glance, she knew, it was carefully positioned and timed as if her lover were laying it all down for Winston to see. She thought she heard Elizabeth gasp. Sylvia looked over at her husband. He was staring straight at Ayo as if processing the information. She knew Winston was an astute man, details would not escape him, but he showed no emotion. Instead, he carefully folded his newspaper and put it aside.

• • •

They drove home from the clubhouse along the compound's paved streets and neatly trimmed lawns.

"You need to watch the children more at the pool after..." Winston didn't finish his sentence. They didn't actually mention the near drowning accident again.

"Of course," she brushed him off. It wasn't a full blown, shouting kind of argument, but it was conflict nevertheless. It was there, beneath the stilted words, the arms crossed over her chest.

"You weren't there when it happened," Winston said quietly. There was accusation in his voice. But was he accusing her of another crime?

She didn't respond, biding her time until he left again for the bush. A pungent stench came from the ripening pods of the tree outside their house. It smelled like rotten fish.

WINSTON

Chapter 23

The next morning, a relative from Simeon's village arrived on Winston's doorstep, pleading for help. Simeon was in trouble and Winston left quickly for his village. He was secretly glad to have an excuse to leave. His wife...he couldn't even think what she might have done. All he wanted to do was run as far away as possible. He drove recklessly down the dirt road despite the potholes. A new colleague, Donna Burns, an American PhD student from Harvard, sat next to him.

"This is some kind of wild ride," Donna said, grinning as she bounced around in her seat.

"What's your dissertation about?" he said, trying to distract himself from his wife and her possible transgressions. Donna looked as if she was actually enjoying the ride, and he stepped on the gas pedal harder.

"It's on the role of women in West African farming. It's going to be titled something like 'The West African farmer and *her* farming practices.'"

She was clad in shorts and a t-shirt, her long, straight hair loose. She was one of those hippies, he thought. He wasn't sure how the traditional village women were going to accept or handle someone like her. In fact, he wasn't sure how *he* was going to accept or handle someone like her accompanying him on these trips. But she was there on ADA orders, and he had agreed that, in principle, they needed to do more outreach to the village women.

When they arrived at Simeon's village, Abike came running toward them.

"He's sick. He's sick, and it's your fault, eh?" Abike shouted at him.

"What's wrong?" Winston said.

"I dunno. His body no move. He throw up. It's de juju spell, he's going to die," Abike wailed.

Donna put her arm around Abike, trying to comfort her. Abike pushed her away, probably wondering who this strange white woman was.

"Wait outside," Winston turned to Donna.

He went with Abike into Simeon's hut. Simeon was lying on the straw mats on the ground. Winston was shocked at what he saw. Simeon seemed paralyzed, his muscles twitched, and he drooled at the mouth.

"I'm going to take him to the hospital," Winston said quickly.

But Abike wailed, "I don't want you take him to hospital. He will die dere. No one ever comes back from de hospital."

"Please let us, doctors might be able to fix this," Winston said.

"No dey can't, it's not a normal illness, eh? It's de curse I tell you," Abike continued to wail.

Despite Abike's resistance, Winston and Donna took Simeon to the dirty, crowded hospital in Ife. Winston covered his nose, the stench of blood, pus, and other bodily fluids overwhelmed him. He noticed, to his surprise, Donna didn't seem particularly bothered by the stench.

The doctor, a Nigerian educated in England, seemed to know what he was doing.

"I found something unusual in his bloodstream, a toxin known as physostigmine. It's found in the local calabar beans. Just one bean is highly poisonous," the doctor said as they stood in the dirty hallway.

"Can you treat it?" Winston said.

"Yes, I'm already doing so with atropine, it works as an antidote, but you have to carefully control the dosage as it can work against you too."

"I don't get it. Did he eat the beans by accident?" Donna asked, wide-eyed.

"It's possible. It happens to children sometimes, there's nothing unusual about these beans that makes it easy to tell them apart from others, but..."

"But?" Winston asked, knowing there was more to it.

"The calabar bean has historically been used here in Nigeria as a poison by juju doctors in various rituals to determine if someone is possessed by evil spirits," the doctor explained.

"Do you think someone tried to poison him?" Winston asked slowly. He looked over at Donna, his young student protégé, but she didn't seem afraid or flustered at all. If anything, he thought, she looked suddenly more intrigued.

"It's possible. It seems unlikely that his wife would cook these beans by mistake," the doctor said, thinking out loud.

"So...you guys think someone tossed a bean or two in Simeon's bowl without him noticing? Why on earth would someone do that?" Donna said.

Winston knew the answer. He suddenly felt queasy. "Should

we report this to the police?"

"Might be a good idea. I'll write up a medical report," the doctor said.

Winston and Donna drove back to the compound from the hospital.

"I'm going to recommend to the ADA that you do less field work. A young girl like you shouldn't be put in harm's way," Winston said.

"First, I'm not a young girl," Donna retorted, seeming offended. "Second, I spent two years in the middle of the jungle in Benin with the Peace Corps. It's not like I haven't come across poisonous beans and witch doctors. It's no big deal."

"Both Simeon and I have had attempts on our lives. It's too dangerous."

"So did you stop working on the project?"

"No, I can't."

She stared back at him. "Look, I came to Africa to make a difference. I'm not going to sit in the compound and twiddle my thumbs. I could do that back at Harvard. I'm going out to the bush with you. Let me decide what risks I want to take."

Winston was silent. He could tell she was a strong woman, stubborn and outspoken for her age, and not particularly respectful to her elders. He guessed she was in her late twenties. Still, he would recommend less fieldwork for her or maybe a transfer to another project. It would be nice to get her off his hands anyway. He didn't want the responsibility of babysitting her with all that was going on.

• • •

After a few days, Simeon recovered from the poison, and Winston brought him back to the village. Abike was glad to see her husband, but she barely nodded a word of thanks to Winston. He knew he would have to tell her the frightening truth.

"It was poison. Calabar beans," Winston said.

"Oh God be crazy," Abike said hysterically. "Poison, eh? Oh no, dis can't be happening."

"Did you see anything suspicious that day?" Winston asked.

"I dunno, I dunno," Abike said.

"I see Oluwa, yes it was him. He go be sneaking around her cooking pot. I see him wit my own eyes," Abike's sister chimed in, but Winston couldn't tell if this was an accusation or a real witness account.

"Dat man, he go try and kill my husband, he go be de devil himself," Abike screamed.

"Oluwa, are you sure?" Winston asked Abike's sister.

"Oh yes I'm sure, I can recognize dat rat face anywhere. He was here."

Winston spent the rest of the afternoon asking other villagers what they had seen. Several other women corroborated Abike's sister's story.

"We should report this to the police. We have witnesses," Winston said.

"De police? What dey going to do?" Abike said as if he were stupid.

Winston felt her animosity, her resentment directed at him. Did his own wife feel that way about him as well?

Later, Winston and Simeon stood in the fields. The maize stood high, full of ripening corn, ready for harvest in a month.

Winston broached the subject. "If you want to quit, I understand. Your wife is not happy."

"Quit? Why would I want to quit, eh? When we a good crop

like dis," Simeon responded, sweeping his arms around at his farm. "Dat's what dey want us to do. Staying in de same mud hut, eating de same chicken. Tst. Dey stupid, eh. Me, I refuse to be like dem. Dey are not going to stop me, those idiots."

"Someone just tried to poison you. Think through this carefully."

"Oluwa and his people just want to frighten me. But can't dey see? Dey can't fight de white man's medicine. I am cured." Simeon stretched his arms out proudly.

"You see, I'm not going to be stopped by Oluwa," Simeon continued. "Ever since we were boys, he try to do betta then me. He wish he was de chief's son. He envy me for dat. He marry my sista, so he can be chief's son. I was betta at English school than him. He hated dat, he left de school and said it was rubbish. Dat's why he hate de English and *O'Ebos* because dey showed how dumb he was. Dis is why he try to hurt me, he don't want to see me so rich and successful like de English. He jealous and he hate. Dat's why."

Winston realized this was really a long-standing childhood battle between Simeon and Oluwa, their egos, the direction they wanted the village to go, each drawing on the power of what they believed in.

"Oluwa told me about a prophecy. About the village being destroyed. Have you heard of this?" Winston asked.

"Oh, dat yes yes. You know you can interpret dese prophecies whicheva way you want. Maybe part of de village has to be destroyed, so we can change. With change, dere is pain. "

"Maybe," Winston said slowly.

"You not getting frightened by dese people?" Simeon sounded worried now. "You have to be with me. Without you, I have no power."

"Of course, I am with you," Winston responded, but he had mixed feelings about Simeon pressing on. He worried about Abike. "I will arrange for the ADA to have several armed guards come here and protect you and your family. I will not take no for answer."

• • •

Winston travelled in the bush for over a month, meandering his way through the dirt roads of the jungle, anything to keep him away from home. After visiting several other villages and farmers, Winston returned in time to help Simeon and Abike with the October harvest.

Winston hired a large truck to help transport Simeon's bountiful harvest to the market in Ife. This year, the market by the large pothole was unusually crowded. Abike was surrounded by other vendors selling ground corn displayed as mounds of yellow powder in colorful enamel bowls. This year's harvest had been particularly good for everyone as increasingly more farmers had adopted the hybrid seeds.

That day it was particularly humid and hot. Flies swarmed Abike's face as she tried to bargain with customers.

"You charge too much, eh," a female buyer said to Abike. "I go find a betta price at de next stand, dey sell de same ting."

The woman walked off to the stall next door, also selling bags of maize, and Abike let her. But after the third woman started walking away, Abike relented.

"Okay, what is your price? Tell me," Abike said.

The woman named her price.

"What? You crazy crazy, eh?" Abike said.

"No, I not crazy woman. Dat's what dey selling it for everywhere today. Go see for yourself, eh."

Winston walked around the market, checking what other bags of maize were selling for at the other stalls. He walked through the labyrinth of narrow muddy alleyways in between the tin-roof bungalows, stepping over puddles and decaying garbage. He dodged vendors carrying huge sacks of rice or ground gari, and his armed guard followed close behind. After talking to someone at every last maize stall, Winston's fear had become a reality. Winston had worried about the local market being flooded with too much corn. Earlier, he had suggested to Abike that they transport the maize further to another, larger market, perhaps even as far as the capital in Lagos. But Abike had ignored Winston, coming to her usual market to gossip and show off to the other women. And so due to the surplus of corn at the local market, the price had dropped, cruelly backfiring on his project's success.

He continued to walk quickly through the market, lost in the maze of his own disappointment. The stench reminded him suddenly of his childhood in Taiwan and the associated feeling of loss. His marriage was falling apart. He knew all of this was partly his own doing, and he couldn't blame his wife. He had kept his heart barricaded against these moments, but still she had pried open the iron gates just enough that he still felt something when he didn't want to feel anything. He could not name the feeling, but it was an aching sensation of loss, a long lost emotion that somehow surfaced again.

He walked quickly among live chickens in cages made of twigs, flattened, pressed dried fish hanging from the stalls and the smell of open sewers. He looked back and saw his armed guard stuck behind a mob of people. Winston didn't wait for him and continued to walk quickly through the rickety stalls with piles of *gari* and rice, white chunks of starch from the cassava, used to starch clothes, and large plastic containers of bright red-yellow palm oil. His guard was lost somewhere in the crowd, but Winston didn't care about his personal safety. It was the last thing on his mind. Simeon had persevered and risked his life for this project, Winston thought, but for what? Was it even worth it? After standing in the hot sun all day, Simeon's wife sold only half her bags and at half the price.

SYLVIA

Chapter 24

"You should leave him. He knows," Ayo said as they lay together under the hazy white mosquito net. The rusty fan was turned off, and she could feel the heat of his body next to hers.

"Winston didn't say anything. He's been gone for over a month," she said.

"He's waiting for you to say something. It's your decision," he paused. "We're all waiting."

She was quiet. She wanted to just stay here in his arms for the rest of her life, lying here next to him, it seemed so easy. She imagined a life with Ayo, working side by side at his clinic making a difference, coming home to his father's house, falling asleep and waking up together. It was the kind of life she had dreamed of as a girl, a unique, meaningful life with someone she loved. How many people had found their calling and their love in the same man?

"Choose happiness, Sylvia," Ayo whispered. "For both of us."

He turned to kiss her on her neck, the side of her face.

He looked at her, his face just a few inches above her. "What do you say?"

"Yes," she said. He kissed her, moving his body on top of hers.

• • •

After about six weeks, by mid-October, Winston returned home, and she prepared his favorite dumplings. While he showered, she set the table. She would tell him tonight she was leaving. On the side table, she noticed the half-opened airmail letter written in Chinese. In all their years, Winston had never received any mail from his family in Taiwan. What could this mean? She could barely read Chinese, but she still picked it up and tried to decipher the characters.

Winston appeared in the living room and saw her holding the letter. She turned to him and saw the pain in his face. He was going to throw her out, she thought. It would make things easier if he did.

"My father is very sick," he said instead. "He might not make it."

"I'm sorry, Winston." She put her hand over her mouth.

"I'm going to leave tomorrow for Taiwan to see him."

He didn't mention her transgression or maybe he had forgotten; he had much more to worry about than her. She would have to wait to tell him. She had waited four years, she could wait another week.

• • •

When Winston returned from Taiwan ten days later, he looked haggard, jet-lagged, and depressed. His father had passed away, and Winston, the eldest son, had held the banner for the funeral procession through the chaotic streets of Taipei. But since his return home, Sylvia sensed something was not quite right with her husband. The first night, he tossed and turned in their bed.

"Are you alright?" she asked in the dark.

There was a silence.

"He died before I got there." His voice sounded off-key, it didn't sound like him at all.

"I'm sorry," she said, not knowing what else to say.

"I never got to apologize to him."

"For what?" she ventured, wondering if he would tell her more. She had been married to him for a decade, yet she knew so little about him, what went on inside his mind, his heart.

"My father didn't want me to go to the West to study for a PhD in chemistry. He wanted me to stay in Taiwan. Study and teach Chinese literature just like him." The darkness seemed to give anonymity to Winston, to let him speak freely. "I felt like those subjects were useless. They were the reason China fell behind the West. I wanted to go to the West and study science. To me, science is real, concrete, built on facts and numbers. I didn't trust literature. It's a thing of the past."

He paused and then continued, "When I left for the UK, he disowned me. We haven't spoken since."

All these years he had been carrying around this burden, a mother lost as a child and now a father who had disowned him. Sylvia felt she understood her husband now just a little bit more. She knew this missed chance to reconcile with his father had taken a toll on Winston. Suddenly, he seemed human and vulnerable to her. She wanted to cross that invisible line in their bed that had separated them for years and hold him, but she remained on her side.

The next day, Winston added his father's photograph to his

mother's on the makeshift altar in the corner of their living room. It was a black and white picture of a serious-looking old man with a wispy beard. Sylvia watched Winston light fresh incense sticks, bow three times, and place a new bowl of tropical fruit in front of his parents' photographs. Tears streamed down his face. He had just lost his father. She knew he had never gotten over his mother's death as a child. And now he must have felt all alone in the world, without family. She was all he had now. How could she leave him now? She felt torn between her two lives.

• • •

Later that afternoon, Lila and Thomas brought their school report cards home and handed them to Winston. He still didn't seem completely himself. Lila was nine now, and Thomas was seven. The children attended a small correspondence school on the compound run by the wives. Pale wooden rulers with the words *Baltimore, Maryland* came with their textbooks on American history and geography. Her children learned more about George Washington and ancient Greece, both remote and unrelated to them, than they knew about the great Nigerian empires of Benin and Oyo or about China, their own country. This school unknowingly reinforced the concrete wall and broken glass between Africa and them.

But Winston took this school seriously. He sat in the living room studying their report cards, his father's scrolls of black ink calligraphy and Chinese mountains behind him.

Winston scanned Lila's report card briefly, a long line of satisfactory B's. He didn't say anything, just a nod, a half-smile— mandatory acknowledgement, received and reviewed. Then he took Thomas' report card. Winston frowned in disappointment. The rounded curves of one solitary "B" tripped up the perfect symmetry of a straight line of A's.

"Thomas, you can do better," Winston said, becoming emotional. "We're from a family of scholars. Your grandfather got top scores in the official examinations in China. I expect you to excel, I got all A's, perfect scores when I was a boy." His voice wavered at the mention of his father.

"Yes, Baba," Thomas said, looking down to hide his tears.

Of course, Winston had nothing to say about Lila's report card. She received neither praise nor disappointment. She was getting used to his distracted mood—downcast eyes, praises unsung, and the heavy, sagging space in place of the words left unsaid in her relationship with her father.

After Winston retreated to his study, Sylvia went over to comfort her children and take them in her arms. She held onto them tightly, she couldn't let go. Thomas was only seven, he was in second grade, how could Winston be so harsh? Lila squeezed her brother's little hand as if to say everything would be okay. Thomas stopped crying. As a typical younger sibling, Sylvia knew he adored his older sister. Ever since he was a toddler, he followed his sister everywhere, holding a crocodile skin handbag just like Lila. He used to sit opposite her, reading the same book upside down.

The children escaped to the kitchen, a place where Winston rarely ventured. They helped Patience prepare the sweet fried plantain, which Sylvia served with salty Chinese food.

"Eh, Patience, my stomach is worrying me, I don't feel like dinner," Lila began.

"Me too," Thomas chimed in.

"Don't worry, eh? I'm sure your stomach go be okay for food," Patience said

"Why does my father not like me?" Lila asked.

"Your fatha loves you, but you are a son, and you are a daughta. It is different with girls and boys. A fatha is different with his daughtas and sons."

The children spoke to Patience in the local *pidgeon* English with a mix of Patience's Cote d'Ivoire patois.

"But eh, why, why are we different?" Lila asked.

"Dat is the way, dat is the way God intended, *comprend?*" Patience said. "But you have each other, eh? Brotha and sista."

Thomas and Lila looked each other, comforted by Patience's words.

Sylvia observed them from the kitchen doorway. It reminded her of the closeness she felt to her eldest brother. As children, her brother took care of her, sharing the pocket money their father had only given to the boys. During the hot summers in the alleyways of Hong Kong, her brother bought her shaved ice with red bean sauce from the street vendors. Her brother had been her only family. She understood that powerful feeling her own children felt, she couldn't tear them apart. If she left Winston, he would keep Thomas, his son. There would be no question. That was custom in Chinese culture, the children belonged to the father, not the mother. But could she willingly separate her children and break their close bond? Could Sylvia be apart from Thomas and leave him with his strict, absent father?

Chapter 25

The next day, Sylvia drove to Ayo's old house in town. But he was not at home, and his steward said he was at the market near the University of Ibadan. She didn't know what she was going to say, the words hadn't taken shape in her mind yet, but she had a vague feeling of what she needed to do. She sat in her car in the usual traffic on Oyo road. The vendors pushing their wares through the window, the smell of exhaust, the heat—all of it made her feel sick to her stomach.

She looked for Ayo at the busy market. She ran through women dressed in lace, children in rags, hanging dried fish and barrels of rubber slippers. She saw Ayo at a tailor stall. The tailor sat behind a black Singer sewing machine wearing an *agbada* and a brand new pair of red Nike tennis shoes. Behind him, colorful *agbadas* hung from rusty nails on the wooden walls of makeshift stall.

As she approached Ayo, he saw her face and seemed to know what she was about to say. He led her away from his tailor and stopped in front of an albino boy's lamp stall, neat rows of little paraffin lamps, each made from a used light bulb.

"I don't know if can," Sylvia said, looking up at her lover.

Ayo closed his eyes briefly as if in pain.

"I'm not sure what a happy ending is," she continued. "If I leave you, Winston would keep Thomas. I don't think I could bear being apart from my child. I can't separate my children from each other either. I can't make my family unhappy, just for my own happiness." And would she even be happy, separated from her son? She had spent so many years guarding her children from danger, how could she now willingly hurt them?

Ayo didn't answer, his face darkened. He of all people understood sacrifice, she knew, it was his whole life.

"We've had our love. We will always have that," she said softly.

"You're already speaking in past tense." There was so much pain in his voice; it hurt her to hear it.

Sylvia looked at her lover in the white light of the harsh African sun. She remembered the day she had first met him at this same market, nine years ago when Lila was a baby. She wanted to reach out and touch his face, but she feared someone would notice. There were too many compound servants shopping at the market, people they didn't know but who knew them. This crowd of strangers was somehow a silent witness to the end of their relationship. It was because of them that she could even say these things to him. He couldn't touch her, take her into his arms, and convince her otherwise. Alone in a room with him, she knew she couldn't be so strong, but she had to find that strength somewhere.

She turned and walked away quickly, losing herself in the crowd. She didn't look back fearing she would change her mind. She thought she was doing the right thing, but she felt like she was closing up, the reverse bloom of a flower in fast-motion, petals closing up into a tiny knot. Tiny wrinkles started to appear around her eyes, barely noticeable, but there.

•••

That night, well past midnight, Ayo came to her house and knocked on the door. She knew he might come. She had waited for him in the living room while Winston slept in the bedroom. Sylvia opened the door. She could smell beer in Ayo's breath. She had never seen him like this. He grabbed her and started kissing her roughly, pushing her against the kitchen counter. She wanted to give in to him, and it took all her will power to push him away.

"Don't," she said. "Not like this."

He let her go. They stood apart in the kitchen, separated by the white beam of moonlight coming across the tiled floor. They did not speak. His eyes were full of sorrow. She wanted to take him in her arms, go back on her decision. She felt caught between her lover and her family. She heard the rustle of the mango trees outside the kitchen window, the sound made her think of flying and farewells.

"Please go," she pleaded, fearing Winston would wake up.

Ayo punched his fist through the kitchen window in anger and frustration. When she heard the glass shatter, she felt like he had punctured her heart and his too. The broken glass cut his hand. His blood dripped onto the white tile floor where they had once made love. She couldn't erase that image in her mind. She grabbed a kitchen towel and wrapped it around his bleeding hand to stop the blood. He looked up at her, but she avoided his gaze. Instead, she turned and opened the door, signaling him to leave. He did not protest but walked slowly out the door.

After he left, she cleaned her lover's blood off the kitchen floor, her own tears washing it away. She called the compound maintenance to come and fix the window, saying a robber had broken the window. Then she went into Winston's study and wrote on the yellow legal pad on his desk: *I have left him. I am here for you and the children.* She hoped he would forgive her.

• • •

The next day, Winston didn't say anything. But she knew he found the note; it was scrunched up in a ball in the trashcan next to his desk. She cooked all his favorite dishes for dinner, *niu ro mien* beef noodles, dumplings, and spicy *ma po tofu*. A feast, this was her apology to him, which he accepted by devouring her dishes. He still didn't say anything, but she could tell by the softened expression on his face, he was appreciative in his silent way. Later that night, she touched him, and he was more than willing.

In the middle of January 1983, a few months later, she enrolled in the Nursing School at the University of Ibadan. As she walked into her first class at the age of thirty-two, she hoped she could start over. For the next six months, she spent her mornings at school and her evenings doing the required homework. She missed Ayo, this she couldn't deny. But what hurt the most was that by the summer of that year, he seemed to have moved on and taken up with the new American woman, Donna. Young love flows like water, but water that has flowed away cannot be brought back. So went a local Nigerian saying.

Donna—single, young, looking to have sex and adventure with a local flavor, wasted no time singling out Ayo, attractive and charming. Sylvia had to endure this long-legged brunette in a short white tennis skirt chase after the ball opposite Ayo. She felt Ayo lost no time either. Did he not care about her feelings? He probably was not used to women discarding him. His ego had been bruised and hurt by her, and this was why he readily accepted

Donna's advances. It felt like a betrayal to her even though she was the one who had left him. He was entitled to move on with his life, it was what she wanted for him, but still it was more than she could bear. One night, Sylvia saw Ayo and Donna leave the clubhouse together, drunk on local Star beers. She felt like someone losing a game of mahjong. She had thrown the woman next to her the winning tile. She was not shrewd enough at the game. She would have to pay double for this. Except the stakes were not plastic colored chips, but love.

Images of Ayo's hands running over the athletic body of that American woman tormented her. She heard Donna leaned on Ayo as her tour guide for the "local scene." She asked him to take her to the tin-roof shantytown bars packed full of perspiring locals dancing to highlife music under red light bulbs. Donna, fearless and full of adventure, drank the local homemade brew of fermented grains rumored to be spiked with fuel and the accidental ingredients of dirty water—rotting rats or underwear.

Sylvia supposed Ayo was glad to fulfill these new roles. It must have been easier for him, dealing with Donna, non-emotional, just in it for the sex. But he never took Donna to his father's old house in town, this much she heard through Patience and her robust network.

SYLVIA/WINSTON

Chapter 26

As Sylvia watched Ayo with Donna from afar, she began to doubt her decision. But how could she go back to Ayo? He had moved on. But she craved seeing him and began to look for a reason to be by his side again. Events in the tumultuous country around them would set the stage, providing her with the perfect opportunity and excuse.

Nigeria, which at the start of the last decade had been drunk on its sleek oil, now woke up in 1983 with a heavy hangover. After having been drenched in crisp *naira* bills pasted on foreheads and arms while they danced, the people discovered the money was never really theirs. Secret pipelines had siphoned valuable foreign exchange to Swiss bank accounts. Schoolteachers had not been paid in months. After the rigged election, people took to the streets in December 1983.

In Oyo state where Sylvia lived, President Shegari's Northern Muslim-dominated party had "won" even though the state was mostly populated by Southern Christians, the opposition party.

Winston was gone, paying no heed to the unrest in the country, visiting Simeon and other rural farmers. Sylvia heard there had been a riot in the town. She knew Ayo's clinic would be overflowing with patients, and he would need any help he could get. It was the morning of New Year's Eve, the day that marked the start of their affair years ago. Suddenly, she had to see him again. A kind of madness compelled her to get into her car and drive through the unsettled streets.

Sylvia turned out of the compound's white gates. She noticed there were more people than usual clustered alongside the road, and the traffic slowed. Despite the air conditioner, it was hot in the car, and her bare legs stuck to the plastic seats. She kept the windows rolled up. Suddenly, there was a loud bang on her window, and she jumped. She looked up and was surprised to see a boy holding a bag of red apples instead of the usual mangos and pineapples. He shouted out an exorbitant price, the apples smuggled in someone's suitcase from the UK, banking on desperate expats craving their favorite fruit for the holidays.

Sylvia drove by the new soccer stadium, the steel structure casting a dark shadow on the cardboard and plastic tarp shacks around it. Precious government oil revenues had been squandered on steel and glass while half-dressed children played in the gutters beneath it. Next to the stadium, she saw the carcass left from a car accident—the wheels, steering wheel, seats, and mirrors already scavenged and reused. Somewhere, a legless man was wheeling around in the front car seat, now attached to bike wheels. A young woman was applying lipstick while gazing into the rear view mirror that now hung above a yellow plastic bucket, her sink and bath.

A block from Ayo's clinic, the traffic stopped moving entirely. She could see the two-story blue and white clinic in the distance, but her car was trapped behind the multitude of cars, mopeds, and carts swarming the road. She got out of the car, not caring that it might be gone in a matter of minutes. She began running toward the clinic, weaving through the crowds and pushing her way through. When she reached the clinic, she was out of breath, her dress drenched in perspiration. She walked through the glass doors and saw Donna sitting behind the small wooden reception table.

• • •

Unaware that his wife was running to Ayo's clinic in the midst of riots, Winston visited Simeon's family on the morning of New Year's Eve. He had brought gifts for the children. The four children smiled at him with dark eyes and white teeth. Simeon's ten-year old son held up a small white goat in his arms. His son was shirtless, and his brown pants were too large for him, rolled up at the waist and at the bottom. Simeon's other two children pulled the youngest child in a pink plastic laundry basket around the dirt ground, the little girl with beads in her hair squealed in delight. Abike stood ironing the children's school uniforms on a wooden plank placed over an empty oil drum, the rusted iron full of burning charcoal. She took pride in ensuring her children were dressed in crisp, clean uniforms every day for school. But today, he could feel the intensity of her rage coming from the hot iron, the way she attacked her ironing with a vengeance.

Now more than ever, he wanted to make it up to Abike, to quell her rage. Winston sat down on a wooden stool next to Simeon. He reached into his bag and pulled out a large manila envelope. This year's harvest had generated enough to replant next season. But it was still not enough to repay Simeon's loans, which Winston knew were multiplying with interest. There

211

had been too many failures. Two harvests ago, Simeon's crop had suffered without the regular supply of fertilizers. This year, despite a decent harvest, the flooded market had driven the price of maize down. Winston knew Simeon was struggling financially.

He placed the envelope into Simeon's hand. Simeon looked inside and saw folded naira bills, a generous amount of Winston's own savings. Simeon looked up at Winston. He seemed surprised and then hurt.

"No, no...dis is not necessary," Simeon said, shaking his head, pushing the envelope back into Winston's hands.

Winston took the money back, embarrassed. He had hurt Simeon's pride. He suddenly wished he had not tried to do such a thing. The gesture had been full of good intentions, and he knew Simeon appreciated this, but it still recalibrated their friendship. He knew it had humiliated Simeon, signaling they were not on equal footing.

Winston got up, embarrassed, and took his leave. He put the small white goat, a gift to him from Simeon, in the back of his jeep. He saw Oluwa standing in the distance, watching them.

"Be careful, sah," was all Simeon said as Winston got into his jeep.

The armed escort drove Winston along the deserted road. Winston looked out the window and felt the isolation. There were no towns along the road, just the bush on both sides. The late afternoon sun lit up the red earth termite mounds, some ten feet high—spiraled towers and castles of dirt, full of underground tunnels. Winston couldn't stop thinking of Simeon's face when he had offered the money. He noticed Simeon's goat was skittish in the back of the jeep, jumping from corner to corner. This nervousness was contagious and Winston felt on edge. He knew bloody skirmishes had occurred between the Muslims and

Christians in the towns. He was glad to have the armed escort, but he didn't know if this was a false sense of security.

After seeing no one for a full hour, he saw something in the distance, a few empty oil drums set out in the middle of the road, some soldiers dressed in camouflage, a military check point. But something didn't seem right. Why in the middle of nowhere was there a military checkpoint? Perhaps a response to the riots and violence in the town, he hoped. The armed escort slowed the jeep.

• • •

The soldier at the checkpoint asked Winston and the armed escort to get out of the jeep and open the trunk. It seemed to be a routine military checkpoint, and in any case, Winston thought, the armed escort was no match against the military. He was merely meant to scare off a few crazy villagers.

Another soldier looked in the trunk and picked up the skittish white goat trying to make its escape.

"Keep it, Happy New Year from me," Winston said, hoping this would be the end of the search. He was worried the soldiers would find the envelope full of cash in his bag. He had shoved the bag under the passenger seat as they had approached the checkpoint.

"Tank you, ma friend," a tall, thin soldier said smiling. "Anyting else you want to give me, eh?" When he smiled, the tribal tattoos on his cheeks, ripples on his skin, seemed to disappear.

Winston shook his head.

"Are you sure?" the tall soldier opened the front door of the jeep and peered inside as if he had been tipped off about the envelope of money.

"You trying to hide something from us, you *O'Ebo*?" the soldier said as he searched the car further. Because of his height, it took some effort for the soldier to reach under the seats, but he soon found the bag. He looked in the bag and pulled out the manila envelope. The soldier's eyes grew large when he saw the amount of cash stuffed in the envelope.

"Keep it too. Another New Year's gift from me," Winston said, suddenly feeling nervous.

"You weren't going to share dis wit me and I thought we was friends. I am hurt, ma friend," the soldier said, holding the cash in his hand.

With his other hand, the soldier hit him in the face. Winston fell to the ground, his mouth full of dirt and the taste of his own blood. With the salty tang of blood in his mouth, Winston suddenly felt afraid. He knew once blood started flowing, who knew if they would stop. These men liked the smell of blood and the scent of fear on their prey. Winston's armed escort reached for his gun, but another solider hit him in the stomach, and he fell to the ground. They put Winston and his armed guard in the back of their truck.

"We taking you to de station for dis deception. Take you to see de boss," said the soldier with the scars.

Winston realized his folly. He should have just given these men the envelope up front. Now, they were going to mess with him.

The soldier drove Winston to the "station," a stifling, three-room cement house under a tin roof. The inside "office" was more for show. Most of the soldiers hung out under the cool of the large tree outside. The soldier introduced him to his captain. Winston sat down at the desk. The Captain, a large overweight man, sat down opposite him and asked for his passport. Winston reluctantly gave his passport to him, but the thought occurred to him that this could be last time he would see it. Being stranded in a country on the verge of political violence without proper identification was not his idea of how to spend New Year's Eve. His passport served as his ticket out of here. He thought of the road they had built on the compound next to the lake, long and wide enough for airplanes to land and takeoff for immediate evacuations.

The Captain read his passport cover page, *Taiwan, the Republic of China,* as he smoked a cigarette. Old cigarette butts were scattered on the cement floor below him.

"China?" he asked. "My brotha he go to China. He is soldier too. He met Chinese girl. She come here with him." The Captain spoke with a scratchy, raspy voice, typical of a chronic, long-term smoker.

The Captain was not smiling, he didn't seem angry either, so Winston couldn't tell if this coincidental family connection was going to be fortuitous for him. Winston wondered what the Captain's brother was doing in China, but this was the Cold War. No doubt Communist China was doing its bit to build "relations" with African countries especially oil-rich ones like Nigeria. Winston didn't bother to explain that he was from Taiwan, the "other China."

The Captain tossed the passport on his desk, and to Winston's dismay, the passport seemed to get lost in the piles of loose papers and bits of oil-stained newspaper once used to wrap the Captain's breakfast. This Chinese woman, Winston realized, whether she had been nice or not nice to the Captain's brother, would decide his fate. She was his only ambassador at this point.

"Let me show you your five stah hotel for tonight," the Captain said, coughing. His voice sounded brittle to Winston. He walked down the short hallway. They passed a cell crammed full of people—the small size of the cell offering barely enough standing room for the crowd. The Captain led Winston to the other cell.

"We prepared dis one just for you," the Captain said. "Courtesy of your good friend."

Winston looked up. This was the first time the Captain had mentioned any other accomplice in his situation.

"What friend?" Winston asked.

"Let's just say we have a friend in common, you and me." The Captain chuckled.

Winston thought only of Oluwa. He had arranged for this? Had he seen the envelope of money Winston had tried to give Simeon and then alerted the Captain to rob him? The money would be payment to the Captain for locking Winston up, serving Oluwa's larger goal to be rid of Winston.

The Captain pushed him into the cell. Winston surveyed his dismal accommodations. The cell was empty. There was a small window up high with bars. The only furniture in the room was a wooden stool and a lidded red bucket in the corner of the room that reeked of urine. The Captain then shouted someone's name. A girl came hurrying in with a bucket of Fanta and Coca-Cola bottles. The Captain handed the girl a stapler. A stapler? What were they going to do to him? But the girl took the stapler and, with the back of the metal, opened a soft drink bottle for Winston. Another soldier came into the cell and threw Winston his suitcase with his toothbrush and change of clothes. Then the barred metal door slammed loudly, and the Captain, soldier, and girl took their leave.

Winston was left alone in the cell. He wasn't sure what had happened to his armed guard. Was he in the cell next to him? Winston felt unbearably hot. There was not much air in the cell. The smell of urine coming from the bucket and the cell itself made him feel sick. He sat down on the stool against the wall strewn with the pockmarks of bullets. Would this be his end, languishing in a Nigerian cell arranged by Oluwa and his juju doctor? He might not make it through the night. He tasted the flavor of his own blood in his mouth. He washed this down with the sweet orange taste of the Fanta soda.

Chapter 27

Sylvia walked through the mass of people overflowing into the hallway, the familiar sour, metallic smell of blood and ammonia greeted her. She noticed some new rusty-red stains on the floor.

"Sylvia," Ayo said, their eyes met. "You came." He showed her into his office at the back of the clinic.

"I came to help out."

"I'm glad to see you," he said softly. "I've missed you." They looked at each other briefly, and she blushed. He was so close to her, she wanted to touch him, lay in his arms again.

"I'll end it, if you come back. She's nothing to me," he said as if reading her mind.

"I should go get changed. I'm sure there's a lot of work to do," she said, suddenly upset. How could he make love to someone and say it was nothing?

Donna poked her head in his office. "Ayo, they need you in room four. Bleeding won't stop." Did he ask all his lovers to become volunteers?

He touched Sylvia's shoulder lightly and left.

Sylvia went to the staff room and changed into a nurse's uniform. She looked down the hallway. Donna was busy in reception writing down patients' symptoms in the spiral notebook with the triage nurse, Sylvia's old job. Sylvia tried to avoid Donna, working instead on attending to the patients already checked in. The lacerations on some of children were grotesque, innocent bystanders in the riots. She help stitch up some of these wounds as best as she could. Others would require surgery.

"Winston told me you were a nurse," Donna said, coming in to her room to watch her work on patients. "That's great that you put yourself to work out here unlike the other wives just sitting by the pool."

"I'm not much into sitting by the pool," Sylvia responded as she finished up stitching a girl's arm.

She hadn't expected a compliment from her, but then again, maybe Donna did not know they were rivals in any way, or perhaps she didn't care given her casual attitude toward sex and relationships. But Sylvia still thought to tread carefully as the woman was also Winston's colleague. The less said, the better, she thought. She ignored Donna and focused instead on another child, picking out pieces of glass from a wound on his leg with a pair of tweezers.

"Well, I can see you're busy. Just wanted to say I admire your work," Donna said as she left the room.

Later around five o'clock, they all climbed into Ayo's car. Sylvia never explained that she had foolishly abandoned her car by the roadside. But they didn't get that far down the road before an angry mob surged forward. Ayo deftly sped the car backwards down the road, but the crowd followed with sticks and metal pipes, whatever they could find. Ayo's new Peugeot, imported and a sign of entitlement, was an easy target for people angry at those robbing them blind. He swerved backwards into the clinic, honking at the gatehouse. His guards, armed with machine guns, let them in and then quickly shut the gates, dispersing the crowd by firing a few shots into the air.

•••

When Sylvia woke up the next morning, lying on the cot in Ayo's office, the country had changed overnight. She could hear the faint sound of military parade music coming from the next room. She worried about her children. Were they safe? They were supposed to have gone to the New Year's Eve party at the clubhouse as a family. Had Winston made it back to the compound?

Sylvia looked over and saw the two chairs Donna had slept on were empty. Sylvia hadn't slept much of the night. She had heard the sounds of Ayo's voice, low and muted, as he did the rounds in his clinic all night long, but somehow she must have drifted off in the early hours of the morning. She looked at herself in her compact mirror and rummaged through the contents of her purse for lipstick, anything to make her look less tired and disheveled.

"You're awake," Ayo came into the room, he seemed worried. "There was a military coup last night. Soldiers descended on the Presidential palace and took over the government, but so far no one has been killed."

"Can…can we go back?" Sylvia said, her voice wavering. She had heard all those stories about expats in Iran after the overthrow of the Shah in 1979, having to flee with whatever clothes they had on them. What about her children? And where was Winston? She felt the juju doctor's misfortune descending on her and her family.

"Don't worry. Your children will be safe in the compound," Ayo said, but he didn't attempt to put his arms around her and instead kept a formal distance. "We'll go back immediately. The guards said the streets outside have calmed down since hearing the news. People are keeping a low profile."

Donna peered in, holding a short-wave radio. "I can't find any more news except the little we heard on the BBC. All the local stations are just playing military marching music." Her hair was tied up in the same ponytail, and she wore no makeup.

They got in Ayo's car again. Donna sat up front while Sylvia climbed into the backseat. Ayo drove through the streets, and everything was eerily quiet. They made decent progress along the road, driving quickly through the empty streets.

"Do you think the people will welcome the military takeover?" Donna said.

"Oddly enough, yes," Ayo said. "I know it's contrary to what you think. But honestly, I think everyone is fed up with so-called democratic government. Shegari's presidency has been the most corrupt ever. People are upset. In spite of the oil, the economy and the ordinary people's lives are worse off."

"I realize that. But how do you know these guys aren't going to do the same thing? I mean steal money from the state's coffers. Especially now since the people have relinquished their right to boot them out," Donna said.

"We don't know. In the past, military leaders have set up free elections and given up control. But yes, it's quite possible, they could hang on, and this could be the beginning of a long line of despots."

"You're willing to take that chance?"

"I suppose I've lost all my idealism. Not sure if democracy worked. Not sure if military dictatorship worked. They were both terrible," Ayo said, sounding defeated. "I'm in the business of worrying about the sick, the children, the injured. Nothing seems to improve under either rule."

Sylvia was quiet, listening to how easily they spoke to each other. She felt jealous and left out of the conversation. She saw something that perhaps Ayo and Donna didn't know yet. Despite his casual attitude toward Donna, Ayo had found his equal in her, something Sylvia felt she could never be.

"This country has so much potential to be great," Donna said. "The people are entrepreneurial, and you have some of the best minds in Africa. If only we could stop the few trying to rob it blind." Donna's face seemed to light up as she talked about Nigeria.

Sylvia looked over at Ayo. He seemed buoyed by Donna's enthusiasm for his country. It would bond them in some inexplicable way, she feared. Suddenly, Sylvia felt claustrophobic in the car with them, she had to get out.

• • •

Ayo dropped Sylvia off first, knowing she was concerned about her children. She got out of the jeep quickly, barely acknowledging Ayo or Donna. The children heard the car pull up, and they ran to the door, looking worried.

"Where were you Mama?" Lila said angrily. "We missed the New Year's Eve party because of you." She was eleven years old, and Thomas was nine.

"Madam, we wait and wait for you. But you not come, so I put de children to bed," Patience explained.

"Winston hasn't come home yet?" Sylvia said as she entered the living room.

Patience shook her head, and the children suddenly looked

frightened. He was supposed to have returned yesterday for the party.

Sylvia looked up frantically at the clock on the wall. It was ten in the morning. "Maybe he is on de way," Patience said, trying to reassure her.

Sylvia turned the TV on. But there was nothing on except the usual colored stripes accompanied by loud, military marching music. She left it on anyway.

She picked up the phone and called Richard.

"Yes, I know there's been a coup…Winston hasn't come back yet…Yes he was supposed to come back last night…A search party?…Do you think he's in trouble?…No, I will try not worry…Yes, sit tight."

She hung up and collapsed on the couch, too tired and anxious to even shower. Patience brought her some tea and toast.

"Madam, you need to eat," Patience said in a maternal way. "Don't worry, everyting will be OK. God will be watching over him."

"Thank you, Patience," Sylvia said, grabbing Patience's hand. "What would I do without you?" There were tears in the corner of Sylvia's eyes as she held Patience's hand. She had been through it all with her—the baby, the spirits, the unraveling marriage, the affair, the juju doctor's spell. Patience had been her friend, her family, the one person that had remained steady and constant in her adult life in Africa. If Patience left her, she would be at a loss.

"Patience, do you like it here?" she asked, suddenly. "I mean, would you one day go home back to Cote d'Ivoire?"

"I cannot go back dere, eh."

"I don't understand."

"I left to go to school in Abijan. But I failed. Only my people dey don't know dat. Dey tink I am a successful businesswoman here in Nigeria. Dey tink I have plenty plenty money. I send dem most of my salary. I can't go home. It's a lie. I have no money."

They both were exiled from their homelands, condemned to wandering a stranger's land.

"You look tired, madam, you should go rest," Patience said.

"Call me Sylvia, not madam."

"I can't, madam, it no feel right eh," Patience said as if she were wary of crossing the imaginary employer-friend boundary. Sylvia realized Patience was her friend, but was she Patience's friend? She had relied on Patience for everything in her life, but had Patience relied on anything from her except her salary?

Disappointed, Sylvia retired to her room. It had been a long day. Sylvia drifted into a quasi-sleep state and had terrible nightmare. It was about Winston. There was blood everywhere. It was another terrible hallucination, one of the many that had seemed to haunt her recently. When she woke up, she felt sick to her stomach.

• • •

Winston did not sleep much that night. His two companions, a giant flying cockroach and a tailless lizard, kept him awake much of the night scuttling around in the cement cell. The lizard chased the cockroach, hoping to make a meal out of it. He listened in the darkness to their battle. He heard the crowd fighting in the cell next to him. Was his armed guard in there too? He knew the prisoners had been crammed together in that tiny cell to accommodate him, an *O'Ebo*. Yet he still wasn't about to open up his cell to them either.

Sometime close to midnight, he heard people cheering outside. He thought it was just the usual New Year's revelry. He didn't know the military had just captured the President and set up shop in the palace. At sunrise, he heard the roosters crowing, and someone opened his cell door.

"It's time to celebrate, ma friend." A man he didn't recognize dressed in civilian clothes came in, smiling, giving him a cold beer for breakfast.

He led him out of the cell. The Captain was nowhere to be seen. The cell next door was empty of its prisoners, the iron door left open.

"Where is everyone?" Winston said as he drank the beer eagerly.

"Everyone is happy. Dat President Shegari robber has been overthrown," the man continued. "De Captain and his soldiers are loyal to Shegari. Dey fled. Before de military come and arrest dem."

Winston nodded, stunned at his sudden freedom.

Winston slowly made his way to the door outside. He figured any sudden movement might cause fingers to bear down on triggers.

"I need my passport," he said, looking through the papers on the Captain's desk. Some beer had spilled onto the passport, but otherwise it was mostly intact. Winston put his passport back into the front pocket of his shirt. He thought a passport from Taiwan held no currency in the counterfeit passport business. Who would want to go there? If it had been an American or British passport, it would not have made it through the night simply lying on the Captain's desk.

"Your man is waiting outside for you," the man said, pointing to his now unarmed guard waiting by the big tree. Winston was relieved to see him.

"My jeep?" Winston asked the man.

"Oh dat, I dunno what happened to it. I tink the Captain and his men take it when dey run in de night."

It didn't matter to Winston, at least he was alive, nothing had happened to him. If it hadn't been for the coup, he wasn't sure what Oluwa and the Captain might have had in store for him. He was safe and free for now. He and his guard managed to find a ride home on the back of a local pickup truck, sitting on top of a mound of cassava tubers.

PART THREE

1984-1986

SYLVIA

Chapter 28

Ayo tried to get in touch with her after the coup, but Sylvia never returned his calls. As the year went by, Ayo and Donna became a full-fledged couple, with Donna moving into Ayo's apartment on the compound. Sylvia had recommitted to Winston, but nothing had changed between them, in fact, he distanced himself even further as if protecting himself from her. *Her*—she had become that kind of woman, an adulteress, but she had nothing to show for it. The love of her life had moved on. Meanwhile, her husband spent more time on the road, far away from her, the curse still looming over his life, not that he seemed to care. But she tried her best to make sure her children were safe. Her daughter was growing up, and as each year went by, Lila moved one step away from the spirit world until one day she finally severed her ties.

When Lila turned twelve in 1984, she became more brooding, sulky toward her mother. Sylvia found her looking through her drawers, perhaps searching for a piece of evidence, any clue about her real father. Lila clearly didn't buy the Portuguese ancestor story Sylvia had spun all those years before to explain her different looks. But Lila's search for her father would change her relationship with the spirit world and this Sylvia welcomed.

One night, Lila had a strange dream. On this particular nightly sojourn to the spirit world, Lila told Sylvia she met a crocodile spirit, half fish and half snake. When she met him, he was angry. Along his river, they were building a modern dam. Its construction would drown the surrounding villages that worshipped him. The crocodile spirit attacked the dam. Several construction workers were buried alive within the dam wall after falling into the wet concrete. But eventually the dam displaced the crocodile spirit and all he stood for. Lila watched as the water rose—people and animals, whole species—were drowned in an effort to bring electricity to darkness. Some tribesman had stayed behind not believing the waters would truly rise. Lila screamed as water filled the lungs of the village children. Lila felt the water rising quickly around her until only her head was free. In a matter of minutes, she feared she would be completely submerged. In his anger, the spirit and his fellow crocodiles feasted on all the corpses left behind.

Suddenly, her father appeared, but the man did not look like Winston, only a hazy version of a stranger whose face she could not see, but somehow Lila knew this man was her real father. The man held his arm out to her to save her from the rising waters. She kept trying to look at his face. Perhaps Lila wanted to see her biological father's face so much she wanted it to be real, and in that moment, Lila realized she was standing in a dream.

It was then that Lila woke up in her bed, drenched in sweat. Sylvia heard her screaming, and like many nights before, she came to her daughter. But something about that night seemed different. Sylvia had come to Lila when she was a young child, hoping to wean her from the visits to the spirit world but to no avail. Tonight her daughter was sitting up in her bed, wide awake.

"I thought I saw my real father," Lila said in a far-off voice. "But it was only a dream." She explained pieces of her dream.

Sylvia held her daughter in her arms. She lay down next to her, holding her until Lila finally fell asleep. Sylvia had waited twelve years for this moment. When a child could finally separate dreams from reality, this was when the child lost all connection and consciousness with the spirit world. Finally, Lila's dreams started to peel away from her reality and with that, at last, the spirit world began to fade away. From that moment on, Lila was no longer a changeling who could move freely between the earthly and spirit worlds. She was fully grounded in this life. The spirits would no longer be able to lure her back to the afterlife. She had grown up.

Sylvia welcomed this shedding of her spirit side with a mixture of relief and apprehension. She was relieved to be rid of the spirits' hold on Lila's life, but at the same time, she was afraid of what had caused it. The timing of it clearly had something to do with her growing suspicions of her biological father.

• • •

With the spirits vanquished, Sylvia seemed to drop her guard. As the weeks went by, Sylvia woke up with dark circles under eyes and wandered around all day in her nightgown. When Winston was away, she didn't bother to cook. Her children ate Skippy peanut butter and passion fruit jam sandwiches for dinner every night while she had nothing but cups of dark coffee. She was overly anxious and erratic, telling her children one minute not to play on the grass outside because of the snakes while the next minute, she sat on the sofa, staring into space, not noticing if they went outside at all. What was wrong with her, she wondered? Was she pining away or was it something worse, a tropical fever of some sort?

"You sick, madam, you need to go to doctor," Patience said, worried.

"I went to the doctor. They can't cure it," Sylvia lied.

"You need to go to Ayo doctor."

"No. Don't you contact him, you hear?"

Sylvia stopped going to the clubhouse and other compound social events or dinner parties. If Lila and Thomas wanted to go swimming, Sylvia sent Patience and the armed guard with the children to the pool. Since Lila had severed her ties with the spirit world, Sylvia was less worried about the threat of water.

The only thing Sylvia did on a weekly basis was to shop at the market in town. She borrowed videos from a makeshift rental place at the back of a furniture store run by an Indian family. In between the Bollywood musicals, the shelves in this small backroom were stocked with TV or rerun movies on blank tapes with hand-written labels, recorded from BBC or ITV by the owner's cousin in the UK—plenty of James Bond, Grace Kelly, and Peter Sellers. She would watch movies all day dressed in her nightgown and robe. VHS had just been invented, and television-starved expats all over Africa were the first to adopt it.

As the weeks progressed, Sylvia began to have increasingly bizarre dreams, hallucinations in vivid clashing colors. She dreamed she planted a sacred silk cotton or *Peregun* tree outside Ayo's father's house. The tree was known to secret a semen-like juice that traditional Yoruba medicine used as an aphrodisiac or love potion. It was used by women seeking special favors from their husbands when rivaling other wives. In her dream, the tree's branches wound its way like snakes throughout Ayo's house.

These horrible dreams haunted Sylvia now every night, and she became an insomniac, afraid to close her eyes. For several nights in a row, she had a reoccurring nightmare. In the dream, she sensed someone scraping a sharp tool against her skull, engraving Chinese oracles into her bones. She felt the cracking of her skull. She didn't need to interpret the cracks—they were predicting death.

WINSTON

Chapter 29

In the fall of 1984, Simeon experienced the worst harvest ever. Winston followed the harvest procession through the sacred part of the forest. This patch of thick, virgin tropical jungle had been preserved and untouched for centuries. It was not a forest Winston could forget. The place still haunted him—perhaps the darkness even in broad daylight or the thickness of the under-growth and vines. He knew it was a sacred grove frequented by spirits, a meeting place for religious chiefs, village ceremonies, or initiation grounds for secret societies. Supposedly, the plants and trees possessed special healing powers. But since the forest was sacred, the inhabitants of the villages nearby guarded it with their lives. No one was permitted to cut down a tree or plant in the forest without special permission. Winston noticed over the years that the neighboring Cole Agribusiness plantation had expanded so that now its chain-link fence bordered this forest.

The harvest procession moved through the forest. Winston

dutifully followed even though every limb in his body wanted to flee in the other direction. Today, few villagers danced. When they reached the shrine deep in the middle of the forest, a village elder, dressed in a white robe, offered a white kola nut and a white pigeon to the shrine along with a few yams and ears of corn from the meager harvest. It was nothing like the mounds of yams and corn offered in years past.

This year the pests had been cruel, leveling the kind of attack that Simeon and the other farmers had never seen before in their lives. The leaves of the maize crop were full of holes, bitten to death by bugs. Simeon desperately sprayed double the amount of pesticide, but this seemed to have little effect. Winston wondered if this was some sort of retaliation against the pesticides themselves. The chemicals were made to kill all in their path. They didn't differentiate. The "good" bugs that might prey on the pests were also killed. This might also explain the sudden spike in the pest population. Had man, in his pursuit to control nature in the end, toppled nature's own finely tuned ways of control? The question lingered in the forefront of Winston's mind.

Winston leaned in with the crowd, turning his attention to the divination rite of the harvest ritual. He hoped that next year would be better. The elder tossed the yams, and the entire village held its breath. But then both yams fell facedown. The crowd seemed to collectively gasp and put their hands over their mouths in fear. Winston knew this signaled the worst was still to come. Not even the prediction of ambiguity. He suddenly thought of his wife. Lately, she seemed sick, depressed even. His wife and his project were unraveling before him, and he felt powerless. The procession walked slowly back to the village, and the crowd congregated for a feast under the thatched canopy, but the mood was somber. This time, Simeon did not invite the village over to his house to watch his television. His house remained half-built, and the generator had broken, Simeon had not bothered to fix it. The television still stood under his porch, orange dust caking its screen.

Winston and Simeon sat alone on his porch next to the dusty television.

"You know, dis spray you give me, it may kill da bug," Simeon said bitterly, "but de bug rise from de dead and come back more of dem. Dey angry at us. We were at peace with dae bug before. Now dey are at war with us."

Winston said nothing. He knew Simeon was losing faith, and Winston himself was beginning to doubt.

"I dunno if I have de money to replant. I borrow, I buy, like you tell me, but I don't sell nothing. Nothing," Simeon continued, he shook his head. "De spell, we can't fight it no more. It's stronger than us." He seemed angry at his defeat. "Dat Oluwa, he wins."

Simeon went into his hut and returned with a pesticide canister. He opened it and took out a crumpled stack of IOU notes. Winston was shocked at how much Simeon owed. It had been his idea for Simeon to borrow the money in the first place. Winston felt the burden of saving Simeon clearly rested on his shoulders.

• • •

The next day, Winston paid a visit to the neighboring plantation managed by Cole Agribusiness. As he drove through the plantation's maize fields, he noticed their leaves were full of holes from bugs as well. He saw the Cole representative Jim McCormack standing outside his office, supervising some men loading farm machinery into a truck. Jim waved at him with his usual misleading smile.

"Howdy," Jim said. "Always pleased to see ADA men."

Of course, he was pleased to see ADA staff, Winston noted with cynicism. Winston had come to save Africa from poverty and hunger, but in reality, he and his other colleagues at the ADA had amounted to nothing more than traveling salesmen for Cole Agribusiness, peddling bags of their seeds under the banner of "third world development."

"The local farmers are having the worst pest year they have ever seen," Winston began. "I see your crop is experiencing a similar fate."

"These African bugs are tough little buggers," Jim responded. "But we'll just spray twice the amount next season. That should fix the problem."

"You think more pesticides are the solution? They could be the cause of the problem." Winston realized a representative of Cole would not admit this, of course. His solution would be to advise an increase in purchases of the pesticides. He was a well-programmed corporate robot, this man Jim.

"Business is good. We're planning to expand," Jim said.

"Really? Expand? Where to? Into that forest? You know it's sacred." Winston pointed toward the forest between the plantation and Simeon's village. At six-foot-four, Jim towered over Winston. Usually, this didn't bother Winston, but today, standing next to the man, he suddenly felt the inferiority of his physical size.

"No, no, of course not," Jim said, but he looked down at the ground.

"Then where?" Winston was worried. Simeon's village was on the other side of the forest.

"Let me give you a word of advice," Jim said, his icy blue eyes looking straight at Winston now. "I know you're trying to help these farmers, but don't worry yourself with things that don't concern you. After the day is done, you and I will be going back to our respective countries."

Winston noticed a framed photograph of Jim's smiling family, little blond children living back in America. Of course Jim wanted to go home. Winston realized there were vast differences between this man and him. Winston couldn't go back to Communist China. He had no plans to go anywhere. Africa was his home now.

Chapter 30

The miracle seeds, brought in the palm of the white man, had displaced centuries of seeds carefully saved by farmers after every harvest, stretching back to the dawn of agriculture. Since his adoption of the Cole Agribusiness maize seeds more than a decade before, Simeon had stopped saving some of the corn kernels from his harvest to replant. Winston told him these hybrid seeds, concocted in the laboratory, were not self-fertile. In fact, replanting these seeds would not produce the same kind of successful plant that would ensure high yields or fast growth. But Simeon had tried replanting these cross-bred seeds and had gotten a crop that reflected a random assortment of genetic traits that bordered on the bizarre. In order to replant, Simeon was forced to purchase new seeds from Cole Agribusiness every year. He had been doing this since 1974 for over a decade now. By planting season in May of 1985, despite his failed crop and growing debt, Simeon had no choice but to purchase another bag of seeds.

Winston and Donna walked along the narrow dirt footpath

in between the tall grass and new maize fields toward Simeon's village.

"Dey were here yesterday," Simeon said, his head hung low. These days, any news seemed to be bad news.

"Who?" Winston asked.

"De plantation people. Our neighbors. Dey tell us dis land and dis forest is not ours, dey showed us paper dat de government owns it and sold it to dem. Dey want us off. But I told dem we are not leaving. We don't have paper, but we live here for many years, my fatha's fatha and his fatha. Dis is our land."

Winston was afraid of what Simeon and his village were up against.

"Those assholes. Who do they think they are?" Donna ranted. She spoke with such confidence and rage, Winston thought, it was infectious. "You guys have lived here for generations, and now they're saying you need papers to prove it. What a scam. This is bullshit."

At Donna's suggestion, Winston agreed to go over to the Cole plantation next door and "get some answers." As they drove up to the Cole office on the plantation, Winston saw the tractors lined up, parked near the warehouse. They knocked on Jim McCormack's door, and not waiting for him to answer, Donna pushed it open.

"I was expecting you," Jim said. He didn't offer them coffee.

"What papers are you flashing at the farmers next door?" Donna wasted no time. She stepped in and leaned on his desk. Winston had always had mixed feelings toward Donna. She was culturally alien to him with her feminism and hippie hair, but now at this moment, he felt oddly aligned with her. She was saying the things he wanted to say, only more brashly with no respect for diplomacy.

"Official government papers," Jim said. This time he was not smiling.

"We don't want to cause any problem. I understand you have official papers. But what about the people you are displacing?" Winston said.

"We're not displacing them. We're modernizing agriculture. Turning this hodge podge of small plots into a more efficient, large scale farm. We'll offer them jobs on our plantation."

"And what if they don't want jobs as slaves on your plantation?" Donna said.

"Whoa. Wait a sec. If they don't want well-paid jobs that include housing and schooling for their kids, that's fine. They can join the rest of the crew migrating to the cities. We're giving them a better option out here."

"Shouldn't you ask them first what they want?" Winston said.

"We did ask them. We've already got one farmer from the village that's signed up to be the manager of all the farm workers. We're building him a proper cement house with electricity. We've thrown in some extra land for him and his family as well. Let me tell you, he's very happy."

"What's his name?" Winston asked.

"I can't remember," Jim said. "Those Nigerian names all sound the same to me. Begins with an O or ends in an O. I can't recall."

Winston and Donna exchanged glances. Oluwa? They hadn't expected him to join Cole.

"I'm not going to let you do this." Donna's voice was quiet, hollow even. "I'll stop you if I have to lie on the ground in front of your bulldozers."

"Be my guest. But if you get hurt, don't tell me I didn't warn you to get out of our way."

"Is that a threat? You threatening me, Jim?"

"Let's go," Winston said, seeing the conversation was spiraling downward.

• • •

As they drove off in their jeep, Donna said, "What do you make of Oluwa's involvement? Why would he partner with Cole? It doesn't make sense."

"I think he's more cunning than we thought. He seems to want to one up Simeon at any cost, even if it means destroying his own village in the process," Winston said.

"Well Oluwa better be careful. He doesn't know who he's just jumped in bed with. I've seen Jim's type before. He's a real jerk, he doesn't care about Africa or its people. He just cares about his own profit and promotion coming down the pipe. Jim probably wants out of this hell-hole place, he's probably already envisioning his corner office in a glass skyscraper back in Chicago if all goes well."

Winston wondered what Cole Agribusiness would do to get what it wanted. The company, motivated by profits and expansion into world markets, and its staff, incentivized through bonuses and raises, might stop at nothing.

"I'm going to contact my journalist friend. Works for National Geographic. This would make a great story and bring international publicity to this problem. Get that asshole back," Donna said.

"Good idea."

It's so frustrating to come out here," Donna continued. "To want to do good and then you meet assholes like him. This is bullshit." She hit the steering wheel with her fist.

"Why are you here, Donna? In Africa?" Winston asked, suddenly curious.

Donna paused and then spoke slowly, "I've come a long way."

"From where?"

"Westchester County. Idyllic countryside suburb near New York City. Beautiful homes on lots of land, wealthy people but dysfunctional lives. I had to get out."

Winston waited for her to continue.

"I was very angry." She took a deep breath. "Angry at my parents. Dad is a Wall Street guy. Mom's an attorney. Both were completely fucked, excuse my language, but that's the only way I can describe it. It ended up in a nasty divorce. I was a product of their dysfunction. And all that money."

"I'm sorry," Winston said. He didn't look at her, but just to the side of her, embarrassed by her language.

She shrugged. "Who gives a shit? I wanted to get away, far away. So after college, I joined the Peace Corps. Got sent to Benin. Thought there'd be, y'know, some fun and adventure."

"Was there?"

"You know the answer."

"What you got was no fun, lots of hard work. It completely changed your perspective on the world and yourself," Winston said. He had heard this story many times. He sometimes felt the value of the Peace Corps was not just the work it did in Africa but its role in educating generations of young Americans about the world.

"Yeah, that's pretty much my story. The Africa-changed-me story. It opened my eyes. Made me realize my own ignorant-rich-girl suffering was pretty stupid, self-imposed indulgence stuff. I felt pretty dumb, considering real suffering was happening here every day. So I went back to get my PhD at Harvard. Now I'm here."

"We need people like you."

Winston was glad that for every Jim McCormack, luckily

there was a Donna Burns. He also realized that Donna's altruism surpassed his. He had wanted to use science to solve world poverty; he was motivated by proving a concept. She, on the other hand, had fallen in love with the country, the whole continent, for that matter. In contrast, she despised her own people. This was evident in the way she spoke about her fellow American, Jim McCormack. It was as if Donna was bearing the burden, the past crimes of her own country, and that was what caused her to act the way she did. It was a kind of apologetic altruism. She wanted to single-handedly make right all that her country had wronged.

SYLVIA

Chapter 31

Bizarre hallucinations continued to traverse the cluttered hall-ways of Sylvia's mind throughout the spring of 1985. She had been sick for over a year now. At dawn, she walked around the garden. Her husband watched her as he ate breakfast under the franjipani tree. The dusty Harmattan sky was a pale pink, a cool dry season morning. The arid wind blowing down from the Sahara scattered the few remaining petals of the orchids on the brown grass.

"Come and eat," he said, sounding worried.

"I'm okay, not hungry yet." She stood among the dead branches of the orchids. These days, she didn't tend to her garden or cut flowers for their table anymore.

"You're looking too thin. Here, eat some eggs." Being told you are thin in Chinese culture was not a compliment, she knew. Saying, "you're so fat" in Chinese was a way to compliment someone for being healthy, happy, and prosperous.

Sylvia shook her head. "I'm fine. I'll eat later. I'm just not hungry first thing in the morning." But she would not eat later.

Winston did not press her. Instead, he dug into the *shefan* rice porridge, loudly slurping with a Chinese spoon. The table was set with the usual little dishes of roasted peanuts, ro-sung dried beef, pickles, tea-leaf eggs, and tofu with soy sauce and cilantro. Winston picked at the dishes with his chopsticks as he ate the *shefan*.

This was one of the few things she kept up for him. Chinese food was the unspoken language of their relationship, nourishing what little existed between them. Over the years, it had been the medium they used to communicate any affection—she by cooking the food and he by eating it. He slurped it down, savoring the food with a vigor and passion that was otherwise absent in their relationship. As her husband ate, he looked up several times at Sylvia, his expression full of compassion and worry. She realized it was not lost on him that despite her depression and illness over the past year, she still prepared Chinese food for him.

"I heard you moving around last night. Did you not sleep well?" he asked.

"It was nothing. Just a bad dream."

"Again?"

"I'm fine. It's nothing."

Winston said no more. He did not send her to the doctor. Was it too much shame, she wondered, to admit she was suffering from some sort of mental illness and worse still, possibly as a result of a love affair? That was her diagnosis, wasn't it?

Perhaps he worried if she went to the compound clinic everyone would soon know their problems, and he wanted to keep things to themselves. Instead, he brewed his own concoction of Chinese herbs, supposedly a cure for insomnia, anxiety, and appetite loss. But Sylvia didn't drink it. The dark-brownish green tea was left sitting by her bedside, growing cold.

• • •

In the summer of 1985, while Winston and Donna were both away, Sylvia saw Ayo at a dinner party at the Scottish couple's house. It was a rare appearance for her at a social event. Earlier that week, the Scottish woman had actually come over and knocked on Sylvia's door to invite her personally. She didn't know if this was at Ayo's bidding since he was their close friend. She didn't want to offend her neighbor, so she went to the dinner party even though she feared seeing Ayo. She arrived late to the party and hoped to leave early, minimizing her contact with him.

The Scottish woman had written name cards with a fountain pen. Sylvia found her name at the table and sat down. She noticed Ayo's name was next to hers. She nervously twisted strands of her long hair. She wanted to be near him, but she just didn't want him to see her this way. When he sat down next her, she didn't look up. They were served an English roast beef, but Sylvia didn't eat much and she hoped Ayo would not notice.

A red-faced Welsh man at their table told humorous stories of his encounters with "the locals" with quite the flourish. Ayo detested these stories, she knew. They were full of overt racism and condescension, exaggerating the locals' ignorance or curiosity or awe, whatever suited the storyteller.

"Are you all right?" he said quietly to her, staring directly at her thin wrists. After spending days measuring children's wrists for signs of malnutrition, she knew, he could see the signs in her. She pulled her arms away from the table and his examining eyes.

"I'm fine," she said, but she sat tightly compressed, arms tucked close to her body as she ate, careful not to touch him. She felt uncomfortable next to him. She knew Donna was a better partner for him. After all, she loved his country unconditionally and just as much as him, perhaps more.

"You don't look...well," he said. "Come and see me...at the clinic." His words hurt. The impersonality of it all, to come and see him at his clinic as if she were simply a patient, not the woman he had loved.

Sylvia rose from the table and walked away, her eyes full of tears, her dinner left unfinished. It was a mistake to tell a woman she didn't look well. Her looks were fading, she thought, and with it, her hold on him. Sylvia was thirty-four years old, and he was with a younger, twenty-something woman. She left the dinner party early, making excuses to her hosts.

Later that night, she heard a knock on the door of her house. She knew it was Ayo, but she didn't go to him. She was in the bathroom in her white silk robe, fumbling with a bottle of pills. She stuffed a handful of pills into her mouth and swallowed them with a glass of water. She kept doing this until she passed out. She must have hit her head on the tile because the last thing she thought was—*there's blood.*

• • •

When Sylvia woke up, she heard the busy midday street outside— the cacophony of vendors hawking their wares, astute mothers arguing the price down, children wailing in the background. She could smell meat cooking on an open fire. She thought she had returned to her childhood home in Shanghai, the home she had left so many years ago when her family had left China. But when she strained her ears, she did not hear the familiar language of her childhood, but the Yoruba of her lover.

She opened her eyes and recognized the peeling, light blue paint, the rusty electric fan, the faded biblical calendar hanging on a nail on the wall, the mahogany four poster bed of his father's house. She didn't want to look at herself in the gilded mirror on the wall opposite the bed. Outside her room in the courtyard, Ayo spoke to his steward. How had she gotten here? Where were her children? And Winston, did he know? She immediately climbed out of bed. She was wearing a white collared shirt of Ayo's, but her legs were bare.

He saw her standing there. She felt embarrassed and looked away.

"You need to get back into bed," he said. He came into the room and helped her climb into bed. She still did not meet his eyes. She was ashamed that she had tried to kill herself, a hopeless attempt with the sleeping pills from her Indian neighbor. She remembered the difficulty breathing, the blood on her head. She knew she hadn't really wanted to die.

He sat down on the bed and touched her hair. "Sylvia, I need to ask you something, something personal." He looked directly at her.

She wanted it to be about love, but she feared he would ask her about her suicide attempt.

"Are you having strange dreams or nervousness or anything like that?"

She paused and then lied, "No." She didn't want him to see her that way. She wanted him to see her as beautiful, not as the depressed, anxiety-ridden woman she had become.

"Right. How about any kind of psychological illness in your family?" He asked these questions matter-of-factly like he was conducting a medical analysis of her, not asking his ex-lover if she had gone mad.

"No," Sylvia said quickly even though she knew her brother was ill. He left their university in England because he had some sort of mental breakdown. Leaving Hong Kong and coming to the West, the shock had been too much pressure for him. Her parents never mentioned him anymore as if they had rewritten the family story, minus one member. She had one brother now, not two, if people asked. He had been erased permanently from the family consciousness. She knew her mother visited him in a home in Hong Kong. But no one else in their family had ever seen him again. It was as if he did not exist anymore.

She knew her family couldn't take it if they found out she was ill too. She was, though, wasn't she? She had been sick for over a year now. She couldn't reveal this to anyone, especially Ayo.

"Winston...does he...?" she said.

"He doesn't know. They're still traveling. They won't be back until next week. You'll stay here for a few days until you're better." She knew by his reference to "they" that he was communicating to her that Donna would also be away.

"And...my children?"

"Patience is with the children. I told her to tell any visitors that you're ill and in bed at home. I pumped your stomach at the hospital yesterday and then brought you here."

He looked at her differently now, his eyes full of not just love but compassion, pity, shock, a desire to understand. She resented the pity. After all these years she had spent working by his side, she didn't like being his patient now. It seemed to put her in a position of weakness. She was no different from those forlorn, bedraggled mothers that frequented his clinic. She couldn't claim superiority over them; she was just like them—helpless, sick, and desperate. She was no angel of nursing like she had imagined, she needed just as much care as them, if not more.

"How did...you..." she asked.

"Patience."

Patience, of course, she knew everything. Patience had probably found her passed out in the bathroom. It was only natural she would call Ayo. Patience had betrayed her, but she knew Patience was also her guardian angel.

"No one knows I'm here?" Sylvia said this slowly as if processing all that had happened.

"No one needs to know."

Did this mean she could just stay here together with him? They could borrow this time held in suspension by her suicide attempt.

He said, "I'm going to have to drop by the clinic. My steward will take care of you if you need anything." He rose and kissed her on the head like she was a child.

• • •

Sylvia got up and wandered around Ayo's house. She noticed the furniture sheathed in dusty, white sheets and the windows shuttered. It was true wasn't it? He had never brought Donna here. The house looked abandoned.

When he returned that evening, Ayo climbed into bed with her and pulled her close, holding her tightly, like he didn't want to lose her.

"I love you. Only you. Please know this," he said as he held her.

"I thought you and Donna..."

"I'm only with her because I can't be with you. I kept this house closed all these years, waiting for you to come back, it's our house."

It felt good to hear those words. She was always his first choice. Living here in his house, she let herself imagine what it would be like if this life belonged to them. She ordered the steward to make passion fruit juice for them and the maid to wash their sheets. She sat under the large breadfruit tree, the spiky hard skins of the large green fruit, almost soccer ball-size, scattered around her. She watched the headless body of a brown chicken run around the courtyard, its bloody head sliced off by the cook. When she was bitten by sandflies, the maid cut off a wedge of the aloe vera plant in the garden. She rubbed the green gel-like insides of the aloe vera onto her skin to soothe the itchiness.

But underneath this charade the real question still hovered. Could she stay here? Was that her cure? What about her husband?

"What's wrong with me?" she whispered in the dark as she lay in his arms.

"You have *tamazai*, it's what the Tuereg, a Saharan desert tribe, call this melancholy," Ayo said, tracing her face with his fingers.

"Tamazai," she repeated slowly.

"The Tuereg believe spirits of solitude are hidden in sand dunes, and they bring illness to the heart and soul. Women struck by these beautiful sounds of the spirit, in the form of mesmerizing drumming, become afflicted. They suffer from melancholy and depression, they are known as the 'people of solitude.' Secret love is considered the cause."

He tried to frame it in beautiful terms, but in reality, he was telling her she was going mad, wasn't he?

"You should stay here with me. You can't go back," he said as if he was somehow the cause of her melancholy.

But was he? She felt it was something deeper than that, something beyond her control. Perhaps Ayo knew this and wanted her close to him, so he could observe her under the microscope of his medical mind. She was afraid of what he would find. She did not want her lover to see her from this viewpoint—magnified into tiny details, revealing more about herself than she cared for him to know. And so, she said nothing but kissed him instead. She tasted the passion fruit, the crunchy black seeds still in his mouth.

WINSTON

Chapter 32

The soil in West Africa was deeply eroded like the edges of Winston's heart. The natural channels, tree roots, and worm tunnels that had once let sustenance trickle to the heart of the soil had closed up under the weight of modern tractors, leaving the soil brittle and defenseless against the temperamental winds of life. It degraded quickly, running down riverbanks toward the sea, clumps of orange dirt that even the wind could churn up into the sky. So much runaway soil that from the sky, it looked like brown rivers pouring into the blue ocean. Winston thought of his wife and his project, if he could just stem the inevitable tide.

"De earth is tired," Simeon said. "De soil no good anymore. It fly away."

In the summer of 1985, Winston and Donna walked with Simeon in his fields. His maize crop was full of holes again although some of the crop had been spared this year. Winston crouched down and scooped up a handful of the ochre dirt.

He felt the infertile, sandy soil, full of quartz in his hands—the soil of Africa. Was this fragile soil vulnerable to the weight of modern farm machinery like tractors, Winston wondered? Were the chemicals that were poured into the soil to stimulate crop growth ultimately impoverishing the soil? They were using tons of fertilizers to make the plants grow, but this also stimulated weed growth, and the farmers had to douse the fields with herbicides. Winston had believed that technology and science could solve hunger and poverty in Africa. But was it instead destroying the soil—the basis of food and life itself?

"Have you heard anything from the plantation next door?" Donna said, sounding worried.

"Dey keep coming here every week telling us to move. We keep telling dem we are no move. We will fight dem. We have to protect de forest from dem," Simeon said. "Oluwa has already left. To join de plantation. Dat cockroach."

"He's left?" Donna said.

"That's not a good sign," Winston said. "Do you think Cole will go so far as to use force?"

"I wouldn't put it past them," Donna said and then she turned to Simeon. "Would you be ready? I mean to fight?"

"We would be ready. I'm not going to let dem take dis land. It belong to my grandfatha, my grandfatha's fatha. It is our land," Simeon said.

Suddenly, the juju doctor with yellowed eyes appeared. He stood in the middle of the village shouting, "Dis is the end of de village, dis is de prophecy!" The villagers shrank back away from him, even Simeon looked afraid. Then the old man disappeared just as quickly as he had appeared.

"You should send the women and children away. Just in case," Winston said. He felt afraid now. The sudden appearance of the juju doctor had unsettled him.

Simeon was silent as they walked back to the village. The women were washing clothes at the river, dipping their large enamel basins in the water. Rows of colorful cloth lay flat to dry on the ground next to the river. A group of young girls carried their toddler siblings on their backs. The girls' dark blue and green batik cloth wrappers contrasted with the ochre backdrop of the village—mud walls and the deeply-rutted orange dirt ground.

Winston and Donna drove off in their jeep, moving slowly along the muddy road destroyed by the rains. They were both silent, deep in thought. Winston worried about the safety of Simeon and his family. He didn't want them to cave to Cole Agribusiness, but he didn't want them to risk their lives either. Could they stop Cole, Oluwa, and the juju doctor? He hoped Simeon would at least send his family away.

And the harvest? There wasn't much to hope for. Winston knew Simeon would probably salvage what he could at harvest time, the little left after the barrage of the pests. This would be enough to feed his family and perhaps have some small surplus to take to the town market. But nothing like Winston had promised him. *The miracle seeds will produce mountains of grain like you have never seen.* The only mountain that had materialized was Simeon's debt—borrowed money used to purchase the seeds, the fertilizers, and the pesticides from Cole Agribusiness.

Everything he had believed in and staked his life on had turned out to be false. Worse yet, he had convinced Simeon to believe those empty promises too. Winston felt he was a liar, no better than the usual charlatans who came out to Africa with the next best thing. He didn't know how he could look at himself in the mirror again.

On his way home, Winston drove by a gleaming, modern Conoil petrol station, but it was empty. The owner still made better money selling petrol on the black market by the roadside in large, yellow jerry cans, the way he had always done.

SYLVIA

Chapter 33

In the end, Sylvia chose *tamazai* or solitude over her secret love. After a week with her lover, suspended in time, outside the boundary of her life, she returned home. She was falling apart and she didn't want her lover to see her this way. She wanted him to remember her the way she had been, beautiful and alive, not as the thin shadow she had become. Ayo came to her house to visit her, but Sylvia refused to see him.

As weeks went by, her illness only worsened. There were days when she could not get out of bed. Winston knew nothing of her suicide attempt. Sylvia didn't want her husband to know how sick she was. He had too much going on with his work to deal with her too. Besides, she could fake it and get out of bed whenever Winston was home. But most of the time, Winston was not home, and she could barricade herself in her room. Sylvia had Patience to bring her trays of toast, Campbell's soup, and Bitter Lemon soda, to keep her house clean, and to care for her children. Sylvia could easily pass a day in bed and then get up for dinner when Winston came home.

Patience took good care of her, but she worried about Sylvia.

"You need to tell Masta, you sick," Patience said.

Sylvia shook her head. "He's already got too much trouble to worry about."

Patience said nothing, but Sylvia could tell she was mulling things over in her mind. Patience knew all of her secrets—the lover, the suicide, the depression. Over the years, Patience had been the mastermind behind all of Sylvia's indiscretions, and Patience had worked hard to cover up Sylvia's lies so that the children and Winston never noticed.

• • •

Sylvia heard the sounds of the drums coming from town at night. The drums began after sundown. A storm was coming. The Yoruba storm spirit *Shango* was restless in the dusky sky. In his anger, he would throw stones down at them.

She was already in bed when Winston came home. He walked into the bedroom.

"Sylvia," he said softly. The smell of the storm assaulted her, that sweet electric smell, the air full of anticipation. She closed her eyes. The sound of the drums grew fainter as the wind filled her ears.

"Sylvia," he tried again, coming closer to the bed. She opened her eyes. Her husband looked tired, gaunt. His normally rigid face had lost its guard, drooping almost into a frown.

"I'm going to take you to the doctor."

"I'm fine."

"I know about…"

The rain started to fall, crashing down on the roof, drowning out his words. She looked up at him, surprised. She saw his face was full of worry. It had been six months since her suicide attempt.

"Patience told me."

She couldn't hear the sound of the drums anymore, only the rain.

• • •

Winston took Sylvia to the compound doctor the next day. They sat together in the clinic room. The newly-hired American doctor offered a clear diagnosis. He was not clouded by love.

"Is she having nightmares?" he said.

"Yes," Winston answered for her.

Sylvia was silent, a prisoner-patient held captive by her husband.

"Is she over-anxious all the time?"

"Yes. She tried to take her life," Winston added in a low voice.

At the mention of her suicide attempt, the doctor's expression turned serious.

"Has she ever had any previous psychological problems or any family history of psychological problems?"

Winston looked over at Sylvia.

She nodded. "My brother is…schizophrenic."

"But you, yourself, have you ever been treated for any psychological issues?"

"No," she said truthfully. Suddenly she wanted the doctor to solve her problems. Could he or was she going mad?

The doctor looked down at his notes and paused.

"I think she might be suffering from neurological side effects of the malaria pills. It's just a guess, but her symptoms all point to this."

"The malaria pills?" Sylvia was surprised when she thought all along she was pining for her lover.

"The ones I've been taking every Sunday for all these years?"
"We're only just discovering that the pills have neurological side effects on some people. Makes them anxious and gives them nightmares or hallucinations."

"I'm going to prescribe a new kind of malaria pill, hopefully it should put a stop to these neurological effects. Still, it will take time for her to recover. But meanwhile, you'll need to keep an eye on her."

The doctor looked directly at Sylvia. "I'm going to recommend a psychologist in town for you to see once a week. Also, I recommend easing all stress."

As they drove home, Winston placed his hand over hers. She was surprised, stunned by this small gesture. Had they been happy? She tried to remember the night they had met, walking together on the cold, dark campus. Back then, she had felt the anticipation of something better, different. But those feelings felt foreign to her now.

The first thing Winston decided was to pack the children off to boarding school. He said Sylvia needed time to recover without having to care for them. But she knew he also wanted them out of the way. He didn't want them to see their mother like this. He asked Richard for a referral to the schools he sent his children to in England. This way, arrangements could be made quickly. Elizabeth, now living in the UK near her children, offered to pick up Thomas and Lila at the Gatwick airport and take them to the school.

• • •

Sylvia said good-bye to her children in the driveway of her house on the day they left for England in September 1985. The snakes in the bamboo bushes near the house were quiet. She hugged them both, tears collecting in her eyes.

"Mama, get better," Lila whispered to her as she hugged her. Sylvia held her tightly not wanting to let her go. Her daughter was thirteen years old now. She had prevented her from returning to the spirit world for all these years, and now she was still losing her to another world.

The children got into the car with Winston and Ige, who would drive them to the airport in Lagos. The children would fly to England as unaccompanied minors, taken care of by an air stewardess until they touched down at Gatwick airport and the stewardess could hand the children over to Elizabeth. Elizabeth promised to send a telex as soon as they arrived. Although most of the children on the compound travelled as unaccompanied minors and clearly nothing had happened to them, Sylvia still worried. She twirled her hair into tangled knots, thinking of her children lost, wandering around in a foreign country.

Without Lila and Thomas, the house felt eerily quiet. Sylvia wandered around from room to room, the empty spaces hollow, soundless. It distilled her life back to where she had begun with just her and Winston in the room.

WINSTON

Chapter 34

Since his wife had stopped taking the malaria pills, she seemed slightly better. But it was a slow recovery. The anxiety decreased somewhat, but Winston knew she still had the nightmares. The doctor had said the nightmares would linger for some time.

One night, after the children had left, his wife screamed in the dark and kicked him in bed. He jumped out of the bed, startled. He shook her out of her dream, and she sat up. She said—*I was dreaming about fire, I had to fight it. It was consuming us.*

Winston stood at the side of her bed. *Lie down and go back to sleep, he said. It was not real. It was just a dream.* He helped her lie down again. He climbed into bed and placed his hand on her shoulder, not knowing what else to do. Then he lay down himself. He fell back into his own nightmarish dreams—there was a fire and the silhouette of a man he recognized.

• • •

In October 1985, thugs hired by the neighboring plantation

came in the night and burned Simeon's village fields. What little was left, bug-eaten, burned to the ground. The laws were on their side. The wealthy plantation farmer could leverage the new land laws to annex poor peasants' plots that bordered his farm, all in the name of modernization and development. Simeon and the other farmers refused to leave the land. But by law, since Simeon had no paperwork to show for it, Simeon didn't own the land that his ancestors had lived on for generations. And so the thugs came and burned his fields just before harvest.

The black smoke whirled around, incensing the villagers, their red eyes stinging. It was not only the fields they burned. Part of the sacred forest next to the village was also torched. This was a virgin forest, untouched for centuries. Simeon's village had promised to guard this village with their lives, and so, led by Simeon, the villagers marched on the plantation with hoes and machetes.

The plantation owner called the police and paramilitary forces to restore order on his farm, to rid him of these intruders. The police were brutal, unnecessarily so.

• • •

Winston and Donna heard the news of the riot at the plantation and the subsequent crushing of the farmers by the police forces. They traveled quickly to Simeon's region, driving the jeep into the night even though they both knew this was dangerous. The number of armed robbers on this lonely road had increased recently. The government had imposed a sunset curfew in part because of the alarming number of highway robbers. In the mid-eighties, Nigeria was becoming more violent, the political machinery was full of thugs, and ordinary people were simply trying to make ends meet. There was a sense of lawlessness. Winston knew Hans, a Swiss colleague, had been held up on the road recently at night. They killed his driver, hit Hans in the head, and drove off in his Peugeot.

Richard had advised them to wait until tomorrow morning when it would be safer to make the drive. But Winston was worried about Simeon and his family. He had heard some farmers had been killed, and many, including women and children, were injured.

In the darkness, they approached Simeon's village. He could not see any of the usual paraffin lamps. Winston tried not to fear the worst. This man had become his friend over the years. As they drove closer, he noticed the village had been burned as well, the mud huts scorched, razed by the paramilitary troops. Winston got out of the car. He could smell the charred stench of desolation.

• • •

Winston and Donna found Simeon at a makeshift clinic, a tent set up by a local doctor. Simeon lay on a blue tarp on the dirt floor along with scores of other injured patients. As Winston came closer, he was shocked when he saw Simeon's leg—a bloody stump in bandages, sliced off by a madmen's machete. Simeon saw Winston approaching and tried to sit up.

"Don't," Winston said, putting his hand on Simeon's shoulder and forcing him to lie back down on the tarp. He crouched down next to him.

"Dey chop my leg off. I am one legged now. De one legged farmer! Look at me!" Simeon said it in a joking manner, but Winston saw the horror behind his eyes. He knew what losing a leg meant for a farmer. He would become an invalid now, a burden to his family.

"We'll fight them," Donna said, undeterred. If anything, he

thought, she seemed further strengthened by the sight of so many bloody and injured people. It gave her license to respond with equal aggression.

For Winston, the stench of the decaying bodies had the opposite effect. It weakened him. It brought up memories he didn't want dug up. But they came to him, flooding his mind whether he wanted them or not—he thought of his dying mother, her lifeless, cold body.

Everyone in his generation had a war story, an escape-from-China story they carried around on their backs like old Chinese peasants, an amorphous cloth bundle smelling of fish and Chinese herbal medicine. Winston liked to think he had shed this bundle from his childhood, but it was there, he could smell it, feel the burden of the thing riding his back. With these old memories bombarding his carefully-controlled mind, Winston stood up and leaned on the post holding up the medical tent. He needed something to prop himself up, he suddenly felt slightly off-balance.

"Your family? How are they?" Donna asked.

"Dey are safe. Dey went to my wife's family village before de riot broke out."

"Can we…take you there?" Winston said, but he could hear the catch in his voice. He knew he should put forward a show of strength. Simeon needed that, but Winston didn't know if he could find it in himself.

Winston and Donna carried Simeon on a stretcher and lay him on the backseat of the jeep.

When the people in his wife's family's village saw Simeon's bloody stump, they put their hands over their mouths or eyes to stem the tears. Abike came running out and started hitting Winston hysterically. Winston let her. He wanted to feel her pain and anger, a public flagellation that he deserved.

As Winston and Donna drove away, Donna said, "Let's go over to the plantation and give that asshole a piece of our mind."

Winston nodded. Suddenly, he felt like Donna, full of rage, ready to deliver a punch at that smiling man in a suit. But when they drove up to the entrance of the plantation, the gates were closed. There were several security men with arms guarding the entrance. Clearly, they did not want any visitors.

• • •

When Winston came home, his wife seemed to be waiting for him. Without the white noise of children filling the silent gaps, their relationship was forced to take shape.

"Are you alright?" she said at dinner as if sensing something was wrong.

"His leg's gone." He stared blankly into space, barely touching his food.

"Oh my god." She put her hand over her mouth.

"I'm afraid—" he began.

She looked up at him.

"Afraid that I won't be able to help him. That it's all my fault." He lowered his head, his hands covering his eyes.

She stood up and put her arm around his shoulders. He let himself succumb to the comfort of being in her arms. He wasn't sure why he had resisted it for so many years. Later that night, for the first time in a long time, he touched his wife. He let those lacquered doors hiding his heart swing open, revealing the deep, inner courtyards of himself to her. He felt exposed, vulnerable, and frightened as a child.

The next day, Winston did not go to his office. Instead, after breakfast, he went to his study and sat down at his desk. The moment had come, the final judgment hour on his project, so to speak. He had to write a report for the ADA about the riots at the plantation. He had two choices. Write it up as an "incident" as they would have seen it. Or write the truth as he saw it. He knew it was far more than just another incident. It undermined the basis of the project itself.

Winston knew the real problem was multinational agribusiness' involvement in development aid work. Cole Agribusiness was not only taking rural farmers' lands to expand their plantations, but they were selling the small farmers everything from seeds to fertilizers to machinery, and this had driven the farmers into debt. Winston had signed on the dotted line of this partnership between Cole and ADA in the name of using modern technology to feed the world's poor. But were they feeding them? Or were they pushing them further into poverty at the expense of a few wealthy men in Chicago?

How to write that diplomatically without potentially losing his job? He thought of Simeon's bloody stump. Was it even a choice? He put took out his paper and let the rage overtake his pen.

The project has failed, Winston wrote. We have imposed Western technology and practices without tailoring them to suit the unique conditions of Africa. In the process, we have overlooked traditional farming practices. He cited the case study of Oluwa's planting of acacia trees in his fields as a natural and traditional way to enrich the soil. The consequences of all this have been dire. Over the last decade, Nigeria has gone from being a net exporter of agricultural products to become a net importer of food. Although many political factors have contributed to the decline of the agricultural sector, the Green Revolution project has made the situation worse. The heavy tractors and chemicals have ruined the fragile African soil. The pesticides have caused the pest population to balloon out of control. Moreover, the technology is beyond the bank accounts of rural farmers, and many farmers are in debt. Multinational agribusiness is the only benefactor.

Winston's Nigerian secretary, Queen, neatly typed the report the next day. The report was hand-delivered in October 1985 to the New York headquarters of the nonprofit ADA by a scientist's wife who happened to be traveling to America. Winston waited for the ADA's response. He hoped they would be willing to acknowledge failure and learn from their mistakes. But would they be bold enough to admit nearly thirteen years of investment in the ADA 2000 Starter Pack program had amounted to nothing?

Chapter 35

The real owners of the land are the ancestors who have farmed here before and who watch over it still. No farmer has worked his land without asking permission of his ancestors first. At the beginning of the rains, a chicken is killed and its blood poured on the ground. The chicken is cooked with plantains or yams and then scattered on the farm. Only the ancestors can decide whether the land will yield a plentiful harvest.

But Winston wondered if the ancestral spirits would follow Simeon and his fellow villagers to protect them? They were landless, cut off from the long line of their ancestors tilling that same dirt. Rootless now, they were a people in transition. They had no protection.

In November 1985, a month after Simeon was pushed off his land, a messenger arrived at the compound gatehouse. A gatehouse guard brought the messenger to Winston's house.

His wife opened the kitchen door and saw a thin man with bloodshot eyes standing in front of her.

"What is it?" Winston said, coming into the kitchen.

"A man is here. He says he's a relative of Simeon's wife," Sylvia said.

"Come in," Winston said to the man. "You must be tired and hungry. Patience will cook something for you. How did you travel here?"

"On top of lorry, sah." The previous night the messenger had travelled sitting on the top of a tarp-covered truck. He had fought off sleep and the risk of tumbling from the truck.

"Simeon, he dead, sah," the man said, still standing outside the kitchen door. He made no move to come inside.

Winston felt a numbness descend on him. He thought of the juju doctor's spell, it was coming true. He still felt nothing—that unadulterated feeling of nothingness, he had worked hard his whole life to achieve this stillness of his heart.

"How?" Winston asked.

"He drink de bottle of pesticide."

• • •

Winston and Donna went that afternoon to Simeon's burial ceremony. They arrived at the village and were ushered into the mud hut that held the body. The body had been washed and was dressed in black and white embroidered cloth. When Winston saw Simeon's body, the reality of it hit him hard. The carefully calibrated numbness he had worked so hard to achieve was suddenly replaced by a rage he did not recognize. Simeon, his friend, was dead. The ADA 2000 Starter Pack project had failed. Thoughts of his mother's dead body invaded his mind. Another death had been his fault, and *he* should have somehow prevented it from happening.

Winston went back outside. A group of women swayed and wailed, a chaotic sound, as they chanted funeral dirges—*Why didn't you tell me you were going? Why are you so silent?* The dissonant sound reminded Winston of the paid mourners and wailers at his mother's funeral. He felt a pain in his chest he had never felt before. He almost doubled over. Donna joined the women, wailing with them. Winston saw Abike with her hands covering her face, wailing as she crouched on the ground. Winston covered his eyes with his hand.

He had the sudden urge to weep. It was an emotion he had not felt in years, not since he was a boy after his mother's death. To assuage his guilt, he had gone on this personal crusade against hunger, a crusade that had crushed and defeated him. With the women wailing around him at Simeon's funeral, all these emotions that he had kept at bay suddenly descended full-force upon him. This was where his project had taken the farmers—to their graves. He felt the tears coming. He walked away from the crowd; he didn't want the others to see him this way.

He wept for everyone he had lost. The list had accumulated over the years—his mother, his estranged father, his friend Simeon, and his wife Sylvia. He knew he could only blame himself for this monumental feeling of loss. If he could change the clock, he wasn't sure which way he would go, into the past or quickly into the future to his own death, which he knew was waiting for him.

• • •

As Simeon's coffin was lowered into the ground, a goat was slaughtered, so its blood could run into the grave. The farmers from the old village, now spread out, came for the funeral. They still saw Simeon as their leader even though he had led them down the wrong path. Simeon's sons stood with their backs to the grave and threw maize pap onto the coffin. With their backs still turned, they filled the grave with dirt. Simeon should have been buried in the sacred grove outside his village, the place of his birth. But the grove had been partially burned, and the forest no longer belonged to them. They should have brought his body back to his birthplace, the rightful place for his burial. But instead, they buried him here near his wife's village. Abike stood at the edge of the group, tears running down her face, she looked up at Winston. There was no anger in her face, just immense grief.

As Winston walked back from the grave, he saw a small shrine made of wood and palm leaves they had built to make offerings of kola nuts and food to Simeon's spirit for many years to come. It was similar to Winston's own shrine of incense sticks and fruit used to honor his mother and father. The chief, old and infirm, was carried to participate in the funeral. But the old man's mind was already lost.

Winston knew Simeon would remain very much part of his family's life. Death was merely a rite of passage into the spirit world, and Simeon's spirit would remain here, hovering over his family. His family members would remember him, leave leftover food in the pot for him, pour drink on the ground, make offerings of food to his shrine, and continue to refer to him, "Simeon's spirit said so and so." The thought comforted Winston, or at least it assuaged his guilt.

• • •

As he drove home with Donna in the jeep, Winston felt exhausted and emotionally drained. The sun was setting outside. He knew they shouldn't drive home in the dark, but Donna didn't seem to care and offered to drive. Along the road, he saw several carcasses of burned cars and a dead animal lying on the side of the road, a dog or goat, he wasn't sure. But as they got closer, he realized it was a human corpse, mutilated and already rotting in the heat. Suddenly, he felt afraid of the violent, struggling country around him and those who were seemingly trying to help it.

"We can still do something," Donna said, her eyes fixed on the empty road in front of her. She didn't seem to notice the dead body lying by the roadside or perhaps she tried not to.

"I'm listening," Winston said, his nerves frayed by the macabre sight along the road.

"Remember that journalist friend? *National Geographic*? He's still planning to come out. Now we've got an even better story here, we've got farmers pushed off their land, riots, maimed farmers, and the evil axis of multinational agribusiness and foreign aid."

"Well-said. You're good at this." This was the story of Simeon's life, Winston thought, depressingly.

"If you're willing to be quoted in the story, it will give it meat," Donna continued. "A senior scientist working on the project, a whistle blower. That'll give it credibility. I'm just a student, so you're who they need."

"He can quote me on whatever he wants."

Winston was desperate, and he held onto this idea of Donna's as his last hope to put things right. But he couldn't shake the image of the dead, rotting body lying on the side of the road. When he returned home, he was haggard, unshaven, and his wife took him in her arms. Finally, he was speaking to her in the form of emotions, which was a language she could understand. She held him close, and he buried himself in her chest like a newborn. He didn't want her to let go.

• • •

The next month in December 1985, Winston and Sylvia went

to a barbecue at the golf clubhouse. Winston stood talking to Richard. Sylvia stayed close by his side. Winston noticed Ayo wander into the party, but she did not go to him. Ayo tried to get her attention, but she avoided looking at him. He turned to focus on what Richard was trying to tell him.

"Look, I'm sorry about Simeon's death too," Richard said. "But…"

Winston simply stared at him. He knew what his colleague was going to say.

"Don't do anything rash. Think about the consequences first. Collaborating with a journalist is bloody risky," Richard continued.

"I haven't heard from the ADA. It's been several months now since I sent the report to them. You'd think they would want to learn from their mistakes. Instead, they ignore them."

"Don't risk your bloody career over this."

"You mean to say one African farmer's death is not worth getting angry about?"

"No. That's not what I meant. I meant—don't destroy everything we've…you've worked for."

"But just what have we been working for?"

Richard was silent.

"Fifteen years of my life I gave to this, and I have nothing to show for it. Except Cole Agribusiness' bottom line just got better while Simeon's only got worse." Winston's tone turned bitter.

"Look, I agree this is all bollocks. But it's not worth sticking your neck out. At least wait until the ADA's annual visit in a few months. Then you can talk to them face-to-face. They won't be able to dodge you then," Richard said, trying to persuade him.

"I've waited too long already."

SYLVIA

Chapter 36

Winston was a changed man. Suddenly, Sylvia saw the emotional, vulnerable side of him, the side she had wanted to find in him for so long. His project had collapsed, and with it, her husband was imploding emotionally. He needed her now, and she wanted to be there for him.

But her daughter was away at school and not a part of this new closeness. Lila had become full of adolescent rage. Every Sunday afternoon at their boarding schools, they had scheduled "letter writing time." They had to sit in the refectory, where they usually ate their meals, and write letters home. On blue stationary, Lila began to write to her mother. At first, her weekly letters were diary-like summaries of what she did every day—woke up, went to Church, went into the village, and bought sweets. I hope you feel better, Mama. But gradually her letters became the forum, the medium for her questions, her hurtful rage. *Dear Mama and Baba—Where did I come from? I have seen so much, yet I know so little. Why is the color of my skin, my hair, not like yours? Why does my father not love me?*

While she was away, Lila turned and lashed out at Sylvia. She was thirteen years old, almost fourteen. Maybe it was just puberty or maybe the distance gave her the space to come out of her shell, far away from her family. While the miles between them let her grow to hate Sylvia, the distance only made Sylvia love her more. She missed her children so much while they were at school that to receive only these letters of anger was hard to bear. She didn't show them to Winston. He had enough going on, she thought. He didn't need to deal with her adolescent rage.

After the first few months at school, Lila and Thomas came back for the Christmas holidays. Their lives were now split in half into two worlds like the Chinese yin-yang symbol—one cold, white; the other hot, black.

Sylvia met them at the airport. Lila looked different. Away from the sun, the brown tan of her skin had faded, revealing a pink-white color underneath, similar to the English girls. But her hair was brown, still brown even after the sunless English sky, not sun-bleached as Sylvia had told her. She realized her daughter had looked at her pink-white skin in the mirror, newly revealed to her in the gray skies of England, and she had hated Sylvia for hiding her true identity. At the airport, Sylvia tried to hug Lila tightly, but she resisted. She had come home to wage war.

For the first few days, neither of them mentioned her letters and their contents. But Sylvia saw Winston's eyes register the paleness of Lila's skin, the revelation of her true colors. She heard the migratory birds flying above their house, flying in a V, coming south for the winter like her daughter. In local beliefs, birds were associated with witches. She knew Lila was drawing on their power to wage war.

• • •

On Saturday, to celebrate the children's arrival for the holidays, the family went to Lucky Dragon Chinese restaurant for lunch.

As they ate their comfort food, Winston asked the children about their new schools. What subjects did they like? Thomas began talking about the science lab and golf course at his all-boys boarding school run by monks. Sylvia noticed Lila said nothing.

Winston continued asking Thomas more questions about school—what was it like? What did he do on the weekends? But Winston never asked Lila anything. Sylvia could tell she was burning with anger.

Suddenly, Lila exploded, "It's a prison. The nuns keep us locked up. It's boring and freezing cold. A stone castle of a prison."

Sylvia felt guilty, aware that it was because of her that they had been sent to such a place.

Lila continued, blurting out the question she had asked so many times in those letters.

"Baba, why do you favor Thomas over me?"

Sylvia shifted uncomfortably in her seat. Winston looked up at Lila. His face seemed fatigued, vulnerable, easy prey to her witch-like anger.

"You...you," she began accusingly. Winston just looked at her, a piercing kind of look studying every inch of her face—as if he was seeing her for the very first time.

Lila continued, "I mean...you...ignore me. You only pay attention to Thomas. It's like...like I barely exist in your mind."

"I...don't mean to—" Winston stuttered.

"Why is that? Why did you do this to me?" Lila interrupted him, throwing the full energy of her attack against him. Sylvia was afraid for the both of them. Lila was too strong, full of anger, and he was too weak, full of pain. Sylvia didn't know who to side with. For years, it had been the other way around: Lila had been the weak one.

"Lila," Sylvia said. "Calm down. This isn't the way--"

But she ignored Sylvia, continuing her adolescent rant. "Why do you hate me? You have made my life miserable! I hate you! What kind of father are you?" She started crying and ran from the table.

"I am not your father," Winston said. He sounded defeated. Lila whipped around and looked at him. Even though she had suspected this her whole life, known it to be the truth, to hear these words out loud from him, it came down hard on her.

Lila ran out the door of the Lucky Dragon onto the dusty streets of Ibadan. Sylvia chased after her daughter, running through crowded market vendors and garbage-filled alleyways between mud-baked walls. Sylvia had a hard time keeping up with Lila, but she didn't want to lose sight of her, not here in the middle of town.

They came to what was once an ancient temple in the middle of town. The modern temple was crammed in between shops and stalls—a shoemaker's sandals hung on its outer walls. Sylvia followed Lila into the dusty inner sanctuary lit by a bare electric bulb hung from a wire, its carved doors and sculptures stolen long ago. Sylvia's eyes adjusted to the semi-darkness, and she looked around the shabby temple. It had once been a labyrinth of chambers and courtyards, carved pillars and doors, a vermilion ceiling, and intricately carved sculptures of monkeys and women. When a lost English explorer had first discovered it years ago, he thought he had found the lost city of Atlantis.

"Lila, I know you're in here, come out. I want to explain everything to you." Sylvia called into the musty sanctuary, fearing that snakes might be taking refuge in the corners somewhere.

"It's a bit late for that," Lila said, hiding behind some rotting wood pillars.

Sylvia tried to tell her about her biological English father, but Lila put her hands over her ears, shouting out loudly, so she couldn't hear her mother's words.

Their family was like this decaying, abandoned shrine. There had been too many secrets. Sylvia's life had been built upon one layer of secrets after another. There were so many things she wanted to tell her daughter, but now Lila was becoming a teenager, she was deaf to her words. Sylvia regretted all those times as a small child, she had been eager to listen, but Sylvia had remained silent.

The next day, Winston left for the bush before dawn. It was better to let them cool off apart, Sylvia thought. Lila got up late, around eleven in the morning, and all through breakfast she said nothing. Sylvia tried to put her arm out to her, to comfort her, but the girl shrugged her away. Her daughter sat at the breakfast table like a guest, a stranger in her own home. Patience served her freshly cut pineapple and toast with homemade guava jam.

When Lila was finished, she got up from table, tossing her batik napkin on her chair carelessly. Sylvia watched her walk out the door, heading to the clubhouse pool where all the other teenagers congregated during the holidays. Since returning from boarding school, it was as if Lila wanted to spend the minimum amount of obligatory time with her family. She hated them, Sylvia thought. Lila was entitled to that, Sylvia could only blame herself.

The tables were turned now. She wanted to spend every minute with her children. She had missed them so much while they were away, but they wanted nothing to do with her now. What had happened to all those years when they were young?

She had squandered that time, Sylvia realized, in her lover's arms.

Winston was not himself lately, which was why he must have just spat out the truth, not caring if it hurt or not. After years of strained relations, how could the two of them—father and daughter—ever repair their relationship? As for Lila, she hid in her room, counting the days until she could return to her other world, the cold one, without them.

WINSTON

Chapter 37

Winston was running now. He kept driving his jeep with no sense of purpose. Lila's outburst had been more than he could bear. She was right, though, he knew. He had somehow mistreated her when all he had ever wanted to do was save her. But he had failed to be a father to her. Winston hadn't wanted to be like his own father, but he had become him.

Winston found himself driving toward what was left of Simeon's village. Nothing made sense to him anymore. He was running on raw emotion now, all his usual restraint and rationality gone. He had let too many people down. As he approached the remains of the village, Winston parked his jeep. He told his armed guard to wait for him. He wanted some time alone. He walked around the burned huts, Simeon's half-built cement house, and the blackened fields. He stopped in front of what was once the chief's house, the painted colors of the wall now blackened by soot. In the distance, he could make out a man standing with the menacing silhouette of a machete hanging from his hand. The land now belonged to Cole Agribusiness, and Winston knew he was trespassing. He quickly started running back toward his jeep. But another man with a machete appeared out of the forest and blocked him. He recognized the hardened face of Oluwa who now worked at the plantation. Winston could hear his own heart thrashing about wildly in his rib cage. Oluwa wore a green Cole Agribusiness cap with the maize insignia. There was only one direction to go now—into the forest. He started running into the jungle, even though he knew it was a trap.

Oluwa and his henchman chased Winston through the sacred forest toward the mud palace, the shrine Simeon's village once used for harvest rituals. Winston ran inside the ruins of the old mud palace, in between the narrow walls of red earth, columns, courtyards, and tall, kapok trees. He saw an empty palm trunk once serving as a beehive, an ancient weapon against outsiders. Bees, familiar with the odor of the family, only became angry around strangers.

Winston looked back and saw the men closing in on him. He ran past what looked like shrines to ancestors—phallic-shaped mounds stained with blood of sacrificed animals. Out of breath, Winston came to a courtyard full of overgrown banana trees. He knew he was finished. There was nowhere else to run. The machete men caught up with him and hit him in the face. Winston lay on the dirt ground, looking up at them.

"You're trespassing, sah," Oluwa said.

"I will go and get de boss. Tie him up," the other man said.

Winston waited in the old earthen palace for about an hour, tied at his feet and ankles by some rough rope. His throat felt parched, his clothes were drenched with sweat. He didn't want to think about what his fate would be this time.

He was surprised to see Jim McCormack walk into the banana

tree courtyard.

"Winston, I'm so sorry. I didn't know it was you. They just said there was trespasser," Jim said. Then he turned to his henchman. "Untie him, please."

Winston stood up, untied now. "I see Oluwa has worked out well as your foreman."

"He has actually. I've promoted him," Jim said. "Listen, let's go back to my office and we'll get you cleaned up and have a nice cold beer. There's something actually I want to chat with you about," Jim said.

"You can say whatever you want to me here," Winston said, declining Jim's material comforts.

"OK, if that's what you want." Jim leaned against the mud walls of the earthen palace and crossed his legs. "Winston, let me ask you one simple question, what do you want in this life?"

"I'm sorry, I don't understand." Winston was confused. Did the man want to discuss his philosophy of life? His henchman had just beaten and tied him up, it was all too bizarre.

"I mean, like everyone else, don't you want to get out of this place?" Jim said. "I can get you American citizenship. For your whole family. A suburban house, even. A brand new car in the garage with keys in it. A nice job with Cole in Chicago. What do you think? Consider it a bonus for all the good work you've done for Cole and the ADA."

Winston couldn't believe what he had just heard and he shook his head. He wondered if Jim knew about Donna's journalist who was finally due to arrive next week. Donna had applied for his visa for "personal reasons," citing his visit as pleasure, not business. If the journalist, with Winston's help, exposed the dysfunctional role of Cole Agribusiness in Africa, he knew Cole could potentially lose millions of dollars in supplier contracts with the ADA and other aid organizations involved in agriculture development.

"You don't want to go to America, live the good life? I thought that's what everyone around here wants," Jim said.

Winston wanted to laugh out loud at Jim's naïve belief in the supremacy of his country, but he restrained himself.

"You can't get me want I want," Winston said instead.

"Try me."

"I want to go back to my home, my estate in China, the way it was before the Japanese war, before Communism." And he wanted his mother back, the chance to rewrite his whole life and begin again as a child.

Jim shifted his feet, knowing he had lost the battle, at least for now.

• • •

That night, Winston's armed guard drove him back to the compound. Again, they drove at night even though they knew the increasing dangers of armed robbers on the prowl. The road was dark, lit only by the headlights of their jeep. There were no street lamps or towns lining that lonely stretch. Further from the road, there was an occasional cluster of huts, but without electricity, they were invisible. Tonight, Winston felt an affinity with the darkness. He liked the anonymity of it. He wanted to hide in this darkness, crawl up into its black hole and never come out again.

Suddenly, Winston saw lights up ahead. He knew here in the dark night, lights along the road were an anomaly, signaling not safety but danger.

"Should we stop, sah?" his armed guard said. "We keep driving. Fast fast." They didn't know if this was a real military checkpoint or an ambush.

"And risk jail time again? We'd better stop," Winston said even though his instincts told him the opposite. *Don't stop.*

They pulled over, recognizing the familiar steel drums of a military checkpoint. A flashlight was thrust into their faces.

"Get out of the car," shouted a man dressed in torn pants with a white undershirt and a gun slung over his shoulder. The casualness of his dress was a warning sign to Winston. The man was not wearing a crisp military uniform. Winston noticed he was surrounded by at least ten men, all armed.

"Give me your gun," the man barked at the armed guard. The guard relinquished his weapon.

"Take my jeep," Winston said to the man.

"What makes you tink we want your jeep? What, we look like beggars?" the man said. "But now you mention it, it's a fine jeep."

The man shoved Winston onto the ground. He felt the hardness of something metal against his chest. Despite the fact he had known death was coming, he had even craved and entertained it at times, now that he was facing it, he suddenly felt frightened. His senses were heightened by the feel of the metal barrel against his chest, and all he could think of was: *I want to live. I want a second chance with my wife. My daughter. My son.*

Out of the corner of his eye, he saw another man come out of the darkness, and he immediately recognized the rasping, smoker's voice.

"Ma friend," the Captain, his former jailer said. "You didn't learn your lesson last time we meet." Clearly, the Captain no longer worked for the military but looked to be running his own armed operation outside the law.

The Captain barked orders in Yoruba to his men. He then turned to Winston's armed guard and said, "Run. If I was you."

The armed guard started running into the night. They fired

a few shots after him, but they did not pursue him. Winston kicked the Captain in the shin. He heard the click of the trigger. And then in an instant, Winston felt an excruciating pain in his chest. His last thought was of his son.

SYLVIA

Chapter 38

Later that night, a woman, most likely a prostitute on her way back from one of the shantytown bars, found Winston in a pool of his own blood. She didn't know if he was dead or alive. There were no cars on the road that late at night. She took her heels off and lifted him up on her back. The walking was difficult, he was heavy and his warm blood stained her dress. A Mercedes drove by, and she tried to wave it down, but the car did not stop. She kept walking, not knowing if her effort was in vain. After a while, she saw a motorbike approaching. She put Winston down and waved madly at the motorbike. The man stopped.

They wedged Winston's body in between, and the three of them rode on the motorbike to the hospital in Ibadan. Since his wallet had been stolen by the armed robbers, they didn't know his name. But when the doctor saw Winston had been shot, he contacted the police, not because the police would catch the armed robber, but because they could at least find the man's family.

The police came to the compound, the place of the foreigners. Winston's armed guard had made it back to the compound to report the incident. When Sylvia saw the police and Winston's armed guard, she knew something had happened to her husband.

• • •

Sylvia found Winston at the local hospital in Ibadan, covered in plastic tubes. He was unconscious or drugged, she didn't know which. The doctor came into the room and introduced himself as Dr. Ogun.

"Your husband was shot in the chest. It punctured his lung and an artery as well. I performed emergency surgery," the doctor said, pausing so Sylvia could take it all in. The doctor was a tall, middle-aged Nigerian man, his black beard graying in parts. He spoke with a hybrid Nigerian and British accent, remnants of medical school in England.

"He's lost a lot of blood," the doctor continued. "We did a blood transfusion, but we've run out of his blood type. He's going to need more blood. I need you to round up as many people to donate as possible." She couldn't help staring at the rust-stained pile of Winston's clothes in the corner of the room.

"I...need to round up...what...?" she said. Because it was her own husband, all her years of nursing experience amounted to nothing. She looked away, his blood made her feel faint.

"There are only fifteen bags of blood left in the bank. They are not your husband's blood type. He is O. It is more uncommon, only other blood types O can donate."

"Go back to your compound. Round up your friends. Look, there isn't much time. You will need to do this quickly."

She noticed Winston had been given a private room. Because

he was a foreigner, they must have assumed he could pay. She had heard of stories of unnecessary death because the family could not afford the *dash* or bribe—something as mundane as the purchase of fuel to fill the tank of the doctor's car. Hardly illegal, it was merely a fee, a fee to prioritize your spot in the never-ending line of patients waiting to see the one doctor. She took out a thick wad of naira bills and handed it to the doctor, but he refused, seemed somewhat offended, and said, "Just get me the donors. Hurry."

She had to enlist Ayo's help to save Winston. The police escorted Sylvia back to her compound. It was still dark outside. Sylvia looked at her watch, four o'clock in the morning. How much time did she have? The car sped through the deserted streets, the speed adding to her critical mission. She knew she had to save her husband. She had to save him just as he had saved her all those years ago.

She knocked on Ayo's apartment door on the compound. Donna answered it, but Sylvia didn't care.

"Winston…" Sylvia choked on her words.

"What's wrong?" Donna said, dressed only in a long t-shirt.

"He's been shot. He's at the main hospital down the road."

"Oh my god, shit. Shit."

"Where's Ayo? Winston needs blood donors. Type O," Sylvia said.

"Ayo's at the clinic tonight. I'll send a driver with a message."

Donna took charge. "You and I had better round up some more folks with O blood type. Let's go over to the compound clinic, they'll have the records of who's O."

Sylvia climbed into Donna's jeep and sat side-by-side with the woman that she had shared both of the men in her life with—her husband and her lover. She studied her rival. She didn't really have a pretty face. Her features were not perfectly proportioned, but Sylvia knew Donna possessed a kind of sex appeal. With her charismatic personality and intelligence, men were drawn to Donna.

Donna put her hand on Sylvia's shoulder and said, "It'll be okay."

Sylvia noticed Donna had tears in her eyes. She knew Donna had been Winston's friend. Donna was a good woman, despite it all. Sylvia didn't want to admit it, but she knew it was true.

Chapter 39

When Sylvia and Donna reached the hospital with the additional blood donors from the compound, it was dawn, and Ayo was already there. Her lover was sitting down while his blood was being drawn into plastic bags to save her husband's life. When Ayo saw them walk into the room, he only motioned mechanically to the nurse and said, "Get the donors prepped. We're going to need to do the transfusion as soon as possible."

Dr. Ogun sat her down and explained, "Your husband's lung collapsed from the gunshot wound. We put a chest tube to drain the fluid and re-expand his lung. But he's bleeding again through the chest tube. I'm going to have to perform surgery again."

Sylvia felt the room spinning around her. She still had not spoken to Winston. She had barely seen him. He was covered in tubes and a respirator mask. She watched the nurses wheel him off to the operating room. All she could see that reminded her of him was the jet black hair on the top of his head.

Ayo followed Dr. Ogun into the surgery room to assist him. The other blood donors returned to the compound. Sylvia sat with Donna outside in the hallway, waiting together.

"They shot him. Those bastards," Donna said.

"The armed robbers?" Sylvia asked, confused.

"Cole wanted him shot." Her voice sounded bitter and angry. "Without him, there's no fucking article, and they know it. Those bastards."

"They would…"

"I don't know. Who knows?" Donna continued, crying now. "I only know Winston is a good man. Please if there is a God up there, help him. Help us."

Ayo came out of the surgery room. He looked tired. Donna and Sylvia both looked up at him.

"Is he…?" Sylvia said.

"Dr. Ogun stopped the bleeding. He's stable. For now," Ayo said.

"That's good to hear," Donna said, breathing with relief.

"Can I see him?" Sylvia said.

"He'll be out in a bit," Ayo said. "He's going to need some bags of IV. We'll need to purchase them from the hospital. Sylvia, you'll need to come with me."

Donna got up and put her hand on Sylvia's shoulder. Then she nodded at Ayo and took her leave. Sylvia followed Ayo down the hallway. They stood alone in the dark elevator, which was partially lit by only one of the three fluorescent light bulbs. The last bulb kept flicking off and on as the elevator moved. In the constant flickering, Ayo's face looked contorted, robot-like, like he was in pain but was trying to cover it up.

"Is Winston going to be—" Sylvia began. She heard her own voice echo against the metal walls of the elevator. It sounded frightening to her, metallic, high-pitched.

"I don't know," he said, turning to look at her. "This is a

critical time."

For so many years, they had worked side by side on many life-threatening cases, and he had always been open and direct with her but not now.

"Please tell me. I need to know," she pleaded.

But he didn't speak. Instead he put his arms around her and held her close. She thought he tried to say something to her, but the elevator doors opened.

At the front desk, she paid for several IV bags, each item was bought in increments of *naira* bills, including the IV equipment itself. She wondered what would happen if a family could only afford one bag of IV solution when the patient needed more. What would happen? She knew what would happen. It was a futile question.

• • •

That evening, Dr. Ogun did not look hopeful. He sat down next to Sylvia and said, "He may not make it through the night."

Winston's body was under sepsis attack, a post-surgery infection. They pumped antibiotics into his blood to try to combat the infection. Ayo stood there, not knowing what to say. Sylvia knew from the downcast expression on Ayo's face that he was frustrated at his inability to save Winston. This infection wouldn't have happened in a hospital in Europe or America. They all knew this, but no one actually said it. Sylvia knew Winston's time had come, and the juju doctor's spell was finally being fulfilled—first Simeon and now Winston.

In the dark bluish light of the hospital room, Sylvia held her husband's limp hand tightly. She started crying. Winston's breath was becoming more labored. In West Africa, the spirit was associated with breathing, and she knew his spirit was struggling to exit his body. Winston had not regained consciousness. Could he hear her? She wanted to ask for his forgiveness, to keep him here in this life, but the words stuck in her throat. How could she stop him from reuniting with his long lost mother? Then she realized maybe he could start over, be born again into a new life, a second chance.

"I need to get my children," Sylvia said, suddenly in a panic.

"You probably shouldn't leave him," Dr. Ogun said.

"They need to see him one last time," Sylvia said. She knew Lila, especially, needed to see him.

"I'll go and get them," Ayo offered.

"No, I have to go. Lila may not come otherwise," Sylvia said, running out the door.

By the time Sylvia returned to the hospital with her children, Winston was gone. His body was covered with a white sheet, the plastic respirator mask and machine off. Sylvia noticed how crisp, how white the sheet was, despite all the blood she had seen earlier. And then the tears came, a long, low moan that she couldn't stop.

Her children started crying, Lila became hysterical, flailing her body around. Sylvia put her arms around her daughter to brace her. Lila would have to live with her last, stinging words to him. Neither Lila nor Sylvia could ever ask for his forgiveness. Sylvia knew this moment would haunt them for years to come. They would have to live with their complicated relationship with Winston—there would be no farewells, no confessions, no forgiveness, just the suddenness of a lifeless body covered in a white sheet.

Chapter 40

Everything about Winston's death remained unfinished. It was a Nigerian belief that after death, the spirit of the departed hovers around the home for several months. Sometimes a second burial must be performed before the spirit can join the ancestors. Neglect of proper burial rites can incur the wrath of the spirit and bring misfortune to the family. But in their haste and confusion, Sylvia had not followed the proper burial rites. According to local Yoruba custom, Winston's body should have been taken back to his birthplace and buried under his old home. But they were in exile, they could not return to their ancestral home in China. Winston's ancestral home had been destroyed. But she didn't know where to bury him. Here in Africa? In Taiwan? Or in their new home—America?

They were leaving for America in a few days. Sylvia had decided to go to America, to her brother's house in Minnesota. And so at Donna's suggestion, for practical purposes, Sylvia cremated Winston's body.

She should have buried him in an elaborate small mausoleum like they do in China—colorful tiled walls, the headstone facing the direction that would bring good fortune to his grandchildren and great grandchildren. They should have burned paper money, the rough yellow squares with gold-red stamps shriveling in the fire next to his grave to ensure his material comfort in the afterlife. They should have symbolically fed him a bowl of rice with chopsticks, so he would never be hungry in the next life. They should have held incense sticks and bowed multiple times to Buddhist chanting. Would Winston's spirit be angry with them for not following the appropriate burial rites of their culture? Would he inflict misfortune on them?

Donna said once they arrived in America they could toss his ashes in the sea or river. So his body and soul could return to the earth. She said, "I think Winston might appreciate his ashes returning to the soil to be recycled into new life." But Sylvia wasn't so sure. It sounded disrespectful to her, like they didn't care. How would they be able to pay their respects to him, then, if he was tossed away like that? Instead, Sylvia put his ashes in a lacquered Chinese box and packed the box in her carry-on Pan Am travel bag.

• • •

The children helped Sylvia sort through Winston's things in the study. This was his room. They had rarely come in here when he was alive. It always felt like an intrusion. Standing in his study, touching his things—his abacus, reports, rock collection—it was the beginning for Sylvia of trying to understand who he really was.

"What should we do with his rock collection?" Thomas asked.

"You should have it. He loved it, he would spend hours categorizing new rocks he found on his trips in these glass cases," Sylvia said.

She picked up one of the older, smaller glass rock cases. The wood of the case was old, a lacquered Chinese rosewood. The rocks in the case did not look familiar; she knew they were not from around here. On the side of the case, she saw an inscription engraved in Chinese characters. She looked carefully at the characters. Even with her limited Chinese, she could guess what it said. *For my precious son, from Mama.*

Sylvia almost choked. She imagined Winston as a boy, clinging to his mother as she was dying. Although Sylvia didn't know the details of his mother's death, she realized he had never fully recovered from this traumatic loss. Death, the vagaries of war, the life of refugees, and a cold, unloving father—all of it had stunted him emotionally. Why hadn't she seen this before in all their years of marriage? Winston had saved Sylvia's life, but he was incapable of loving her. Love had been taken from him at such a young age. Why hadn't she been able to help him love again? She saw her marriage now as a missed opportunity. He had starved himself of love, and she could have cured him. She packed the glass cases with his rocks carefully in boxes to ship to America.

• • •

A week before Sylvia left, Donna and Richard organized a memorial service for Winston at the compound conference center. Colleagues of his on the compound came onto the stage and spoke one-by-one at the microphone. They said so many wonderful things about him. *Another great man has passed. He gave his life to reducing poverty in Africa. He was a man that I have felt honored to know.*

As they walked out of the conference center, Sylvia looked into the distance—the silver granite rock of the hillside, the tall palm trees standing high above the green bush and the banana trees. She hoped his spirit would rest in peace. She hoped he would rejoin his mother. She hoped he would be reborn into a better life and learn to love.

• • •

Richard and Elizabeth, who was home for the Christmas holidays, threw a farewell gathering for Sylvia. It was a small group, mostly compound residents and colleagues wishing her well. Even though she had not been close with many of them, during the fifteen years of their lives on the compound, their children had attended the same school, and they had shared milestones together. Soon Sylvia knew she would be completely out of their lives, their acquaintance relegated to annual Christmas cards with exotic stamps. Most of the residents of the compound would eventually return to their homes in Europe, America, or Asia.

As the party dispersed, Ayo stood apart in the garden, leaning against the tree, waiting for her. They were free to be together, finally, after all these years. She thought of her husband. She was leaving for America. But what of this man leaning against the tree, the man she loved?

"I'm coming with you," Ayo said.

Sylvia looked at him questioningly. She walked toward him under the feathery leaves of the tamarind tree, the long hard pods crunching under her feet.

"To America," he said. They were standing face-to-face now, close but not touching.

"You would leave Nigeria?" she said. He knew she couldn't stay here. After Winston's death, it wasn't safe. She also had to consider her illness caused by the malaria pills and her children's future.

"If that's what it takes for us to finally be together, yes." He looked off into the distance as he said this to her.

Sylvia wondered if he was becoming disillusioned with his beloved country. She thought of Ayo's Nigerian doctor friend who had recently left for the UK after a group of armed robbers had descended on his house in town. The man had four daughters and a wife. It was no longer safe here. Nigeria had deteriorated since 1970 when Ayo had come back, medical degree in hand, full of optimism. Now in 1985, the country was worse off, descending into political chaos and violence.

She placed her hand on the side of his face, but she said nothing.

• • •

A week later, Sylvia drove to Ayo's father's house. He stood outside in the carved doorway, waiting for her. It was New Year's Eve 1985.

"Are you sure…you want to come to America?" Sylvia said, walking up to the rust-stained house. Purple dragonflies darted around them.

He looked at her, his expression confused.

"You could live in England," she continued. "You're half English, but you chose to come back to Nigeria. You love your country. I've always known this. It means so much to you, perhaps more than us."

"Not more than us. You're everything to me."

"And your work?" Sylvia continued, not entirely believing him. "I know times are hard right now. But you would regret leaving even more. I know you so well. You don't want to be like them. Running to the comforts of the West. Running away from the problems of your country instead of trying solving them. You would hate yourself for it. And perhaps even me a little too."

"I didn't wait all these years for you to not be with you."

Hearing his words, she closed her eyes. She loved him so much. But would a love like theirs travel well? She felt it belonged here in this time and place, not across the ocean on another continent. She thought of her cousin in Hong Kong who had fallen in love with and married an American. After they had come to live in America, her accent and cultural eccentricities, what had once seemed exotic to her husband in Hong Kong, suddenly became an embarrassment to him. Their marriage had failed within a year.

"Do you really think you could wake up in a comfortable suburban house in America and know that every day children are dying here?" she said.

Ayo did not respond, and she knew she was right.

"Stay here. At least you have somewhere you can call your own." She drew him close and kissed him.

Sylvia thought of her own nomadic life, her constant running further away from her home, crossing continent after continent—first Europe, then Africa, and now America. She missed Shanghai and Hong Kong. But now she had been gone so long, she couldn't return. Her children didn't speak the language. She had to consider their future. She couldn't go back, so she kept going forward.

Chapter 41

In January 1986, the day Sylvia and her children left Nigeria, the air was full of sand. Dust from the Sahara filled the skies so that a pinkish-brown haze hung over the mud huts, the palm trees, and the muddy river. Sylvia said her farewells to the few remaining friends in her life. Richard and Elizabeth came over to her house to stay goodbye.

"Donna and I picked up the journalist at the airport a few days ago. He's going to quote me instead for the article," Richard said as he hugged her. "Winston's death will not be in vain."

"Thank you, Richard," Sylvia said, realizing the Englishman must have had a change of heart in the wake of Winston's death. "You're a good friend."

"I also have something for Simeon's family. Will you give it to his wife?" She handed him Winston's worn leather satchel stuffed full of naira bills. She had drained their savings account. She had Winston's life insurance to fall back on, but Simeon's wife and children had no such thing. "Winston would want them to have it."

"I'll give it to Abike," Richard said quietly.

"Take care of yourself darling, we'll be thinking of you in America. We might even come and visit, won't we Richard?" Elizabeth said.

After Richard and Elizabeth left, Ayo came over with the minibus to drive them to Lagos. They packed the van with their belongings.

Sylvia turned to Patience and hugged her, full of tears.

"Come on, madam, you be going to a nice place, America," Patience said, dry-eyed.

"Patience, I have a gift for you." She handed Patience another satchel of naira bills, the other half of her and Winston's savings account. "I want you to go home and retire in your village as a successful business woman." Sylvia gave her the money.

Patience was stunned as she looked inside the satchel. "No, madam, I can't accept dis."

"Take it. I have no use for it. What am I going to do with it? No one will change all these naira bills into US dollars." Sylvia did not explain that she had just done the opposite—changed all this money from US dollars into naira bills, just for these gifts for Patience and Simeon's family.

"If you say so, madam. But what am I going to do wit all dis money?" Patience laughed.

"Go home, Patience. It's time," Sylvia said. Since she couldn't go back to China, at least one of them should return home.

Sylvia climbed into the minibus and sat next to Ayo. As she looked back at Patience standing there in her driveway, she said to Ayo, "Take care of her, will you? Make sure she makes it home, back to Cote d'Ivoire."

"Don't worry about Patience. She will find her way."

The drive to Lagos would take two or three hours, depending

on the traffic. Sylvia sat next to her ex-lover while the armed escorts drove the minibus to the airport in the capital. The children sat in the back row. It reminded Sylvia of when Ayo had rescued her from running away all those years ago. The night they had first met. Only Lila had been a baby back then, and now she was almost a teenager, watching, probably aware of Sylvia's sins. And this time, Sylvia was really leaving. Their Pan-Am flight to New York departed at midnight, but they would reach the airport before dark. The sun was setting, and they were almost there.

Her leg almost touched Ayo's. There was not much space, but she kept her leg taut, away from him. Was she doing the right thing, telling him not to come with her to America? Could she live without him? She turned and looked at his profile—the eyelashes, the angular jaw, the broad shoulders, and the deep brown of his skin. Ayo stared intently ahead, watching for any signs of armed robbers. She noticed his neck muscles were tight as he craned to look at the darkening sky. She wanted to touch his neck, the place where she knew he held all his stress.

• • •

When they reached the airport, a group of suspicious men mobbed them as they got out of the van. Ayo and the armed guards waved them off. The airport had an air of lawlessness as if air travel was the new medium for pirates. There were rumors of gangs of robbers hiding underneath the airport, snatching suitcases as they came up the conveyor belt. Recently, robbers had also attacked planes taxiing on the runaway, driving their jeeps up to the planes and opening the baggage holds from underneath. Armed robbers also frequently killed people on the road to the airport, a shot in the head for your car or the money in your wallet.

While the driver unloaded the luggage, Ayo escorted Sylvia and the children through the crowd of modern pirates filling the airport hall. At the check-in desk, the Pan-Am representative informed them the flight to New York had been delayed due to mechanical problems. They would fix the plane with parts flown in on a later flight coming in that night. Their flight would not leave until morning. Sylvia thought she might never really leave Nigeria. Something would happen, something would prevent her.

Ayo told the armed escorts to drive them to the Sheraton, one of the few five-star Western hotels in Lagos. On the cement walls surrounding the hotel, a vendor had hung an array of stolen silver hubcaps for sale. Shacks used to crowd the alleyways behind the hotel, but the owners had bulldozed them off the property. They didn't want the guests to see or smell the shantytown from their windows above. Nevertheless the bits of cardboard, wood, and tin were slowly growing again.

It was a new hotel, built only a year before, and the air-conditioned, chandelier-lit marble lobby was a welcome respite after the long, dusty drive to the airport. At the front desk, Ayo paid for three rooms—one for the children, one for Sylvia, and one for himself. The armed escorts would sleep in the minibus.

The four of them had dinner downstairs in the restaurant. Even though the hotel was new, it already showed signs of tropical decay. The white napkins, although painstakingly starched, were frayed at the edges. The children wanted to order ice cream, but the waiter said, "de ice cream machine it done broken." There was something about the humidity that rusted machine parts quickly, and the remoteness that made them difficult to replace. Things from the West simply aged rapidly in Africa. They were not cut out for the weather or the grittiness of the orange dust.

Still, the hotel restaurant was full with delayed passengers. The loud chatter of the other guests distracted Sylvia from the silence at their table. She felt uncomfortable sitting with Ayo and the children as if they were a family, it didn't seem right. It was like a glimpse of what could have been. Her teenage children were full of animosity toward Ayo. When he spoke to them, they did not say much, only nodding or shaking their heads. They probably knew of Ayo and her betrayal of their father. They would never accept Ayo as a father now. Sylvia knew then she had made the right decision.

That night, Sylvia lay awake in her room. They had three adjoining rooms with Sylvia's in the middle. She heard the regular breathing of the children. She got up and quietly closed the door between their rooms. Her husband had been killed. Tomorrow, she was leaving her lover forever for a new country. She stared at the closed door separating her room from Ayo's. She could see the light was still on under the door. She knew he was not sleeping. But she also knew he would not come to her room.

She thought of the years she had known him, worked by his side, the affair. For almost a decade of her youth, she had loved him, and she felt that in this life she would only love once. She was thirty-five years old now. Would another man love her like this? She didn't know if life could be that generous.

She got up and knocked on the door to Ayo's room. He opened the door, but he was not surprised to see her.

She sat down on the bed and lay down, fully clothed. He lay down next to her and put his arm around her, but he did not touch her. She closed her eyes. She could hear his heart beating next to hers. She recalled the first time they had made love against the wall of the mechanical room under the swimming pool. She tried to remember every detail—her grass skirt, his hands—so that the first and last night would be intertwined in her memory.

• • •

The next morning at the airport Sylvia said good-bye to Ayo on the tarmac. They embraced and he held onto her tightly, not letting her go. She took in the bittersweet smell of him, the feeling of being in his arms, the touch of his skin. When she climbed up the stairs, she turned back to look at him. He waved at her, but he was not smiling. She gazed beyond the airport at the green bush, the orange dust, the white egrets, and the twirls of smoke. Then she turned and walked onto the plane.

EPILOGUE

From Sand to Ice

Sylvia was suspended in air, flying above the icebergs of the North Pole, passing through time zones, lost between continents. She had just crossed the Sahara from above—zigzag tracks carved by camel caravans, the occasional rectangular outline of a homestead made from rocks, a lonely, isolated life in all that golden sand, and then nothing, no life, just endless ripples in the sand made by the wind. And now, below her, that other vast barren tract of land, flying over ice, an infinite white, a no man's land. She thought of people living cutoff from the world in lonely igloos. She wanted to communicate to them way down below her. She was no different than they were. She felt their isolation, the numbing cold of leaving, her heart wrenched out and hastily transplanted from sand to ice.

• • •

They came to America in the winter of 1986. Her brother and his wife picked them up at the airport. They arrived in

Minnesota, and snow still covered the ground. They would live with her brother's family until Sylvia could get her bearings.

Her brother lived in a new mansion now. He had started his own successful software company. His house had soft carpet from wall to wall. The kitchen cabinets were a pale wood. The walls were painted a soft yellow. Winston had spoken of these houses made of paper, or pre-fab, as they were called. Sylvia could hear her husband's voice—*a house made of paper, only in the richest country in the world.*

Sylvia lay in her new bed. It was so cold here. The room smelled of chemicals. The smell of the new carpets made her feel sick. Did Winston's spirit know they had come here, she wondered? Could he find them? She didn't think so—it was too far, too bewildering, even for the living. Was his spirit still in Africa, hovering over the home they had left so hastily?

His ashes still lay in the lacquered box inside her Pan Am travel bag in the closet.

• • •

Sylvia applied for a transfer to nursing schools at nearby universities in Minneapolis. Upon acceptance, she received a student visa to live in the US with Lila as her dependent. Thomas was already a US citizen since he had been born in America. Due to a shortage of nurses in America, the school administration told Sylvia it would be easy after graduation to receive a work visa and ultimately a Green Card to stay in the US. In so many ways, she knew she had been given a second chance to begin her life again. Finally, Sylvia would finish her degree and become a real nurse.

She received a check for a million dollars from Winston's life insurance. With some of the money, Sylvia bought a modest, suburban house in her brother's town. The neighborhood, her brother said, was in excellent school district for her kids. She knew Winston would have wanted good schools for them. In her new house, she unpacked the lacquered box with Winston's ashes and placed it on the fake marble mantelpiece along with a photograph of him and some incense sticks. She didn't want to bury him in the ground because that felt too permanent and rooted for her nomadic life. Who knew where she might go next? She couldn't abandon Winston in a lonely grave in a random American town.

In her bedroom drawer, she kept a small photo album of her and Ayo. In the evenings sometimes, she took out the album and looked at pictures of him. She missed him at first, it hurt so much. She felt rudely reincarnated into a new life, everything that had happened before felt like another lifetime, long ago. It was hard to believe she was the same person. She wrote to Ayo even though she knew some of her letters would get lost or never arrive. But he wrote back, turning their relationship into the written word, where they could share their fears, their joys, and their thoughts. In this way, she still kept him in her life.

She also received a letter from Patience through Ayo. She had retired with much fanfare to her native Beng village in the remote forests of Cote d'Ivoire. There she built a cement house with an electric generator and became the pride of her family. Patience also bought a continuous supply of antibiotics, Tylenol, and other medicine and gradually her house began to double as an informal clinic. She used her knowledge of Western medicine, gleaned from years of caring for foreign children, to fight the spirits, so her village children could live beyond seven years. Sylvia smiled, thinking that both she and Patience were now working as nurses in a way. They were both angels, inspired by Ayo.

Sylvia found work at a hospital in one of the poorest

neighborhoods in Minneapolis even though it was a long commute from her home. Because she bought their modest house outright with Winston's life insurance money, they had no mortgage and were able to live comfortably on her nurse's salary. She sent the children to the local public high school and saved the rest of Winston's life insurance money for their college education. She knew Winston would want them to attend good universities. Thomas, particularly, excelled at school.

But Sylvia never quite fully recovered from Winston's death. She never got the chance to say goodbye to her husband or to ask for his forgiveness, and this held her back, prevented her from beginning her life entirely anew. Several men asked her out on dates at the hospital, but she declined them all. She could not forget the two men in her life, one who was the love of her life and one who needed her love to live.

• • •

In 1996, after ten years in America, Sylvia went back to Africa to honor her husband. She knew she had to go back, everything felt unfinished because she had left so hastily. The ADA had invited her to accept an award on Winston's behalf. They were naming a new conference center in his honor. Now ten years later, they were remembering him. A life lost, she thought, and only now did they memorialize him. Sylvia knew it was Donna's doing; she was now director at the ADA. But she didn't know if she could face Ayo, now married to Donna. He had written about their three children, two were adopted orphans and one was their own child.

Lila accompanied her on the trip. Thomas had just started a PhD program at Harvard, busy doing medical research on tropical diseases, and could not leave. But Lila was in a limbo period after college and was searching for her "roots"—something that Sylvia knew was her fault. Lila had just returned from teaching English in China, and she desperately wanted to come with Sylvia. Sylvia knew it would be good for her. Her daughter needed closure too.

Lila was now twenty-three years old, close to the same age that Sylvia had been when she had first arrived in Africa. Her daughter possessed that unique, dark Eurasian beauty that boys shied away from but men fell for. Lila was dating a British archeologist-adventurer type in his forties she had met in China. Sylvia wasn't happy about the age difference, but she knew it was related to Lila's desire for a father figure.

They were met at the Lagos airport by a group of ten armed escorts sent by the ADA. Nigeria had been through a dark period during the early 1990s. But recently, the previous dictator Abacha had been deposed, and things were gradually improving. Still it wasn't safe, and Sylvia was glad to have this small army of guards.

The next morning, the driver and armed escorts brought them several hours inland to Ibadan. Everything was as Sylvia had remembered it—the rusty-tin roof houses and swarming street vendors; the lush banana trees in the distance; the thickness of the tropical grass, each blade wide and thick. For a moment, she felt like she had never left but was venturing into town to do her shopping.

As she drove, she looked down at the bag on the car seat between her and Lila. It held the lacquered box of Winston's ashes. They had sat on their living room mantelpiece for ten years in suburban America. They didn't belong there.

They arrived at the white gates and royal palms of the compound. This was her old home—a place she had tried to escape, even hated once, but now she felt only fondness and nostalgia. They drove up to the clubhouse and guesthouse where they would stay.

Ayo came to see Sylvia, and she waited for him inside the clubhouse. She saw him as he came through the glass doors. He still possessed the same athletic physique, but she noticed his hairline was receding. He was in his early fifties.

"Sylvia." He came up to her and gave her a hug. He smelled the same to her, that faint bittersweet scent. She stepped back a little, feeling dizzy, and looked up at him. Despite his fading looks, she was still drawn to him. Deep down, she knew she would always love him even though they had gone their separate ways. She was forty-five years old now.

"You look fabulous," Ayo said, smiling at her. "You look exactly the same, not a day older. Except you cut your hair." He touched her short, stylish bob as if he missed her long hair and the decade that had passed.

• • •

The next day, Sylvia and Lila attended the naming ceremony in Winston's honor at the new *Winston Soong Conference Center.* Donna went up to the stage to give a speech. She looked older, more mature now. She was no longer a free-loving hippie student but a sophisticated, powerful middle-aged woman. *Winston Soong, my friend and colleague, was a pioneer, she said. He did not lose his life in vain. Without him, we would not be where we are today.* As Sylvia listened, she wondered what had happened to Simeon's family.

Winston's efforts had been the beginning of change, Donna continued. Development aid had become much more wary of too much involvement by multinational agribusiness. Indigenous farming practices were now being integrated into agriculture development. The use of tractors was banned on African soil. The world was becoming increasingly environmentally conscious and was moving away from chemical and energy-intensive industrial agriculture. Instead, small scale, pesticide-free organic farming with low energy input was on the rise. It was the beginning of a new, greener Green Revolution. Through Donna, the ADA had become a leader in this new approach. But still, she warned, with the advent of biotechnology in the late 1990s, genetically engineered seeds were replacing the old hybrid miracle seeds, and multinational agribusiness was becoming an even more formidable force. The fight would continue.

• • •

Sylvia and Lila returned to their old house on the compound, now empty. After they had left, a string of families living in their house had all witnessed snakes coming into various rooms. Their former home had become infamously known as "the snake house." No one wanted to live in it. The gardeners cut down the dense, snake-infested bamboo bushes near the house—the presumed reason for the snakes—but still no one dared move in.

Sylvia and Lila walked around the house to the back garden. The garden was much the same except all the trees and bushes were bigger, more overgrown. They walked under the frangipani tree near the screened porch dining room—a place where so many attempts at family life had failed to happen.

Sylvia took out the lacquered box that had held Winston's ashes these last ten years. She opened the box and motioned to Lila. She wanted to return him to the African soil—the dusty orange dirt he had worked so hard to turn into a miracle. She tossed a handful of Winston's ashes under the frangipani tree, onto the thick blades of tropical grass layered with white blossoms. Then she and Lila walked around and tossed his ashes around the garden, under the thin papaya trees, the spot where the vegetable garden used to be, once full of leafy Chinese greens.

After they had spread his ashes around their old garden and there was nothing left in the box, Sylvia bent down and grabbed a clump of the ochre dirt. She thought—so this was the soil he gave us up for. This was the soil that had driven him in life. Suddenly, Sylvia felt she had to understand it. She felt the coarse unforgiving dirt in her hands. It was part of her husband. She held her fist tight as some of the dirt fell from between her fingers. So this was what he had been all about. Some people were meant to make a mark on this world. Others were meant to love. She turned around and tossed it back, letting it fall on the green lawn next to the fallen white frangipani blossoms. *White was the Chinese color of death.*

Lila took out a worn piece of paper from her pocket and began reading a poem by a Senegalese poet named Birago Diop. The dead are not dead, she read, the dead are never gone. They are not under the earth. They are in the forest, they are in the house. They are in the child that is wailing. The dead are not dead. Sylvia hoped her daughter would find peace at last.

Then Sylvia closed the lacquer box. She knew this would have to be her farewell. Her relationship with Winston would remain unfinished. She would never be able to ask for his forgiveness, but she suddenly felt her burden lighten a little. She had finally returned him to the soil where he belonged. Perhaps one day she would find his spirit or he would be reincarnated in the form of Thomas' child, and then they could meet again.

Sylvia broke off a white frangipani blossom from the tree. Its milky white blood stained her skin. White was the color of milk, semen, and water. Life. Sylvia was Chinese, she was African, she was American. She was from everywhere. She was from nowhere.

She tucked the white frangipani blossom in her hair and walked back to the car. White was the color of purity. Her life could begin again.

• • •

A woman emerged from a hut. She went to the well to pump water for her family. The water sloshed against the sides of her plastic bucket, splashing her face. The sun was still rising, halfway up the sky, its rays filtered through the acacia trees in front of the hut. The woman boiled the water in a large blackened pot over an open fire, preparing *ogi*, a breakfast porridge made from corn, ground into a powder, and then mixed with water.

The corn came from the small plot adjacent to the cluster of huts. She had planted and tilled it herself, just as she and other women have done for decades. On the plot, she also planted vegetables—tomatoes, peppers, cowpeas, and cassava. Simeon's wife, Abike, was part of a rural women's farming cooperative that practiced agro-ecological methods, a natural push-pull system of farming, integrating traditional farming techniques with cutting-edge science. On her farm, Abike planted her crops in between nitrogen-fixing plants that naturally enriched the soil. She cultivated special plants that naturally repelled pests through scent or by trapping them in sticky grasses. To conserve and improve her soil, she laid dead leaves and branches on the ground along with wild animal manure that her children collected in small containers. Her children also helped find rocks to construct stone bunds or rock barriers to prevent soil erosion.

Abike also planted shea trees as part of the rural women's cooperative, founded by a local Nigerian woman, a new leader in development. Using traditional methods of extracting the shea butter by hand and without the use of chemicals, the co-op made pure skin care products, much in demand in the West.

Her husband had killed himself many years ago, but Abike had used Winston's money to send all her children to school. Her eldest son would be graduating next year from the University of Ife with a degree in accounting.

Next to their village there had once been a plantation owned by a government official. He had long since lost favor and fled to London to become a corner shopkeeper in Brixton. The plantation land had since been abandoned. The women in the co-op reclaimed the land by replanting local trees on the razed and barren farmland. The trees grew fast, the foliage hiding the metal carcass of an abandoned tractor. All that remained were the broken headlights, peering out of the bush.

THE END

ABOUT THE AUTHOR

Jennifer Juo is Chinese-American but was born and raised in Nigeria, West Africa. She attended boarding school in England, and moved to America at the age of seventeen. She has lived in San Francisco and Seattle for the past seventeen years. She currently lives in Singapore with her husband and two sons.

www.jenniferjuo.com
www.facebook.com/seedsofplenty
www.twitter.com/jenjuo

ACKNOWLEDGEMENTS

Thank you to Julie Mosow, my editor who worked and re-worked the manuscript and story with me until it was ready to be in print. I am greatly indebted to my writers group, friends, and family in Seattle who spent years with me as I wrote and researched this novel. I appreciate your constant feedback and reading and rereading of my manuscript. So much gratitude to my writers group—Nancy Brenner, Elizabeth Coulter, Karen Heileson, Laura Swindlehurst, Lori Whittaker, and our dear friend, Kathy Medak, who we lost to cancer. Thanks also to my other writer colleagues, good friends, and family who endured reading drafts as well: Diane Owens, Joe Richardson, Margaret Rodenberg, Ingrid Olsen, Alicia Trochalakis, Jodi Nishioka, Melissa Sebastien, Krista Lewis, Melissa Tarun, Cam Bradley, Jasmine Juo, Peter Juo, my mother, Rosalind Juo and my University of Washington instructor Scott Driscoll. Finally, special thanks to my husband, Garth Bradley, for all his support and love on this project.

I did extensive research to write this novel. In particular, anthropologist Alma Gottlieb's book, *The Afterlife is Where We Come From: The Culture of Infancy in West Africa,* inspired many rich details about the spirit world and village life. Thank you also to David Sewell and Stan Claassen, colleagues of my father. My father and his colleagues dedicated their life's work to agricultural aid in Africa. Stan provided clarifications on some of the agricultural details and David, a pilot, kindly hosted me in Nigeria in 2007 but recently lost his life when his plane crashed in the African bush. Finally, this novel is dedicated to my late father Anthony Juo who showed me the world and gave me the perspective to write about it.